Cremains

Rob Johnson

XERIKA PUBLISHING

CREMAINS COPYRIGHT

Published by Xerika Publishing

Copyright © Rob Johnson 2019

Cover artwork by Penny Philcox from an original design by Patrick Woodgate.

First published 2019 by Xerika Publishing
10 The Croft, Bamford, Hope Valley,
Derbyshire S33 0AP

ISBN: 978-1-9161289-0-3

http://www.rob-johnson.org.uk

For Nicco.

Glad all over.

So glad you're here.

ACKNOWLEDGEMENTS

I am indebted to the following people for helping to make this book better than it would have been without their advice, technical knowhow and support:

Nuala Forde; Rob Johnson (a different one); Penny Philcox; Dan Varndell; Chris Wallbridge; Nick Whitton; Patrick and Heidi Woodgate.

And last but not least, my eternal gratitude to my wife, Penny, for her unfailing support, encouragement and belief.

COVER DESIGN BY PENNY PHILCOX AND PATRICK WOODGATE

Special thanks as always to Penny Philcox for the cover artwork and to Patrick Woodgate for the original design.

GREEK LANGUAGE NOTE

There are a few Greek words and phrases used in the text, and these have been transliterated into the Latin alphabet. Where a word has more than one syllable, an accent shows which is the stressed syllable. For instance, the Greek word *póso* (meaning "how much") is pronounced with the stress on the first "o".

When you address someone directly by name in Greek and their name ends in an "s", the "s" is omitted. For instance, a man called Nikos would be addressed as Niko. For the sake of simplicity, however, this rule has not always been observed in the text, and for some of the male Greek characters the "s" has been dropped altogether.

1

It's not every day that you see some old granny crushed to death under a baby grand piano, and I'm truly grateful for that. I really am. But the even bigger shock was that this woman – a complete stranger – would be coming back to haunt me in the days to come. Not in a spooky, walking-through-walls kind of way but something a lot more real and far more dangerous.

The inevitable small crowd had gathered round on the pavement to have a good gawp, of course, and not one of them was lifting so much as a finger to get the poor cow out from under the wreckage. Probably too late anyway. All that was visible of her was her blue rinse and one arm of a slightly less blue housecoat.

Two blokes in orange overalls were standing a few feet away from the ghoul brigade and staring up at a second-floor window of the four-storey apartment block. There was some kind of winch arrangement just above the window with about ten feet of rope dangling from it. At the bottom of the rope, half a dozen strips of webbing swayed gently in the breeze. Best guess?

The two blokes in Guantanamo jumpsuits had been delivering or removing the joanna, and the old biddy had been standing right underneath it when the harness snapped. Wham, bam, and raspberry jam.

I'm not a great one for too much of the blood and gore, as it happens, so I carried on up the opposite side of the street without breaking stride. Second turning on the left and glad to see the BMW in its usual spot and with all its wheels still attached. Not that this is the sort of area where even the Rottweilers go round in pairs. Far from it, in fact, and I've got the mortgage repayments to prove it. On the other hand, leafy suburbia is exactly the type of place that some of the thieving little ne'er-do-wells like to target in the hope of richer spoils. Well, they can count me out on that score for a start 'cos I'm totally bloody skint right at this moment, although I'm expecting my fortunes to improve quite dramatically in a few short hours from now. Unless, that is, Alan and Scratch have made a complete bollocks of things, which, based on past experience, is not at all beyond the realms of possibility.

I took the rolled-up copy of *The Times* from under my arm and dropped it into a bin on the corner of the street, noticing that I'd built up quite a collection since it had last been emptied. Lazy bastards. It's not as if they don't get a shitload out of me in Council Tax.

I fished the plastic clicker thing out of my suit jacket and scored a direct hit on the Beamer's rear window, causing the usual clunking sound as the doors unlocked, and the hazard lights flashed. What do they call them? Smart keys, isn't it? Not so bloody smart the time when the battery ran out on the stupid piece of crap and locked me out until I remembered the strip of metal inside it that worked like some kind of pretend key. Late forties hardly qualifies me as one of those grumpy old gits who's constantly moaning on about how much better everything used to be in *their* day, but you knew where you were with a proper key, didn't you? Smarmy gimp at the showroom told me this was a top-of-the-range BMW and I couldn't have a proper ordinary key even if I paid extra. Told me if I was dead set on having a car with a key, 'Perhaps sir might want to consider a second-hand Morris Minor instead.' Cheeky twat.

I climbed in behind the wheel, plonked the briefcase on the passenger seat and tossed the rolled umbrella over into the back. Haven't needed it for days now, but it helps me look the part, that's for sure.

I fired up the engine. Nice purr. Almost worth the obscene amount of cash I had to fork out every month just for that sound. Carla would have had a blue fit if she knew I even *had* a Beamer, never mind that I was already way behind on the payments. As far as she was concerned, all we'd got was a four-year-old Honda Civic that spends most of its time sitting in the driveway. Still, there's a fair old bit that Carla doesn't know, and I'm definitely aiming to keep it that way.

2

I deliberately walked straight past the shop without so much as a sideways glance and stopped in front of the next one. The plan was to pretend to be checking out the contents of the window display while I listened for any undue noise. But then I realised I was staring at a window that had been completely blanked out and remembered it was one of those sex shops – private shops, they call them nowadays – so I carried on to the hairdresser's next door. Not much to see here either except for a bunch of women getting their weekend hairdos done. Better not hang around here too long or one of them might clock me for a peeping tom with a shampoo and blow-dry fetish and call the cops.

I couldn't hear what I'd been listening out for from this distance, so I doubled back to the shop I'd ignored and took the key out of my pocket. A proper key. Still no noise out of the ordinary, so I shoved the key into the lock and turned it. Except it wouldn't. Turn, that is. I tried the handle, and the door swung open with the slightest of creaks. Christ almighty, the bloody idiots hadn't even bothered to lock it.

Once upon a time, the shop had been a gents' outfitters, but it had gone bust months ago. Presumably, the modern world hadn't any need for gents' outfitters any more, or maybe there just weren't enough gents left to be outfitted. Either way, I'd taken out a short lease on the place a few weeks ago in the name of a bogus company I'd set up specifically for the purpose. Not that I ever had any plans to run it as a shop, of course. God, no. I had something else in mind altogether, and this was going to make me a whole lot richer than flogging a bunch of ties and the occasional suit.

The light was dim inside the shop, partly because I'd had the door and window completely obscured with sheets of newspaper – from the copies of *The Times* I hadn't binned – and partly because the air was so thick with dust, you could have grown spuds in it.

Better get out of these togs sharpish or Carla will go into meltdown if she has to take another suit to the dry cleaner's.

I ducked down behind the counter that butted up at right-angles to the window and pulled out a bulging carrier bag. I was just about to take off the suit jacket and lay it on the counter top when I spotted the half-inch layer of dust that had settled on it. I scanned the rest of the shop for somewhere I could temporarily deposit the jacket, but apart from a few shelves bolted to the wall and also covered with dust, there was nothing. Not so much as a hanging rail with a bunch of coat hangers that must have been here when the gents' outfitters was still up and running. Bailiffs must have cleared pretty much everything that wasn't nailed down – and probably quite a lot of the stuff that was, apart from the counter.

I considered my options for a couple of seconds. Not even for that long because there was only one. If I didn't want the suit to end up making me look like a nuclear fallout survivor, I'd just have to put the overalls on over the top and hope to Christ I didn't roast down there. So, out they came from the carrier bag – grease monkey green rather than Guantanamo orange – and I had them on and buttoned up to the neck in a flash. Well, not quite a flash exactly, on account of twice nearly falling flat on my arse when each shoe got snagged up in a trouser leg.

Making for the far corner of the shop, I noticed several pairs of footprints in the carpet of dust, leading in both directions between the front door and where I was heading. Buggers must have been in and out a fair few times since I left them here last night. They'd better not have been sat swilling ale in some club or other instead of getting on with the job in hand. The sound I'd been listening for earlier was clearly audible now and getting louder with every step I took, so they obviously hadn't finished yet.

The swirling dust was getting even thicker too, most of it coming from the top of the metal spiral staircase that led down into the basement. These things are lethal at the best of times, never mind when you can hardly see a hand in front of your face, so I grabbed the handrail tight and took the steps one at a very steady time. At the bottom, I pushed through the heavy blankets we'd hung up the night before to muffle as much of the noise as possible, but they hadn't created enough of a seal to stop some of the dust escaping.

My eyes had already begun to sting like crazy, and the air was almost unbreathable down here, so I whipped out my handkerchief and clamped it over my nose and mouth. I squinted through the haze and my streaming tears to see Alan sitting on the floor with his back against the wall nearest me and Scratch on his knees, drilling into the wall on the opposite side of the basement.

'Bloody hell, you two,' I shouted. 'What if I'd been the cops? You hadn't even locked the sodding door.'

But even Alan, who was only six feet away, didn't hear me over the din of Scratch's massive drill.

I yelled a second time and then went over to Alan and tapped him on the shoulder. Dozy sod nearly jumped out of his skin, and as his head spun round, his left hand flew up to his neck and he let out what sounded like a yelp of pain.

'What's up?' I said.

He pulled down the paper breathing mask to expose the only part of his face that wasn't encrusted with a thick film of cement dust. His lips moved, but I couldn't make out a single word.

'Knock it off a minute,' I yelled at Scratch's back.

Nothing doing, so I picked up a small piece of rubble and chucked it at him. Got him right between the shoulder blades, but whether it was the vibration from the drill or not, he didn't even flinch. Another piece of rubble – a lot bigger than before – and this time he lowered the drill and turned to face me.

He pulled down his own mask, and you didn't have to be much of a lipreader to make out the "fuck d'you do that for?" part of what he said.

I gestured to him to switch off the drill, and moments later, the sound of silence filled the basement with an almost eerie calm.

I looked back down at Alan. 'So what is it?'

'Done my bloody neck in, haven't I?' he said with an extra wince and giving his neck a bit of a rub, presumably to emphasise the point.

'Again?' I said. 'You're always doing your neck in.'

'Bloody martyr to it, I am.'

Scratch snorted. 'Martyr to being a lazy little bastard, more like.'

It was a remark that didn't make much sense, but the gist was clear enough. And it was true. Alan would swing the lead any chance he got whenever any manual labour was involved. He was about the same age as me and probably a fair bit fitter. A couple of inches on the short side and built like a weightlifter. No great coincidence, of course, because that's what he used to do in his younger days. Claimed that's where his neck problems first started and why he had to give it up. But bad neck or not, there was work to be done.

I gave Alan a sympathetic pat on the shoulder, which sent up a fresh cloud of dust from his overalls, and went over to check on the progress.

'What's the story then?' I said, stooping to get a good look at the hole for myself.

Scratch cleared his throat like he was trying to dislodge something the size of the piece of rubble I'd thrown at him. 'Another half hour or so should do it, I reckon.'

The hole in the wall was roughly circular, a couple of feet in diameter and about the same deep.

'It'll have to be bigger than that if you're gonna get through there,' I said.

'Off you go then, Max,' said Scratch, and he laid the drill down and pushed himself upright.

Now, I'm about average height for a bloke, but Scratch has got a good head and shoulders on me and a physique that's totally in proportion to his height. The man is bloody enormous, and what with the shaved head – a vain attempt to disguise the rapidly advancing baldness – and a busted nose, looks like a right thug that you really wouldn't want to run into in a dark alley. But that's where you'd be wrong because Scratch wouldn't hurt a fly. Not unless provoked. And if that happened, you – or the fly – would be in serious trouble. Come to think of it, though, the fly would probably be OK since it's unlikely that Scratch would risk being within swatting distance of it in case he was allergic. For a guy of his impressive stature, it had always struck me as weird that he should have so many allergies. Whatever it was, if you could touch it, smell it or swallow it, it was odds on that Scratch would come out in a rash. Hence the nickname. Apparently, however, he didn't have too much of a problem with cement dust.

'Any spare masks?' I said.

Scratch shook his head and took off his own. 'You'll have to use mine.'

It was already thick with caked-on dust and probably well past its usefulness, but I guessed it was better than a handkerchief, so I slipped it on and picked up the drill. Christ, it weighed a ton, and the vibration when I started in on the hole made my brain rattle. This was the first time I'd used the thing on account of having to get off home soon after we'd got everything set up the night before. Both being single, Alan and Scratch didn't have a Carla waiting to give them an earful about being late for their tea, but I'd promised them I'd do my share when I came back today.

Mind you, what did Scratch reckon? Another half hour or so? Jesus, I doubted I'd last more than five minutes.

3

At bloody last. Finally there was light at the end of the tunnel – or at least an opening the size of my fist at the far end of the hole. Scratch's "half hour or so" had turned out to be well over double that, even though we'd worked non-stop in shifts. Alan had moaned like hell all the while he was having his go, of course, but thanks to the din of the drilling, Scratch and I could hardly hear him.

'Here, I'll take over,' said Scratch, presumably fired up with renewed enthusiasm now that the job was almost done.

Even so, I wasn't about to object, and I gladly handed him the drill.

The work was a lot easier from then on with Scratch chipping away at the far end of the hole and pausing every so often so I could pull out the loose rubble or push it through the other side. Ten minutes later and the hole was about the size of my head. Ten more and it was big enough for me to get my shoulders through with a bit of wriggling. The dust began to clear, and my eyes swept across the pile of rubble in front of me.

Holy shit. What the—? Feet. Human feet. In shiny black leather. The sharp points pointing straight at me. Thin stiletto heels nearly six inches long. My gaze crept stealthily upwards, eventually reaching the tops of the black leather boots and the pale skin of a pair of thighs. Then more black leather with little straps and buckles at regular intervals. Twin bulges of white flesh trying to force their way out, partially obscured by forearms clad in long black gloves. A coiled whip in one hand being slowly and rhythmically tapped against the palm of the other. Thick, black leather collar studded with viciously long spikes. Glossy scarlet lips, pouting slightly. Black leather eye mask and a bob of gleaming black hair.

Jesus Christ, what was she doing here?

Panicked, I darted my eyes to left and right. Wood and metal contraptions everywhere with ropes or chains dangling from most of them. A wooden X-shaped frame with a man strapped to it, spreadeagled and totally starkers apart from a black rubber hood that covered his face and head completely. Red welts criss-crossed his massive man-boobs and equally enormous belly.

I switched my focus back to peering upwards at the pouting red lips and the black eye mask. But the lips were no longer pouting. Instead, they'd spread into a kind of lopsided, leering grin.

'Who's been a naughty boy then?' said the lips, and there was a sharp "*krakk!*" as the business end of the whip struck the floor of what was pretty obviously not the vault of a bank.

4

It was, without a doubt, the best sleep I'd had in days. Weeks even. Snug as a bug in a rug, I was. The generous velvet padding saw to that with the added advantage of the complete and utter silence. Or it would have been complete and utter silence if it hadn't been for the ringing in my ears that had only now started to wear off nearly a week after all the drilling. Next time – if there was a next time – I'd remember to take ear defenders.

The intensity of the darkness was another bonus. For some reason only known to herself, Carla always insisted on leaving her bedside light on all night, and I had to resort to one of those stupid blackout masks or I'd never get a wink of sleep.

But the very thought of a black mask – leather or otherwise – brought back a memory I really didn't want, so I tried to think of something else. Something comfy and reassuring like... like a... Oh, Christ on a bike. Now all I had was an all too vivid image of the old woman who'd been crushed to death under a baby grand piano.

'You need to relax,' the voice in my head was telling me. 'Try and think of something calm and soothing.'

'What the fuck d'you think I'm doing?'

I didn't say it out loud, of course. I'm not that crazy. And just because I hear voices in my head doesn't make me crazy either. Anyway, it's only the one voice, and I'd spent almost my entire life without even hearing the slightest whisper from it until about eighteen months ago. That was when my financial situation had taken a turn for the disastrous and I decided to take matters into my own hands. As a bank manager, you'd think I would have had a better grasp on my incomings and outgoings, but that would be ignoring a crucial part of the equation – a wife who could spend money like there was no tomorrow.

'Are you sure this is wise?'

Those were the very first words the voice had said to me as I'd filled in the paperwork for the first bogus account. I'd got the idea from watching a Philip Seymour Hoffman movie called *Owning Mahowny*, which was based on a true story about a Canadian guy who worked in a bank and embezzled millions. He'd set up a pretty complicated scam involving fake loans, bearer bonds and so on to feed his gambling habit, but I didn't need anywhere near the kind of money that the Hoffman character syphoned off, so I went for something a lot simpler. I didn't have an expensive gambling habit, only an expensive wife.

Creating a fictitious account was a piece of cake for someone in my position. No need for any proof of identity documents. Just tick the boxes and there's your new account, Mr Jeremy Wickham. Then it was simply a case of adding some funds to Mr Wickham's account. A hundred from here, a couple of hundred from there. Always from accounts with balances of six figures or more where the customer would be most unlikely to spot the occasional small transfer. Besides, if you were rich enough to leave that kind of cash sitting in a bank and earning bugger all interest, you deserved to have a wee bit of your wealth redistributed. OK, so I could hardly claim that my pocket counted as a genuinely worthy cause, but Mr Wickham's shiny new debit card didn't seem to mind.

The extra income certainly helped, but I was still struggling to keep up with the pace of Carla's spending sprees, so I had a few other imaginary customers open accounts at various intervals.

'Are you sure this is wise?' became the voice's mantra on every occasion that I started filling in a form for a new account – with the increasing addition of some other choice phrases concerning my mental health. But that was nothing compared to what it was yelling at me after I started to increase the size and frequency of the transfers from the bank's obscenely well-to-do. 'For God's sake, what the hell do you think you're doing? It was risky enough before when you were only taking small amounts at a time, and quite frankly, I'm amazed you've got away with it so far, but this is just madness. How long do you reckon it'll be till somebody realises what's been going on and how long after that till they figure out who's responsible?'

That was one of the most annoying things about the voice. It was more often right than wrong, and this was no exception. Less than a month after I'd begun to raise the stakes, some miserly bastard with an eye for detail had queried a couple of transfers on his latest statement. Not with me, though. If he'd have come to me, I could have given him some blather about a computer error, refunded his money and sent him happily on his way. But when one of his regular golfing partners happens to be the regional fucking manager, that's who he'd have a moan to first, right? And when that regional manager considers him to be among the bank's most valued customers, they're going to promise him all kinds of shit like a "rigorous and comprehensive investigation" or some other twaddle.

Except it didn't turn out to be twaddle at all as I discovered one morning when a pair of suits turned up at the bank, looking stern and disconcertingly efficient. After that, it was only a matter of time before they unearthed some "serious anomalies", all of which had my signature on them.

Citing Carla's extravagant tastes wasn't likely to get me very far in the way of mitigating circumstances, but what did count in my favour – big time – was that while I was shitting myself about the thought of a lengthy prison sentence, the much-higher-ups in the bank's food chain were also shitting themselves for a very different reason.

Even though a few quid over sixteen grand was a piss in the ocean – as far as *they* were concerned – the bank had a "Your money's safe with us" reputation to uphold, of course, and that would have taken a massive dent if it ever got out that one of its own managers had been caught with his fingers in the till. So that's when they decided to offer me a deal. Well, not exactly a deal. More of an ultimatum really. Keep my trap shut, pay back the money I'd nicked within a month, and they wouldn't press charges. Oh yes, and my services as manager would no longer be required.

Not unnaturally, it was an ultimatum I couldn't refuse, but where the fuck was I going to lay my hands on sixteen grand in a *month*? Carla had already spent every last penny of my ill-gotten gains as well as my legitimate earnings, and I wasn't in much of a position to ask for a bank loan.

As soon as I'd been escorted off the premises of the bank, I headed straight for the nearest pub with two specific intentions – (1) to try and conjure up a solution to my financially challenged predicament, and (2) to get absolutely steaming ratarsed.

I was about two thirds of the way to achieving the second of these objectives but still without the ghost of an idea how to tackle my financial problem when the voice in my head came out with something useful for a change. 'How about Danny Bishop?'

'Danny Bishop. You know what? I think you might well have something there.' Being moderately bladdered by then, I did actually say this aloud, which got me a few weird looks from the rather more sober of the pub's customers, but so what? The voice had come up trumps – or so I'd thought at the time – and this was why, less than a year later, I now found myself lying inside a closed coffin with the very same voice reverting to type and irritating the hell out of me.

'I've lost count of the number of times I warned you about stealing from the bank,' it was saying. 'But did you listen? Of course you didn't. So it's hardly my fault that you've ended up…'

While the voice carried on lecturing me on my stupidity, I heard the lid of the coffin being lifted off, and a blaze of light seared into my eyeballs even though my eyes were still tight shut. And I kept them that way. Didn't move a muscle. Kept my arms folded diagonally across my chest as they had been the whole time I'd been in here.

There was a few seconds' pause and then a voice I knew even better than the one in my head. 'Max? You all right, Max?'

I didn't even breathe. Serve the bastard right.

A shorter pause this time and then: 'Oh, Jesus. Don't tell me you've—'

Quick as you like, I flashed open both eyes. Danny Bishop's ugly mug was inches above my face. Close enough that I could feel the heat of his breath and smell the whiskey on it.

His head jackknifed back as he shot himself upright. 'God almighty, Max. I thought you'd gone and croaked on me.'

"Croaked" was hardly a word I'd expect to hear from an undertaker – especially one with a posh accent like Danny's – and I told him so, but before he could answer, another face loomed over the side of the coffin.

'Not dead but sleeping, eh?' said the dark-skinned face with the pathetic attempt at a moustache.

'Shut up, Sanjeev,' said Danny and sent the lad off to get on with polishing the other display coffins.

'Surprisingly comfortable, these things,' I said, uncrossing my arms and giving the coffin's velvet lining a stroke.

'Top of the range, this little beauty,' said Danny with a grin so smug it was as if he'd given birth to it himself.

'Nothing but the best for me, eh, Danny?'

'Absolutely. But do try not to get the upholstery

grubby, there's a good chap.'

Cheeky sod. I wasn't having that, so I said, 'How much?'

'How much what?'

'For the coffin.'

'For the Highgrove Deluxe?'

'If that's what you call it, yeah. This one,' I said, and I gave the inside of the coffin a gentle rap with my knuckles.

'You couldn't afford it,' said Danny, his smug grin having morphed into a kind of condescending sneer.

'How do *you* know?'

'How do I *know*?'

'Yeah.'

'Because you still owe me half of the sixteen thousand I lent you nearly a year ago – not to mention the couple of grand I stumped up to fund your most recent bank robbery debacle – and you keep telling me how you can't pay up. That's how I *know*.'

'Oh yeah. That's right.'

'"Oh yeah. That's right"? What do you mean, "Oh yeah. That's right"? It's why I put you in there, for Christ's sake.'

'Oh yeah,' I said again and eased myself into a sitting position with an almighty yawn and a good old stretch. Winding Danny up had always been a pushover, but I never could resist an opportunity. 'Sorry, Danny. Not quite with it yet. "A gentle reminder", I think you said.'

'And don't forget the sinister cackle,' said Sanjeev, who may or may not have finished his coffin polishing duties but had reappeared anyway. 'There was definitely a sinister cackle that went with it when you told him, boss.'

'Sanjeev,' said Danny with the half-closed eyes of someone struggling to suppress an almost overwhelming urge to commit an act of extreme violence, 'if you've got nothing better to do, why don't you go and pop the kettle on, eh?'

It very obviously wasn't a question at all, so Sanjeev gave a barely noticeable one-shouldered shrug and trudged his way through the impressive assortment of display coffins towards the front of the shop.

'As we were saying,' said Danny. 'A gentle reminder of what's going to happen if you don't pay me back what you owe me.'

'You mean you'll shove me in a coffin for real? Kill me?'

There was a worrying pause while Danny seemed to be giving the possibility some serious consideration.

'Not necessarily,' he said at last and then slammed his fist down hard on the rim of the coffin. 'Dammit, Max, you were supposed to freak out in there.'

'Oh?'

'Claustrophobia.'

'Doesn't bother me. In fact, I actually preferred it *before* you took the lid off.'

'Of course it bothers you. You told me once. Back when we were kids.'

'Not me, mate. *Osmo*-phobia maybe, but not *claustro*-phobia.'

Danny raised a quizzical eyebrow.

'Fear of bad smells,' I said. 'If you'd locked me in some underground public toilet or shut me in this coffin with an overactive skunk and some week-old roadkill, then that'd be a different matter altogether.'

'Well, it must have been somebody else we were at

school with who had claustrophobia.'

'Dave Morgan, was it? I remember him going totally off his head once when Kev Parry locked him in a broom cupboard.'

'Oh yes, you're right. – You know he died recently, did you? Kev, that is.'

'You're joking.'

'I'm surprised you hadn't heard. Gruesome murder like that was all over the news.'

'He was *murdered*?'

'Indeed he was. And since it was only a few weeks after Chris Delaney was stabbed to death—'

'Chris from school?'

'The very same, old boy. Which is why there was a lot of chat about there being a serial killer on the loose. Both being from the same school, as it were. Perhaps you and I had better watch out in case we're next.'

Danny said the last bit with a hint of a smile, but I was fairly sure he wasn't kidding about the rest of it. So how come I hadn't heard about it? Not that I followed the news that much, although if the murders had happened locally... Or maybe they didn't live around here any more. But both of them within a few weeks of each other was more than a coincidence, wasn't it? Kev *and* Chris? Yeah, but the pair of them were always getting into trouble when we were at school, so perhaps they'd carried on the same way. Got involved in gangs or whatever and there'd been some sort of feud.

I started to ask Danny what else he knew about the murders, but I was interrupted by the electronic "*bing bong*" sound of the shop door being opened and Danny saying, 'Shit.'

'Customer,' he added by way of unnecessary explanation. 'Stay where you are. I haven't finished with you yet.'

'Can't Sanjeev deal with it?' I said. 'I mean, I'm pretty keen to find out where this little chat of ours is leading.'

'The less my clientele has to deal with that useless waste of space, the better,' said Danny. 'Lord alone knows why I keep him on, to be honest. Misplaced sense of charity perhaps? You know, the very first customer I let him attend to was a young widow whose husband had passed away well before his time, and while Sanjeev was speaking to her, his mobile phone went off. No big deal in itself, but I bet you can't guess what the ringtone was.'

'*Stayin' Alive*?'

Danny's mouth dropped open. 'How on earth did you know that?'

'Lucky guess, I suppose.'

'Still, I have to admit that he does make a really rather good cup of tea,' said Danny, recovering his composure after I'd ruined his punchline. 'But, hey-ho, duty calls, eh?'

'Yeah, well, do you think you could hurry it along a bit? The wife'll do her nut if I'm late for dinner again.'

'Somewhat under the old thumb, are we, Max?'

'Piss off, Danny. It's just that I don't want to give her any more reasons to get suspicious.'

'What, she thinks you're having an affair?'

'No, she thinks I'm still the manager of a fucking bank.'

Danny's face looked like it couldn't decide between shock and amusement. 'You never told her?'

'How could I? Christ, I get enough stick for getting home late. Can you imagine what she'd be like if she knew I'd been sacked for embezzling money from the bank?'

'So how have you kept it a secret all this time?'

'Set off every morning like I've still got a job to go to.'

Danny let out a low whistle and scratched the back of his head. 'Well, aren't you the sly one, eh?'

'Hello?'

A woman's voice from near the front of the shop reminded him that he had a customer to attend to, and his features rapidly moulded themselves into an expression that was both sombre and comfortingly sympathetic at the same time. Your standard undertaker look, in fact.

I watched him as he set off towards the front of the shop, his hands clasped behind his back, and straight away the voice in my head started up again. 'What the fuck are you waiting for? Get yourself out of that box and leg it out the back way.'

The voice had a point, of course. By now, Danny was twenty yards away, being sombre and sympathetic with a tearful-looking woman by the front door, so I'd have had more than enough time to do a runner. On the other hand, the fact remained that I still owed the bastard ten grand, and he was bound to catch up with me sooner or later. Sooner probably, so I might as well stay put and get it over with – whatever the "it" was that Danny-boy had in mind.

Another yawn and a stretch, and I lay back down in the Highgrove Deluxe for another kip, although my mind was still reeling from the news about Kev and Chris, so it was doubtful I'd get much sleep. I closed my eyes anyway, but the light still bothered me. Maybe Sanjeev'd be along in a minute and I could get him to pop the lid back on.

5

Bernard Pemberton turned his head to the side and stared through the pub window at nothing in particular while he tried to forget about the table. But it was no use. Less than half a minute later, he gave it another nudge. Not that he expected that some kind of divine intervention had miraculously stopped the damned thing from rocking since the last time he'd tried it. Rather, it was a scratch that had to be itched and equally as infuriating.

Why in God's name they can't make decent tables any more is utterly beyond me, he thought. Or maybe it's the floor that's wonky. Probably both, more than likely.

He knew perfectly well that the sensible thing would be to wait for Tess to fix it when she got back from the bar, but he couldn't put up with the wobbling table for a second longer. Grabbing a beermat, he slid his backside off the wooden settle and onto a threadbare carpet that looked like it had been laid before he'd even been born. All fours wasn't an option as the pain in his knees would have sent him through the roof, so he stayed sitting on his arse with his legs splayed out in front of him. Predictably, the table leg furthest from him seemed to be the main culprit, dangling uselessly about a quarter of an inch off the floor. Buttock by buttock, Bernard shuffled himself towards it, then folded the beermat roughly into four and rammed it into the gap.

'Granddad? What on earth are you doing down there?'

At the sound of Tess's voice, Bernard's head shot up and smacked itself against the underside of the table, partially dislodging the beermat.

'Bloody wonky table driving me mad,' he said, replacing the beermat and shuffling backwards until he was clear of the table.

'Well, that's not exactly going to do your knees a lot of good, is it?' said Tess as she reached down to help him to his feet. 'Why didn't you wait till I got back?'

Bernard muttered incomprehensibly and eased himself back onto the settle with a sigh like a rapidly deflating tyre. He gave the edge of the table a prod with his finger. If anything, the rocking was even worse than before.

'Oh, for goodness' sake.'

He picked up his half pint of bitter, some of which had slopped onto the tabletop, and took a tentative sip. Tess squeezed in beside him and mopped up the spilt beer with a tissue from her pocket.

'Do you want me to have a go?' she said.

'No, leave it. Damn thing's beyond redemption, if you ask me.'

Tess swirled the ice around in her glass of orange juice. 'It's not really that big a problem, you know,

Granddad.'

'Shoddy workmanship is what it is. I mean, why can't—?'

'I wasn't talking about the wonky table.'

Bernard followed her gaze to the slim, plastic folder which lay before them in the centre of the table. "The Last Will and Testament of Dorothy Jane Pemberton".

'She couldn't even *play* the ruddy piano. Said she'd always wanted to learn. Seventy-eight years old and she wants to take up the piano. "It'll keep my mind active," she said. "Stop me getting Alzheimer's". Silly mare.'

'Well, I did read somewhere that—'

'Why not the clarinet, for heaven's sake? Or the bassoon even? I don't think I've ever heard of anyone being crushed to death by a bassoon before.'

He felt the light touch of Tess's hand on his forearm, and he turned to face her. No makeup as usual, and the shoulder-length dark hair didn't look like it had seen a comb in days. Dottie always said she could be a real beauty if she put in a bit of effort. Said it was probably why she'd never managed to find herself a husband. Utter rubbish, of course. Tess had had more than her fair share of boyfriends over the years – lived together with a couple of them – but the settling down kind of life had never seemed to suit her. Not that Bernard minded as long as she was happy. The only drawback, of course, was that he'd have loved to have had a great-grandchild or two. True, she was only in her mid thirties, so there was plenty of time, but would he himself still be around to witness the happy event? What was beyond any question, though, was that Dottie certainly wouldn't be.

'You OK, Granddad?'

He felt the squeeze of Tess's hand on his arm. 'Hmm?'

'It's just you seem to have gone into a bit of a trance.'

'What?' said Bernard, willing into submission the tears that had begun to form and hoping that Tess hadn't noticed. 'Sorry, sweetheart. Miles away there for a minute.'

'In Scotland perhaps?'

There was the faintest suggestion of a wicked glint in her eyes as she spoke, which Bernard found mildly irritating in the circumstances.

'Oh, bloody hell. Don't remind me.'

Tess smiled at him, no longer even a trace of the wicked glint. 'Like I said, though, it's really not that big a deal.'

'Not that big a deal?' Bernard snatched up the folder, rocking the table as he did so, and flicked it open to the last of the pages. 'Here it is in black and white, look.' He jabbed at the paper with his finger. 'Traipse all the way up to bloody Scotland to scatter her ashes on top of some bloody mountain just because it's close to where she happened to be born.'

'I'm not sure that's the exact wording, Granddad.'

'I notice it doesn't say the bit about "being of sound mind" at the beginning. Perhaps she wasn't. Perhaps she was totally bonkers when she had that bit added in.' He slapped the folder back down onto the table, causing it to rock even more wildly than before. 'That's it. I'll contest the will is what I'll do.'

'I really don't think you—'

'Good grief, she didn't even tell me she'd *made* another will. Never even told me about this ash scattering nonsense. Thought I'd more than likely pop off before she did, I suppose.'

'Doesn't seem like it,' said Tess, and she leaned across and read aloud from the page. '"To be carried out by my beloved husband, Bernard".'

'Tuh!'

'"Even though he'll moan like hell about it".'

Bernard brought the document closer to his face so it was in sharper focus. 'It doesn't say that, does it?'

'Of course it doesn't. But it might just as well have done.'

'Ha ha, very amusing,' said Bernard and sipped at his beer. 'But I very much doubt there'll be much to laugh about once I've scaled the heights of Mount MacEverest – very probably in a howling gale and torrential bloody rain.'

'So once we get there, we can wait for a fine day. It's not as if there's a deadline or anything.'

'We?'

'You don't think I'd let you loose up there on your own, do you? We can take the camper van. Make a trip of it.'

'What about your job?'

'It'll be half term in a couple of weeks. Perfect.'

Bernard wasn't entirely convinced that he'd be able to cope with such a road trip at his age. As far as he was aware, there wasn't even a toilet in the van, and the washing facilities were probably not up to much either. But to hell with all that. At least he'd be able to spend a few precious days with his granddaughter, and besides, it would be a welcome break from rattling around in the flat on his own without Dottie.

Tess was holding up her glass of orange juice, and he obligingly clinked his beer mug against it. As he put his mug back down, the table produced its customary wobble. This time, however, he didn't even notice.

6

I'd no idea why a mortuary slab would need to have thick leather straps attached to it, but there I was, pinned flat on my back and barely able to move a muscle. Maybe it was in case they ever got a stiff that wasn't quite stiff after all and the straps were to stop it sitting bolt upright all of a sudden and scaring the crap out of whoever happened to be down here. I'd read about that kind of thing happening sometimes, and it made my flesh creep just thinking about it. Imagine that, eh? Six feet under and waking up inside a wooden box. Jesus.

As well as the straps being so tight they were almost cutting off the circulation to my hands and feet, I was also freezing my arse off. Strictly speaking, though, my arse was a degree or two less frozen than the rest of me on account of being stark naked except for my modesty-preserving Calvin Kleins. If it hadn't been for the thin white towel beneath me, the cold would probably have welded my skin to the stainless steel surface of the slab, and I'd have died of hypothermia within minutes. Still, I suppose I couldn't have been in a better place if the Grim Reaper *had* happened to come calling.

Then there was the appalling stink. It was playing havoc with my osmophobia, so my head was pounding like a bastard, but I couldn't properly identify what it was. The general stench of death perhaps? Not rotting corpses as such. It was too bloody cold in here for that, and from what Danny had told me, they had this dirty great fridge where they kept the less recently croaked. No, it was more sort of "chemically". Definitely more than a whiff of formaldehyde in amongst it, and the only reason I knew that was because it reminded me of our old school biology lab. Reeked of the stuff, it did, what with all the jars of dead frogs and what looked a lot like human foetuses the biology teacher insisted on having on display around the place. No coincidence he got the nickname Frankenstein. That was probably about the first time I discovered I'd got this osmophobia thing, so I jacked biology as soon as I could and did German instead. Dull but with a far more pleasant aroma. Danny had loved his double biology lessons, though, and hadn't given a toss about the stink. Put a dead animal in front of him and a scalpel in his hand and he'd be happy as Larry for hours. Maybe that's when he'd first decided to go into the dead body business as a career.

I swivelled my head to the left – about the only part of me that I could move with any degree of freedom – and checked out the other three slabs. Well, not so much slabs really but more like body-sized, stainless steel tables with raised edges and mounted on wheels. Pretty much the same as the one I was on, in fact, but with one significant difference. The two tables nearest me were empty, and as far as I could see, totally strapless. I couldn't tell whether the one at the far end had straps or not because there was a body on it and a woman in a white lab coat was obscuring most of my view. She had her back to me and was bending over the corpse, doing God knows what to it.

'Your one got straps on it?' I said, but she either didn't hear me or chose to ignore me, so I tried again, a bit louder.

This time, I got a snappy 'What?' in response but still the same view of the back of the lab coat and the glimpse of dyed blonde hair above it.

'I was just wondering how come this table I'm on has got straps and the others don't.'

'Ask Danny. I'm busy.'

I obviously wasn't going to get any further striking up a conversation with her than I would have done with the stiff she was messing about with. Instead, I was left to contemplate my immediate future with only the voice in my head for company, constantly bleating on about how I wouldn't be in this mess at all if I'd heeded its warnings in the first place.

Danny had made it abundantly clear when he'd brought me down here to the basement that it wasn't part of some guided tour and that there'd be a certain amount of unpleasantness involved. Predictably, there'd been the standard guff that I'd heard in every Guy Ritchie movie I'd ever seen about having to set an example and not letting anyone think he was a soft touch, blah, blah, blah. But as to the precise details of the example-setting, he'd been disturbingly vague.

Not that I'd have to wait too much longer to find out, judging by the clip-clopping of footsteps echoing down the steps and then a cheery 'Sorry to keep you waiting, Max. Needs must, as they say.'

'That's all right, Danny,' I said, not doing too bad a job of matching his cheery tone. 'I'm not in any hurry.'

Danny's chuckle was as unconvincing as a sitcom laughter track. 'Glad to know your sense of humour hasn't deserted you despite the... difficulty of the circumstances.'

Looking up at Danny's mug looming over me as I lay flat on my back was becoming a habit, and a habit that I'd have little problem in kicking as soon as I got the opportunity. There was definitely an argument in favour of getting this over and done with, but then again, I'd always been a great one for procrastination whenever pain is on the agenda.

'About these straps,' I said.

'A little tight, are they?'

'A bit on the snug side, yes, but I was just wondering why this is the only table that's got 'em.'

'Because this is my *special* table. Surely you don't think you're the first transgressor that I've had to... reprimand, do you? Only a couple of weeks ago I had Fancyboy Flannagan laid out exactly where you are now and, oh my word, you should have heard the screams. You see, what I did was I—'

'Yeah, thanks, Danny. I think you can spare me the details.'

'As you wish, dear boy. As you wish.'

I was beginning to feel distinctly queasy now and was starting to sweat from every pore despite the icebox-like temperature. Doing deals with God was hardly my style, partly because it was unlikely that anybody'd be listening and partly because I knew I'd never stick to my side of the bargain. All the same, I figured it would at least be worth a shot, but before I could get any further with my silent prayer than "Listen, God, I know I'm not your favourite person", there was a loud rattling sound. Metal on metal, and it was getting closer.

I twisted my head to the right to see where the noise was coming from. Sanjeev was wheeling a stainless steel trolley towards me, and he brought it to a halt next to the slab. The top tier was cluttered with a whole range of evil-looking shit. Knives of every type and size gleamed under the harsh glare of the strip-lights, and mingled in amongst them were a couple of pairs of pliers, a few different kinds of saw, a monkey wrench and a variety of other items that didn't look like they belonged in your average mortuary toolkit.

'Fuck's sake, Danny. You're not gonna use all of them, are you?'

'I'm not a sadist, you know,' he said with a smirk that had more than a hint of the sadistic to it. 'I merely asked Sanjeev to bring me a selection so I could choose something which would have the maximum deterrent effect whilst causing you the minimum amount of pain.'

'Thoughtful.'

'Max, my friend, if it wasn't for the fact that we've known each other since we were knee-high to a grasshopper, your fingernails would be all over this floor by now.'

I didn't doubt it, but whichever implement he decided to use, the "minimum amount of pain" was still probably going to be a lot more than I could handle. I wasn't going to beg, but...

'Look, Danny,' I said, squinting up at him against the glare of the strip-light directly above his head. 'I'd pay you if I could. You know that. But like I told you a fortnight ago when you had me banged up in that coffin, I'm totally and utterly skint.'

'And as I recall, that was why I gave you another two weeks to come up with the rest of the money you owe me.'

'So where was I supposed to find ten grand in two weeks?'

'Rob another bank perhaps?'

'Oh, come on, Danny. You know as well as I do that these things take more than a couple of weeks to put together.'

'And, I might add, a certain degree of competence.'

Danny's less than subtle gibe about my abilities as a bank robber was harsh but fair. Apart from the most recent catastrophe, Scratch, Alan and I had only managed to pull off two other jobs in the ten months since I'd been sacked, and neither had been a spectacular success.

I hadn't switched from bank manager to bank robber overnight, of course, but there weren't a whole lot of opportunities open to me. Without a reference, the best I was likely to get was some shit-paid job as a barman or cleaner or somesuch, and that wasn't going to bring in anything close to the income I needed. Not only that, but Carla would want to know why my working hours had suddenly changed and why I stank of stale beer or bleach every time I got home.

It was Alan who'd first come up with the idea of robbing banks as we'd sat in the pub one Friday evening like he, Scratch and I had done almost every week for more years than I care to remember. We'd had a few by then, so Scratch and I thought he was having a laugh.

'No, I'm serious,' he'd said. 'There's me and

Scratch scraping along on the dole and you tearing your hair out about how you're ever gonna make ends meet. And you know what the real clincher is?' He'd paused for effect, knowing full well that he wasn't going to get an answer. Then he'd planted a hand on my shoulder, and his voice dropped to not much above a whisper. 'Inside knowledge. That's what we've got, my friends. Inside fucking knowledge.'

I obviously knew what he was getting at but he was way off the mark.

'Alan, mate,' I'd said. 'There's a big bloody difference between knowing how to *run* a bank and how to rob one.'

'So how come you got the sack then?'

'That's hardly the same thing as bursting into a bank wearing a ski mask and waving a gun about, shouting "Hand over the money and nobody gets hurt".'

Alan had drained his pint, smacked his lips and wiped the back of his hand across his mouth. 'All I'm saying is give it some thought. Makes perfect sense to me – unless of course you both want to carry on like paupers for the rest of your natural. Your round, innit, Scratch?'

Not much else was said on the subject after that, but a couple of weeks later the bills had started stacking up at such a rate that I was getting desperate.

'You know that idea you had about the bank thing, Alan,' I'd said as we'd settled down at our usual table at the back of the pub.

And that's how it all began, although with much more of a whimper than a bang.

The first attempt had yielded precisely zilch.

We'd picked out one of the smaller, less popular

banks and then waited till there was no more than a couple of customers inside. Balaclavas on, Alan and I marched up to the counter while Scratch kept watch at the door. There were two tellers on duty – a young guy and a middle-aged woman – so Alan and I picked one each and held up our identical cards to the glass: "KEEP YOUR HANDS WHERE I CAN SEE THEM. SET OFF AN ALARM AND YOU'RE DEAD". The young guy in front of me read the card like it was the most normal thing in the world, and I was just about to flip it over to show him the bit about handing over the money when he said, 'So if I set off an alarm, you're going to kill me, yeah?'

It wasn't the reaction I'd expected, especially as I knew that most banks instructed all their employees to comply with any and all demands in the event of a robbery because they didn't want any dead heroes on their hands. But as it had been a crucial part of our plan that none of us should speak a single word once we were inside the bank, all I could do was nod back at him.

'And what are you going to kill me *with*?' he said.

Even though the question couldn't have been any less ambiguous, I raised an eyebrow to indicate that I hadn't understood, but then realised the eyebrow would have been hidden under the balaclava.

So, unaware that I'd made any response at all, the guy apparently decided that I needed a little more detail. 'You got a gun or something?'

I nodded again and patted the bulge in the pocket of the long dark overcoat I was wearing.

'OK, show me.'

'What?'

Shit, as if this hadn't been going badly enough

already, I'd now gone and broken the vow of silence. And what was I supposed to do? Reach into my pocket and threaten him with a fucking aubergine?

In desperation, I glanced across at Alan to see how he was getting on. – A lot better than I was by the look of things because his teller had her cash drawer open and was starting to pull out bundles of notes.

'I think you can put that away again now, Margaret.'

The woman's hands froze, and she turned towards her younger colleague. The little prick's face was a picture of smug self-satisfaction that was begging to be slapped.

'Have a nice day,' he said with a treacle-oozing smile, and that's when the alarm kicked off.

Fortunately, our escape had been meticulously planned and, unlike the robbery itself, was entirely free of unwelcome surprises.

After that, it had taken several weeks before Alan, Scratch and I could summon up the bottle to even *think* of giving it another go and another month or so to scour half the country for a bank that was likely to be a much softer target than the last one. In particular, we were on the lookout for another backwater branch that was especially quiet at certain times and days of the week. Above all, though, it had to be a bank with no more than two tellers, both of whom had to be as close to pension age as possible. That way, with retirement and a cushy pension just around the corner, there was very little likelihood that they'd have the slightest interest in taking their chances at becoming have-a-go heroes.

And we were right. Everything went off exactly as we'd planned, and the guns had stayed firmly in our pockets from start to finish. That was the added extra this time. No fruit and veg, but proper weapons. None of us had been at all keen on the idea, but there was no way we were ever going to get caught out again with nothing more than an aubergine to back up our death threats. But to make sure there weren't any accidents, all of the guns were loaded with blanks.

OK, so it hadn't been what you might call the haul of the century, but after we'd shared out the loot, I'd had enough to pay off all of my outstanding bills and most of what Carla had run up since I'd been fired from the bank. Most, but not all, because I'd also had to pay Danny half of the sixteen grand I owed him to keep him off my back for a while longer. The remaining unpaid half, of course – plus the extra two grand he'd lent me to fund our most recent job – was why I was now strapped to a mortuary slab in Danny's basement and not having the faintest idea what he was on about when he asked me if I played any musical instruments.

'What?'

'Don't worry. I'm not going to go mad,' said Danny, picking up some kind of surgical secateurs from the trolley. 'Just one of the little pinkies perhaps. Or maybe both. And if I pack them in ice afterwards and you get yourself to the hospital quick enough, they might even be able to sew them back on for you.'

He ran his thumb over the blade of the secateurs' cutting edge, and apparently satisfied of its sharpness, told Sanjeev to grab hold of my wrist and keep it steady.

'Which one?' Sanjeev asked.

'Doesn't matter. We'll be doing both anyway.'

Sanjeev stepped forward and took a firm grip of my

left wrist, which was strapped tight against my hip, but I could still clench my fists, so that's what I did.

'Oh, come on, Max,' Danny sighed. 'Let's not make this any more difficult than it already is. After all, there *are* other appendages I could remove that you wouldn't be able to hide from me.'

I let Sanjeev prise open my fingers and closed my eyes as tight shut as they'd go. There was no point putting it off any longer. Prolonging the agony? That part hadn't even started.

A whiff of Danny's hot, whiskey breath as he bends over me. The touch of the secateur blades at the base of my little finger. Teeth clenched. Body so rigid, my back arches a couple of inches up off the slab. Hail Mary, mother of— Shit, I'm not even Catholic, but any port in a—

'Boss?'

'What?'

All of a sudden, my finger is released from the grip of the secateurs.

'Is this one supposed to be open or closed casket?'

Even from the few words I'd heard her speak earlier, I recognise the voice, and I peel open one eyelid after another. Danny's standing upright, secateurs in hand, looking off to my left. I follow his gaze and see the lab-coat woman's face for the first time. Mid twenties, and although she's still over by the stiff she's been working on, she's near enough for me to make out the excessive facial piercings and the gum chewing.

'Open,' says Danny.

'You're kidding, right?' says the woman, taking the gum from her mouth and slapping it onto the underside of her slab.

'It's not something I'd generally joke about, Alice, no.'

Alice thumbs back over her shoulder towards the corpse. 'It's only that this one looks like a grand piano landed on her.'

'*Baby* grand, actually.'

'Eh?'

'Just get on with it, will you? I've got my own business to attend to.'

Alice shoves a fresh piece of gum into her gob and turns her back, muttering something inaudible.

Baby grand piano? Either this was a freak coincidence or death by piano is a lot more common than I'd have expected.

'Now then. Where were we?' says Danny with a fat, cheesy grin.

'As I recall, you were about to undo these straps while Sanjeev here went and fetched me a nice cup of tea.'

The cheesy grin fades instantly. 'Always the joker, eh, Max? Always the joker.'

Once again, he leans forward and takes aim with the secateurs.

'I don't suppose you've got any anaesthetic, have you?' I say, but Danny's starting to get pissy.

'Max, this is a mortuary. Not Saint Thomas's fucking Hospital. Now hold still and let's get this done, shall we?'

7

The Acropolis Restaurant on Tower Street was only about half full and not nearly as busy as it should have been for this time on a Friday night. Not that Dimitri cared one bit. The fewer customers there were, the fewer the orders he had to take and the less often he had to scurry back and forth with overloaded trays of food and drink. As long as Uncle Nikos paid him at the end of each week and the business didn't go totally bust, who cared whether the place was half full or crammed to the rafters? Of course, if the restaurant did have to close, it would be difficult to find another job, but that would hardly matter as long as his plan worked out. That, however, depended entirely on being able to convince Uncle Nikos to play his part.

As always when the restaurant was open, Nikos was sitting at his usual table in the corner, stuffing his face with yet another plateful of whatever he'd summoned from the kitchen. Dimitri took a deep breath and set off towards him, threading his way through the intervening tables and ignoring one of the punters who had his hand raised and spoke the words "Excuse me,

waiter" like it was an apology. Too bloody polite for
their own good, these English, thought Dimitri and
then went back to rehearsing what he was going to say
to his uncle. He'd been putting this moment off for
days now, but the fat pig had seemed to be in a
slightly better mood than normal that evening, so he'd
decided to take advantage of the opportunity while it
lasted.

Nikos's face was barely six inches above his plate,
and he was forking spaghetti into his mouth with such
speed that it was as if he was afraid someone was
about to steal it from him.

'You got a minute, Uncle Niko?' said Dimitri,
directing his question at the wispy black comb-over on
the top of the man's head.

Nikos looked up, a forkful of spaghetti halfway to
his mouth and several half-eaten strands of it dangling
from beneath his thick, droopy moustache.

'Whassup?' he said. 'You got no work to do?'

'I'm on my break.'

Nikos grunted his disapproval and sent the forkful
of spaghetti on the rest of its journey down into his
massive gut. Plenty of doctors had warned him of the
likely consequences of his obesity, particularly after
his heart bypass a couple of years ago, but he'd simply
told them to piss off and mind their own business. But
even more than the great rolls of fat that blubbered
over the top of his long since invisible waistband, it
was the constant sweating that Dimitri found most
repulsive. Whatever the temperature, he always looked
like he'd just stepped fully clothed out of the shower
with his customary open-necked shirt more grey than
white with the damp.

'I just need to... ask your advice about something,'

Dimitri faltered.

This time, Nikos didn't bother to suspend his eating, but wafted a podgy, heavily ringed hand in the general direction of the chair opposite him and, through a mouthful of food, told his nephew to 'Sit then, for Christ's sake. You're putting me off my *makarónia*.'

Dimitri sat, uncertain whether this meant that he was supposed to stay silent until Nikos had finished his meal.

Apparently not, because a few seconds later, his uncle glanced up at him and said, 'Speak then. I don't got all frickin' day.'

Dimitri cleared his throat. 'The point is, I've been seeing this woman and—'

'Yeah, woman trouble. I shoulda guessed.'

'Not exactly woman trouble, no, but I—'

'Whassa matter? Can't get it up?'

Says the fat fuck who hasn't seen his own dick in years, thought Dimitri, but he bristled nevertheless.

'Hell, no,' he said. 'No problems in that area. No problems at all.'

'Good to hear it,' said Nikos, swallowing the last of his spaghetti. 'Most of the family was thinking you was *poústis*.'

'What?' Dimitri felt his cheeks flush with rage. 'That's bullshit. I've had more women than—'

He broke off at Nikos's guffaw of laughter. '*Káno pláka*. I joking with you. Everybody know what a stud you are.'

'Yeah, well...'

The heat in Dimitri's cheeks began to cool, and he fiddled with the salt and pepper set on the table in front of him to avoid the sight of Uncle Nikos holding his empty plate up to his face and licking it clean.

'So, you gonna tell me 'bout this woman or what?' said Nikos, putting his plate down and setting about his front teeth with a wooden toothpick.

'She's a bit older than me. Not much. Just a bit. And she's not bad looking. Nice tits, you know?'

Nikos nodded his approval and made the predictable gesture with his cupped hands in front of his own breasts, which were far larger than most women's that Dimitri had ever seen.

'Anyway,' he continued, 'I've been thinking of getting her to marry me, but there's a—'

Nikos almost swallowed his toothpick. 'Married? You?'

'What's wrong with that?'

'She Greek?'

'English.'

'And how old, you say?'

Dimitri shrugged. 'Forty-two? Forty-three?'

'Christ, boy. You outta your frickin' mind? She old enough to be your mother. Why you not find someone your own age? You such a stud like you say, you could have your pick and choose.'

'Chicks my age don't have no dough, and I don't actually *want* to marry her, but er… if things kind of… work out, sort of thing, she's gonna come into quite a lot of money.'

Nikos stared at his nephew for several seconds until the severity of his expression gradually transformed itself into a wry smile of understanding.

'Ah, so now Uncle Nikos sees your little game. Maybe you not as stupid as you look.'

'Thank you,' said Dimitri, realising a fraction of a second too late that this wasn't much of a compliment, but his mind was otherwise engaged with a far more important matter. How best to phrase the next part of what he had to say. The part that was almost guaranteed to wipe the grin off his uncle's fat, sweaty chops.

Nikos poured himself a glass of red wine from an almost empty half-litre carafe and drained it in one.

'So,' he said, dabbing at his moustache with a paper napkin, 'what is this advice you want from me?'

'Well, there's a bit of a problem, you see. About us getting married, I mean.'

Nikos arched an eyebrow, his grin already beginning to fade.

'She's, er... She's kind of already married to someone else.'

'"Kind of"? What you mean "kind of"? Either she's frickin' married or she's not.'

'She's married, yes. Definitely married.'

'Holy mother of God, boy,' said Nikos, slamming both of his meaty fists down onto the table so hard that everything on it leapt an inch into the air. 'You *are* as stupid as you look.'

'No, but here's the thing. She can't stand the sight of him. Her husband, yeah? He's a bank manager or something. Boring as shit, you know? But she doesn't want to get a divorce because the silly bitch signed some sort of agreement, so everything's in *his* name. You want me to marry a pauper?'

'A what?'

'Er... someone with no money.'

'You frickin' idiot, I no want you to marry this woman even if she richest woman in world. Your mother know 'bout this bullshit? She go crazy if she knew.'

'No, but—'

'Anyways, if she no get a divorce, how the hell you gonna marry her?'

Dimitri began to fiddle with the salt and pepper pots again as he struggled to find the right words. 'Well, er... that's the thing I wanted to ask you about. You know, if there was any way you might be able to, er...'

Unable to finish the sentence, he looked up and met his uncle's eyes. They were blazing with fury, making it abundantly clear that he'd understood perfectly what Dimitri was getting at and also how he felt about the idea.

'You saying you want me to get rid of the husband? Is that it?'

'Well, it's not as if you haven't—'

'That's different. That's a business thing. This kinda bullshit? Frickin' insane.'

'I don't see why it's so—'

'Enough!' yelled Nikos, mopping some of the excess sweat from his brow with a fresh paper napkin. 'I no wanna hear another word. So piss off and get back to your work.'

Dimitri caught the sodden napkin one-handed and, mercifully, avoided it hitting him full in the face. He eased back his chair and slowly got to his feet. 'But you'll give it some thought, yeah?'

This time, only one of Nikos's fists hammered down onto the tabletop. 'No, I won't give it some frickin' thought. Now get your arse back in that kitchen and fetch me some baklava. In fact, get one of the others to bring it. I no wanna see your stupid face no more for rest of the day.'

As soon as Dimitri turned and began to slouch his way between the tables, he became aware that the entire restaurant was utterly silent apart from the piped bouzouki music. Every diner was sitting with knives and forks raised in a state of suspended animation and gazing up at him as he passed or glancing furtively in the direction of Uncle Nikos.

Uncle Nikos, however, was totally oblivious to their attentions, busy as he was with attempting to extricate a particularly stubborn piece of meat with his toothpick as he muttered, 'Who he think I am? Al frickin' Capone?'

8

'Of course,' said Danny, 'there might be a way of avoiding all this... unpleasantness.' I popped open one eye. Danny was standing upright, having once again released my left-hand pinkie from the grip of the secateurs. 'A way you could pay me what you owe me *and* keep all your fingers.'

This sounded interesting enough to pop open the other eye, but Danny gave a slight shake of his head and drew air in through his teeth.

'No, no, that wouldn't work,' he said. 'I remember now that you've got... scruples about that kind of thing. What on earth was I thinking?'

Scruples be damned, I thought, as he leaned forward again with the secateurs.

'What kind of thing?' I said with a vain attempt to minimise the eagerness in my voice.

'Oh, only a little job that I— No, I'm sorry, Max. I shouldn't even have mentioned it. I have far too much respect for your moral principles.'

'Bollocks to moral principles,' I said without the slightest attempt to disguise my eagerness. 'What sort of "little job" are you talking about?'

The pause that followed and the furrowed brow were presumably supposed to convey that Danny was giving serious consideration to whether he should tell me or not. Far more likely, though, was that he was toying with me and loving every moment of it.

'As you know,' he said at last, 'I sometimes have occasion to dabble in the pharmaceutical trade.'

'Peddle dope, you mean.'

'A rose by any other name, Max. A rose by any other name.'

Danny had been dealing for years, and not just as a "little sideline" as he liked to put it. He was into it big time and at the heavier end of the market too. He'd even tried to get me involved when he'd first started, but I'd turned him down flat. I'm no saint by any stretch of the imagination, but when you're twelve years old and watched your older brother almost croak from an overdose of smack, you tend to take a rather different view of the whole druggie scene.

Still, desperate times call for desperate measures. And besides, I could always say no if I didn't like the sound of what he had in mind.

'So, what is it you'd want me to do?' I said, silently promising myself that there was no way I was going to do anything that involved swallowing a load of condoms or shoving anything up my arse.

'Very well then,' said Danny after a much shorter pause than the last one. 'There happens to be a certain erstwhile business associate of mine by the name of Nikos Spiropoulos who – for reasons you don't need to know – has decided to curtail our previously fruitful commercial arrangement.'

'In English?'

'Fucker says he's not going to buy from me any more, which is somewhat of a shame as I shall soon be taking delivery of some particularly fine cocaine. And although I already have buyers for most of the consignment, I still have a couple of kilos I need to find a home for. Prior to our recent little... contretemps, Nick the Greek would have bitten my hand off, but now alas...'

He let the sentence hang, but I was still none the wiser where I came into the picture. 'So what is it you want me to do about it?'

'Sell him the charlie without him knowing it came from me. Simple really.'

Simple? Jesus Christ alive. Even if I could swallow my principles for a couple of hours or whatever it took, this was some heavy duty shit I'd be getting myself into. Two kilos of coke was some pretty big league stuff, and I knew full well what some of these people would do to you if they found out you'd put one over on them. Never mind losing a couple of pinkies, those sort of scumbags wouldn't blink at taking the whole fucking arm – and that's if they were feeling charitable.

'But no,' said Danny. 'I can see that you find the very notion of it utterly repugnant. Forget I even mentioned it.'

For the umpteenth time, I felt the touch of the secateurs' blades against the base of my little finger, and once again my eyes reacted instinctively and screwed themselves shut. Apparently, there were no more "Get Out Of Jail Free" cards left in the pack.

9

Fur coat and no knickers. That's what my dad would have said about us if he'd still been alive, and it was a phrase that often sprang to mind whenever I walked up the driveway to our detached, four-bedroomed piece of suburbia. Neatly mown lawns on either side with well stocked and weed-free flower beds – all courtesy of the gardener we couldn't afford but Carla insisted on "because we're not going to be the only ones in the avenue who do it all ourselves". On the plus side, though, it meant that I never had to lift a finger in the never-ending battle with Mother Nature.

Lift a finger? Considering what I'd just been through, the very thought made me wince. But so also did the almighty din and the meat-heavy cooking smells that greeted me as soon as I opened the front door. As always, the din was coming from two distinct sources. Blaring telly from the living room and shit-awful music – if you could call it music – booming out at eleven loud from upstairs.

No point calling out "I'm home" because (a) nobody would have heard me above the racket, and

(b) nobody would give a toss whether I was home or taking a long walk in the Hindu Kush. Except when I was late for meals, of course, and then Carla would definitely notice my arrival. Before I lost my job, I used to have to work late on a fairly regular basis, so nowadays I sometimes stayed out late deliberately to avoid suspicion.

I checked my watch and braced my eardrums for the anticipated barrage as I stepped into the kitchen.

Yet more evidence of the fur coat and no knickers variety. The room ran from the front of the house to the back with glass patio doors overlooking the absurdly large garden at the rear. And just this side of the glass, a ridiculously large dining table that must have left an unnecessarily big hole in the Amazon rainforest.

'What do we need a dining table that size for?' I'd asked Carla when I'd spotted the price tag in the furniture shop. 'Or are we going to use it as a helicopter landing pad?'

'It's for when we have dinner parties,' she'd said.

Dinner parties? That was a laugh. In the six or so years we'd had the damn thing, we'd had precisely two. And they were only at Christmas when Carla's family inflicted themselves on us. The only blessing was that Carla couldn't come out with the stereotypically ambitious wife thing and insist on me inviting the boss and his missus round for dinner. As far as she was concerned, I *was* the boss – at work anyway.

The whole dinner party justification was also the reason we had to have the top of the range of everything. And I mean *everything*. Plates, cutlery, pots, pans, right down to the silver bloody napkin rings. Every last item had been bought for the specific purpose of impressing our imaginary dinner guests.

In the middle of the kitchen area was one of those designer "island" things. A big rectangular block of cupboards with a dirty great slab of polished granite on the top. Carla had been determined to have one ever since she'd seen something similar on one of those desperately dull home makeover programmes on the telly.

'It'll give us extra storage and work surface space,' she'd said, 'and we can also use it for mealtimes when it's just the four of us.'

Yeah, right. On one of those rare occasions when we didn't have a shitload of dinner guests.

I loosened my tie and hung my suit jacket over the back of one of the four wooden bar stools at the island. Carla had her back to me, standing over the enormous gas cooker that would have made Heston Blumenthal's eyes bleed with envy. She was stirring something on the hob with one hand and glugging away at a glass of white wine with the other. A half empty bottle close by on the worktop. No point putting it back in the fridge. It wouldn't be there long enough to take the chill off.

Her blonde hair hung in loose ringlets down to her shoulders, whereas normally when she was cooking she had it scraped back so tight into a ponytail that it stretched her face into what looked like a permanent grin. And what were those thin strands of pinky red? As far as I could remember, they hadn't been there when I'd left this morning, so she'd presumably been to the hairdresser's again. More bloody expense.

She turned to the wine bottle for a refill, and as she did so, clocked me out of the corner of her eye.

'Oh, hello, darling,' she said, all smiles. 'I didn't hear you come in over all the din.'

Darling? *Darling*? How much had she had to drink? Or was it something else? Something crazy expensive that she'd ordered and couldn't possibly live without? Or no, hang on a sec. She'd got the blue eye shadow on and the pale red lippy. That was it. She'd been shagging again. The cheery "hello, darling" and the makeup were always a dead giveaway. She might as well have worn a T-shirt that said: "Yes, I've been with my lover again, and we've been screwing each other's brains out all afternoon".

I'd no idea who the unlucky bastard was – or maybe there was more than one unlucky bastard – and I really didn't care. If it meant she was getting her oats elsewhere, that was absolutely fine by me. Like with the gardening, that was me off the hook in the conjugal duties department for the foreseeable future. Another plus was that I got a brief respite from the usual moaning and complaining – at least till her afterglow had begun to wear off.

'Beer?' she said, handing me an opened bottle of Fuller's London Pride and a glass.

Christ, she must have been on a right shag-fest.

She watched as I poured the beer. 'Dinner's ready when you are. It was actually ready an hour ago, but I think it'll still be OK.'

So, none of the expected "Where the hell have you been? Dinner's ruined" then.

I decided to make the most of the truce while it lasted. 'Yeah, sorry about that. I was a bit tied up... at the bank.'

'Oh well, never mind. You're home now.'

'Yeah.'

'Still, I'd better keep an eye on the food. It's your favourite.'

Favourite? I wasn't even aware I had a favourite.

Carla was about to head back to the cooker when she seemed to spot something behind me, and the sickly have-a-nice-day smile vanished in an instant. 'You're not going to leave that there, are you?'

I glanced over my shoulder but couldn't see anything out of the ordinary. 'Leave what where?'

'That,' she said, pointing to the back of my stool as if a giant turd had suddenly appeared over the waistband of my trousers.

'My jacket?'

'Your jacket.'

'But I always hang my jacket on the—'

'And I'm always having to take them to the dry cleaner's every time you splatter food all over them.'

So that was it, was it? The shortest ceasefire in the field of modern warfare.

Wait a minute, though. The smile was forcing itself back like a slow-spreading rash.

'Why don't you hang it on the rack in the hallway, eh?' she said. 'And while you're there, give Emma a shout, will you? Tell her dinner's on the table.'

Out in the hallway, I was about to hang the jacket on the coat rack by the front door but changed my mind. Overcome by an urge to commit a childishly pointless act of rebellion, I draped it roughly over the banister rail at the foot of the stairs.

Equally pointless was my first attempt to make myself heard over the ear-shattering decibels coming from my daughter's room to tell her that dinner was ready. As expected, there was no response, which could have meant she hadn't heard *me* or I hadn't

65

heard *her* – if in fact she'd bothered to answer at all.

With two teenage kids in the house, I knew all about selective hearing and curled lips, and the pair of them were only marginally better with Carla. I sometimes wondered if I'd get a bit more respect from them if they knew what I really did now and that I wasn't just Boring Old Bank Manager Dad any more. But it wasn't something I was going to put to the test any time soon.

I climbed three of the stairs and waited for a pause in the so-called music. Fortunately, I didn't have to suffer for very long.

'Emma?' I yelled. 'Dinner's on the table.'

No response.

'Emma!'

The "ma" part was drowned out by the next track on her playlist-from-hell kicking off, and it suddenly increased in volume to sonic boom proportions. Wonder of wonders, she'd actually opened her bedroom door. I craned my neck, but her room was too far along the landing for me to see her.

'What?'

I didn't need to see her. The scowl in her tone was perfectly clear.

'Food's ready.'

'Yeah, I heard you the first time.'

'And do you think you could turn down the—?'

To be fair, the volume did instantly drop back down to a little over eleven loud but only because Emma had slammed the door to her room.

I hovered for a few seconds to see if she'd make an appearance at the top of the stairs. She didn't. Oh well, I'd passed on the message, so that was job done as far as I was concerned.

Back in the kitchen, Carla was dishing up from a vast Le Creuset pan on the hob. Part of a set. "Flame orange" I think it was called.

'Is she coming then?' she said over her shoulder.

'Not sure, to be honest.'

'You did tell her, I suppose?'

'Uh-huh.'

I grabbed my beer and drained the glass.

'Give Brad a shout, will you?'

I contemplated saying something sarcastic about not being a messenger boy and why didn't we just buy a very loud dinner gong but decided it wasn't worth breaking the already fragile truce. In any case, Brad arrived at that very moment and saved me the bother of going to fetch him.

'All right, Dad?'

Christ alive. Three actual words. He hadn't been shagging as well, had he?

At the ripe old age of thirteen, he was two years younger than Emma so was still only a fledgling parent-hater. He was certainly working on it, though, but he was noticeably at his most polite when his frequently empty belly needed replenishing.

'Dinner ready yet? I'm starving.'

By way of response to Brad's question, Carla transferred three steaming plates of food onto the island unit. Spaghetti Bolognese. So that was my favourite, was it? News to me.

What wasn't news was that the portions varied considerably from plate to plate. By far the largest was Brad's and mine the smallest with Carla's somewhere in between. It was like an upside-down version of *Goldilocks and the Three Bears* with me as Baby Bear. Another of Carla's little digs about my waistline.

Brad grabbed his plate and set off back to the living room. Not surprisingly, there was still no sign of Emma, so Carla and I sat opposite each other and began to eat.

'By the way,' she said after several seconds of silence, and I could tell immediately that all the smiles and the hello darlings weren't just about the shagging. 'Melanie rang.'

Here we go. Carla's older and only slightly more bearable sister.

'Oh?' I said.

'Toby has to do some work experience thing for school.'

'Oh?'

'I told her you'd take him on.'

I dropped my knife and fork and stared at her. 'Take him on?'

'At the bank.'

Oh, Jesus, tell me this isn't really happening.

'Listen, Carla, I'd like to help of course, but I can't just—'

'Can't what?'

'I'd need to check if it'd be OK for one thing.'

'Check with who? You're the manager, aren't you?'

'Yes, I know, but—'

'Anyway, there's no time for that now. He's meeting you at the station on Monday morning.'

Holy shit. Now what? If Toby found out I wasn't a bank manager at all – as he surely would – he was bound to blab to his mum, and she'd be straight on the phone to Carla. Maybe I could bribe him to keep his mouth shut. Kids of his age would do pretty much anything for a few quid. But I couldn't just let him tag along either. I had stuff to do that he really shouldn't know about. Maybe I could bung him a bit extra to take himself off for a few hours a day for however long this work experience thing was supposed to last.

'What's the matter with your hands?'

I was so caught up in trying to think of a way out of the impending disaster that I barely registered Carla's question. 'Uh?'

'Every time I look at you, you're staring at your hands. Like you're counting your fingers or something.'

I was only vaguely aware I'd been doing it – repeatedly checking to reassure myself that all ten were still there. Amazing the little things you learn to appreciate when you've almost lost them.

10

It's hardly the world's best kept secret, of course, but the vast majority of people in the so-called "civilised" world hate, loathe and despise Monday mornings with a vengeance. The Boomtown Rats even did a song about it. In my line of business, though, the days of the week didn't make a blind bit of difference, except on this particular Monday morning.

There I was, trudging towards the railway station amongst a gaggle of pasty-faced, besuited commuters – both men and women – every single one of them looking like they'd lost a shilling and found sixpence, as my dad would have put it. I was no exception, and like many of the other commuters, I was suitably accessorised with briefcase, brolly and copy of *The Times* tucked under my arm. Today they were going to be needed. Unlike my fellow lambs to the slaughter, however, my own brand of dread had nothing to do with the soul crushing expectation of yet another mind-numbingly tedious week at "the office". Mine was a rapidly mounting anxiety – almost to the point of a panic attack – over what the fuck I was going to do about Toby. I'd already dispensed with the idea of trying to bribe him as this would have involved telling him at least part of the truth about my real occupation, and I couldn't be certain that he'd keep his trap shut anyway. Besides, there was no guarantee that he wouldn't branch out into full-scale blackmail and bleed me dry for the rest of my life.

By the time I spotted him sitting alone on a bench in front of the station, I'd decided on a strategy that had always served me well in the past. Procrastinate like crazy until something like a workable solution presented itself. Well, maybe it hadn't *always* done the trick, but I wasn't exactly flush with alternatives right now.

'Hi, Uncle Simon. All right?'

Two seconds in, and there was the first of my problems. A simple enough question, sure, but if I was going to have Toby clinging on to my coat tails over the next few days, we were bound to bump into somebody who'd call me Max, and the kid would more than likely smell a rat straight off. To pretty much everybody in *my* world – the non-Carla, non-suburbia type world – I wasn't Simon, I was Max. Max Dempsey. Why? Because very early on, I decided that if I wanted to be taken seriously within the criminal fraternity, Simon Golightly just wasn't going to hack it.

Toby stood up. Sixteen years old and nearly as tall as me. Almost obligatory smattering of teenage zits. Blonde like his mum. More than a dab of gel.

'All right, Toby? How's things?'

'Yeah, cool, thanks.'

The flicker of an unconvincing smile clearly belied the fact that he felt anything but cool, and who could blame him? If I'd been his age and about to spend a week as an unpaid dogsbody in a bank of all places, I'd have hardly been thrilled to bits either.

I looked at my watch, having had the foresight to check out train times on the Internet the night before. 'OK, we'd better get a move on. Train leaves in ten minutes, and we need to get tickets first.'

'Don't you have a season ticket then?'

'A what?' I knew exactly what he was getting at, of course, but the little sod had already caught me out on my first mistake.

'Season ticket. You do this trip every day, don't you?'

'Every day, yeah. Bit of a rush this morning, though. Must have left it at home.'

It was about as believable as his "cool" remark, but it was the best I could come up with at short notice. Things were definitely not getting off to the greatest of starts, which is no doubt why the voice in my head seemed to think it was time to chip in with some advice on how to extricate myself from what was going to be a very tricky situation indeed.

'Just a little nudge in the back, that's all,' it said as Toby and I stood side by side on the edge of the platform. 'Couple of seconds before the train pulls in and Bob's your uncle. Or, to put it another way, the kid's no longer your nephew. Problem solved.'

'Are you *completely* out of your mind?' I didn't say out loud. 'You can't seriously be telling me to murder my own nephew.'

'Shit, man, everybody'll think it was just a tragic accident. Happens all the time.'

Desperate though I was, nephewcide – or whatever it's called – was never going to be an option, and when our train arrived, we climbed into the nearest carriage with both of us still possessed of life and limb.

This being a commuter train, the carriage was packed solid, and despite my attempts to engineer it otherwise, Toby and I ended up sitting opposite each other. The last thing I needed right now was to have to face a whole load of questions he might fire at me about the bank and what he'd be doing there. As it turned out, though, I needn't have worried, because we spent most of the twenty minute journey in almost total silence. No great surprise, I guess, since Toby was obviously as unenthusiastic about the day ahead as I was to have to try and answer questions about it. But just in case he got the urge, my copy of *The Times* came in very handy as a tabloid-sized Do Not Disturb sign.

* * *

'Well, what was I supposed to do? Shove him under a train?'

As prearranged when I'd found out I was being lumbered with my nephew for the week, I was sitting in a greasy spoon caff with Alan and Scratch facing me across a red Formica-topped table. I'd reckoned that three heads might be better than one when trying to come up with a solution to the Toby problem – even though the additional two heads happened to belong to Alan and Scratch.

To buy myself time to conduct this emergency meeting of the What The Fuck Do We Do? think-tank, I'd taken Toby to a random NatWest bank that was just around the corner from the caff and sat him down in the waiting area. I'd told him that I needed to nip straight out again to see an important customer about a loan and that I'd be back in about half an hour. The kid had seemed satisfied with that and had already got his head buried in his smartphone before I was out of the door.

'All I'm saying,' said Alan, 'is that there's no way we can take him along with us. Today of all days.'

'Christ, Alan, tell me something I *don't* know. I mean, that's the whole point of having this chat so you can help me sort something out.'

'Well, one thing's for sure,' said Scratch. 'You can't just leave him in the bank all day.'

I closed my eyes and counted to ten. This was fast becoming a case of a problem shared being a problem trebled. I'd known these two since as far back as when we'd all attended the same youth club, and neither of them was as thick as they often seemed to appear. On this occasion, however, they were excelling themselves with a perfect impersonation of two short planks.

'You could always try bribing him,' said Alan.

At last a sensible suggestion, but I shook my head. 'Thought of that already, but how can I know for sure that he won't go blabbing his mouth off?'

Alan shrugged. 'He's *your* nephew.'

'Yeah, but I don't really know him that well, and if he's inherited any of Carla's genes – especially the ones that have got anything to do with trust – then we'd be totally screwed.'

'No, I think *you'd* be totally screwed, Max. Not "we".'

I slumped back in my wobbly plastic chair and sighed. 'Oh, thanks for the support, *mate*. Always good to know you guys have got my back.'

'Hey, come on, Max. We're the three musketeers, right? Always have been and always will be. One for all and all for one. That kind of shit, yeah?'

Scratch's little speech was barely intelligible through the mouthful of whatever it was he was chomping on that he apparently wasn't allergic to, but I got the gist.

'Good to know,' I said without much conviction after Alan's remark, and I glanced up at the plastic clock on the grease encrusted wall. 'But we need to get this sorted fast. I've been gone half an hour already, and I told him I'd be back by now.'

* * *

Having utterly failed to come up with anything approaching a workable solution to the Toby problem, I plodded back round to the bank knowing that bribery was the only possible option. I'd just have to hope to Christ the kid had at least enough of a sense of honour about him that he didn't rat me out to his mum and Carla. All these months of leading my secret double life to have it pissed up against the wall by a zit-faced teenager? It was way too cruel to even contemplate.

I was still trying to decide what my opening offer would be when I turned the corner and spotted Toby leaning with his back against the wall outside the bank. Probably popped out for a crafty fag, I thought, but as I got closer, I could see that he was looking straight at me with an expression that I could only describe as a cross between a puzzled frown and a smug grin.

'All right, Toby?' I said when I came within

earshot. 'What's going on?'

There was a pause while he seemed to find something fascinating on the pavement between his feet. Then he slowly raised his head again and fixed his eyes on mine. 'Good question, Unc. But maybe it's one that you might want to answer first.'

'You what?'

Oh Jesus, don't tell me the kid had twigged something already.

'The thing is, Unc, I'd been sitting in the reception area for quite a while, and one of the tellers kept giving me the once-over. Then I saw her get on the phone, and the next minute, this oldish bloke in a suit comes over and asks me if I'm waiting for someone.

'"Yes," I said. "I'm waiting for my uncle."

'So the guy has a glance round the place and asks me if my uncle's a customer.

'"No," I said. "He's the manager."

'Then he gives me this very weird look and says, "I'm sorry, but there must be some mistake. You see, *I'm* the manager of this bank. Perhaps you've come to the wrong branch."

'"I can't have done," I said, "because he brought me here not half an hour ago. Maybe he's the assistant manager or deputy or something."

'So he asks me what your name is, I tell him it's Simon Golightly, and he shakes his head and tells me there's no-one of that name who works there at all. To be honest, Unc, it's all left me a little confused.'

11

In addition to having almost every allergy known to medical science, Scratch also has a phobia about anything to do with death and dying, and I had to almost drag him through the door when we got to Danny's funeral parlour.

There was no sign of Danny or Sanjeev, but a youngish woman was sitting this side of the reception desk on one of the two chairs provided for customers. Or was it "clients" Danny called them? She turned towards us at the "*bing bong*" sound of the door being opened, gave us a fleeting half-smile and went back to tapping out a text on a fairly ancient-looking mobile.

Not bad looking, I thought, based on the split second I'd had to check her out. Bit of makeup wouldn't have gone amiss, and the long dark hair could have done with a good brushing. Definitely not the type to spend a small fortune at the hairdresser's like some I could mention.

I scanned the rest of the shop, but instead of Danny or Sanjeev, there was just some old geezer with a walking stick hobbling around amongst the display coffins. Every so often, he'd stoop to get a better look at a particular box that seemed to take his fancy, and each time, the reaction was pretty much the same. At this distance, it was hard to tell if he actually tutted, but there was certainly a disapproving shake of the head. Presumably, he'd spotted the price.

'Sorry to keep you, madam.'

It was Sanjeev, making his appearance through the open doorway behind the desk, a buff-coloured pocket folder in one hand and a large transparent Ziploc bag in the other. Inside the bag was a simple-looking cremation urn like some kind of small trophy but in greeny beige china. Narrow at the base, it doubled in width to a kind of shoulder before narrowing again at the neck and was topped off with a dome-shaped lid.

Barely acknowledging our presence, Sanjeev set the urn down carefully on the desk and plonked himself down onto the big black swivel chair behind it. He took some papers out of the folder and sifted through them until he found the one he wanted.

'So, all I need from you now is your signature,' he said, sliding the piece of paper across the desk and leaning forward to point at the bottom of the page.

'Do you have a pen?' said the woman.

'Yes, of course,' said Sanjeev and rummaged around in one of the desk drawers before producing a cheap biro with a heavily chewed cap.

'Here we are,' he said, removing the cap and palming it.

The woman took the pen and skim-read the document.

Sanjeev gave a slight frown, then got up and came round to her side of the desk to peer over her shoulder. 'It's just to say that you've received the er...'

The woman signed and handed him back the pen.

'Nice tattoo,' he said.

The woman was wearing a brightly striped singlet, and Sanjeev was gawping at a small tattoo on her left shoulder. She half-heartedly turned her head as if to check what he was talking about.

'Horse, is it?' said Sanjeev.

'Dragon,' said the woman with a hint of a sigh as if she'd had to correct this mistake many times before.

'Oh, like in the—'

'Actually,' she said, scraping back her chair and getting to her feet, 'I had it done probably before the book was even written.'

Sanjeev opened his mouth to speak but clearly had no idea how to respond.

'We done yet, Tess?'

Saved by the old geezer with the walking stick, who'd presumably grown tired of tutting at the prices of the display coffins.

'I think so,' said the woman – Tess, apparently – and looked to Sanjeev for confirmation.

'Yes indeed,' he said with an obsequious smile. 'Unless of course there's anything else I can help you with?'

'Not quite yet, thanks, son. I dare say my granddaughter will let you know when the time comes.'

'Well, sir, I'm sure we can—'

'That her then, is it?' the old man interrupted, pointing at the cremation urn on the desk with the tip of his walking stick.

'Grandma Dottie,' said Tess and picked up the urn.

Her granddad grunted. 'Not much to show after nearly eighty years, is it?'

Tess smiled at him and took him gently by the arm.

'Come on,' she said. 'We've got packing to do.'

Another grunt from the old man, and after his granddaughter exchanged the usual pleasantries with Sanjeev, the pair of them left the shop.

'Well, Sanjeev,' I said when I was sure they were out of earshot, 'I'd never have thought you had it in you.'

'What?'

'Flirting away like a good'un, wouldn't you say, Scratch?'

'Oh yeah,' said Scratch. 'Quite blatant, it was.'

'All that "nice tattoo" stuff. I reckon you could be in there, you know.'

'Don't be ridiculous,' said Sanjeev, all flustered and jaw muscles tensing as he went back to his side of the desk. 'Customer relations, that's all. Danny always says that—'

'And speaking of which,' I cut in, 'the boss off on a jolly somewhere, is he?'

'He's... attending to business elsewhere if you must know.'

Oops. Looks like the lad's got the hump. Better tone it down a bit, I guess.

'Fair enough,' I said, 'but we're supposed to be collecting a package.'

'Yes, I know,' said Sanjeev, softening a little. 'Hang on there, and I'll fetch it.'

'Thanks, pal.'

'Hurry it up, for God's sake,' Scratch muttered after Sanjeev had disappeared through the doorway behind the desk. 'This place gives me the willies.'

'You should see what they've got down in the basement,' I said. 'That's where all the stiffs are, and when they get a fresh one in, they—'

'Shut up, Max.'

I'd told Scratch and Alan all about my near-amputation ordeal in the mortuary, of course. I didn't really have a lot of choice, given that they knew all about my anti-drugs views and wanted to know why I'd changed my mind all of a sudden. Even then, they'd taken some convincing to get involved in Danny's "little job". Neither of them were any more keen on the whole druggie thing than I was. Alan had been no stranger to "performance enhancing" drugs back in his weightlifting days, and both of them had plenty of experience in getting out of their skulls on booze, but when it came to uppers, downers, Colombian marching powder and all that shit, it was a definite no-no.

What swung it in the end, though, was when I reminded them that the ten grand I owed Danny was as much down to them as me. The last bank job was supposed to have paid that off with a more than handsome profit for the three of us on top, but Alan had screwed that up big time. Dozy twat reckoned he'd got confused by the spiral staircase and ended up drilling into the wrong fucking wall.

'Here it is then,' said Sanjeev breezily as he came back in through the doorway and handed me a china cremation urn in a transparent Ziploc bag.

As far as I could tell, it was identical to the one he'd given the Tess woman and her granddad.

'What the fuck is this?' I said.

'A cremation urn?'

I could have slapped him for the obvious "duh" in his tone but managed to restrain myself. 'Yes, I know what it is. What I don't know is "why?".'

'The boss always uses them for this kind of... transaction. Says it's less conspicuous.'

'Oh yes, of course. I mean, what could be more normal than wandering around with somebody's fucking ashes tucked under your arm? And in any case, I thought the whole point of this deal was that the Greek guy doesn't suss that it's Danny's coke I'm selling him. You think somehow he might just smell a rat when I turn up with what is very obviously a bloody cremation urn?'

Sanjeev held up his palms in mock surrender. 'Hey, don't shoot me. I'm only the messenger.'

And speaking of messengers getting shot – or worse – we were already running late for our appointment with Nick "The Greek" Spiropoulos. This was because I'd had to spend the best part of an hour trying to dig myself out of a very big hole with nephew Toby. The months I'd managed to keep Carla in the dark, and this bloody kid had caught me out in a matter of minutes. The best I'd been able to come up with was a load of flannel about working for the government and it all being very hush-hush, etcetera, but it was totally unrehearsed with far too many ums, ers and general waffling to be in the least convincing, and Toby wasn't buying any of it. So the upshot was that I couldn't see any way out of the hole other than to come clean with him. Well, not completely, of course. There was plenty of detail that I left out, but the kid was sharp enough to figure out that most of what I did was not entirely legal.

Amazingly, all my attempts to bribe the little bugger fell on stony ground, even when I offered him two hundred quid to keep his mouth shut and spend the rest of the week hanging around in caffs or wherever till his work experience bullshit came to an end. When I'd been his age and somebody'd bunged me a couple of hundred quid to doss about for a week, I'd have bitten their bloody hand off. Christ, I'd've done it for a tenner. But, oh no, not our Toby.

'You know, Unc,' he'd said in a smarmy kind of voice like he was patronising *me*, 'on balance, I think it'd be a lot more fun to tag along with you for the rest of the week... If that's OK with you, that is.'

OK with me? Of course it wasn't OK with me, for fuck's sake, but the kid had me over a barrel, and he bloody knew it. So there I was, about to do a major coke deal with a bunch of Greek gangsters and with my sixteen-year-old nephew in tow.

Let joy be unconfined.

12

The Acropolis Restaurant wasn't open for business yet, so I rang the bell and waited, hoping to hell that nobody was going to frisk us on the way in. It was only on the rarest of occasions that any of us carried a gun – and hardly ever when they were loaded with live rounds – but it was a surefire bet that these guys would be tooled up, and I didn't want us to get caught with our pants down if things went pear-shaped.

The door was opened by a man in his early thirties who was a dead ringer for a moustacheless Freddie Mercury, and as it happened, he was far more interested in the flesh-coloured padded collar round Alan's neck than finding out if we were carrying any weapons.

'What's that?' he said, pointing at it.

'Neck brace,' said Alan. 'I've got a dodgy neck.'

The guy clicked his tongue and asked if we'd brought "the stuff". I held up the cremation urn – minus its Ziploc bag – and his brow furrowed. This was the first indication that bringing the coke in one of these things was a major mistake. Spiropoulos was bound to spot the connection with Danny Bishop, which wouldn't be the best of starts to the sales pitch. I'd briefly considered tipping the stuff into some other container, but we were already late for our appointment and I'd decided we'd just have to wing it.

'Follow me,' said Freddie. 'My father is waiting.'

Alan, Scratch and I trailed along behind him as he led the way through the empty restaurant to a dimly lit room at the back. A store-room-cum office, it was cluttered with surplus furniture from the restaurant, a few broken chairs, several towers of bottle crates and a whole load of cardboard boxes. At the far end of the room was a fire exit – a single metal door with a crash bar – which hopefully led out onto the alleyway at the back of the restaurant where we'd left the Beamer in the event that we might have to beat a hasty retreat. Toby had wanted to come with us, of course, but I'd managed to convince him that, this being a notoriously rough area, somebody needed to stay with the car to make sure it wasn't up on bricks by the time we came out.

Against the wall on our left, two metal filing cabinets and a large, free-standing safe. In front of these was an impressively big desk, the top mounted on a pair of drawer stacks. Behind it sat a seriously overweight man with a wispy black comb-over and a thick black moustache.

Standing at his shoulder was a guy of about the same age as the one who'd let us in, and a third man was about ten feet away, his elbow resting on one of the crate towers. All three of the younger men were well built and had remarkably similar dark features. Brothers probably.

I stepped forward and held out my hand to the

lardarse behind the desk, concentrating on keeping it as steady as I could.

'Mr Spiropoulos?' I said, forcing a smile.

The fat man gave me a barely perceptible nod but didn't smile back. Nor did he show any sign of wanting to shake my hand, so I withdrew it and surreptitiously wiped the sweating palm on my trousers. Sweat? Huh, that was nothing compared to the torrents that were pouring down Nick the Greek's bloated cheeks.

'Well?' he said, drumming his sausage fingers on the desktop. 'You got it or not?'

'Certainly,' I said and placed the cremation urn on the desk.

He leaned forward to inspect it more closely. 'What the frick is this? Your dead mother?'

'It's the er... merchandise,' I said. 'Like we discussed.'

'So where it from?'

'Colombia, I think.'

'No, you dickwadge. Your supplier. Who is it?'

Shit. I'd been so fixated on convincing him that the coke hadn't come from Danny that it had never occurred to me to think up an alternative, and I fumbled around in my brain for a suitable answer. Blurting out some guff about not being able to reveal my sources probably wasn't going to cut it with this guy, and he'd probably know the names of every supplier in the western hemisphere and beyond, so it was unlikely he'd fall for a made-up name like Nasty MacBastard or Micky the Crackhead either. Fortunately, though, and as I'd expected, he seemed far more interested in who the supplier wasn't than who it was.

'Because,' Nikos went on, 'if it from that frickin' Danny Bishop *maláka*, you can take it right back to that little arsewipe and tell him to—'

'No, no, no,' I said. 'Danny Bishop? God, no.'

I briefly considered laying it on a bit thicker. Something along the lines of what a total wanker I thought Danny was and how I wouldn't do business with him in a million years, but I lost my nerve when Nikos fixed me with a gut-churning stare.

'You know what I do to anyone who lie to me?' he said.

I had a pretty good idea, of course, but it was clearly a rhetorical question, and I braced myself for the gory details.

'About same as I do to anyone who cross-double me,' said Nikos.

Thank Christ for that. Nothing explicit after all.

'Except...' he said, holding up his index sausage for emphasis.

Oh right, here it comes.

'Liars, I let them keep their *archídia* – their balls. Or one of them anyway. It depend. *Katálaves*?'

I guessed he was asking me if I'd got the message, so I gave him what I intended to be a "quite right too" kind of nod and hoped he hadn't spotted my bobbing Adam's apple as I swallowed hard.

'And you wanna know *why* I think you lying to me? Is because you bring me charlie in a frickin' funeral jar, and guess what? That Danny son-of-a-bitch-whore Bishop, he is...'

He presumably couldn't remember the word wanted in English because he turned to the guy at his shoulder and said something in Greek.

'Undertaker,' said the younger guy, and Nikos

snapped his fingers, except the abundant flesh of his finger and thumb muffled the sound almost completely.

'Undertaker,' he repeated. 'And he got frickin' funeral jars comin' outta his frickin' arsehole.'

'Urns,' said Alan, who was standing a couple of feet to my right.

Nikos switched his malevolent glare from me to Alan. 'What?'

'It's not funeral *jars*. It's funeral *urns*,' said Alan. 'And, strictly speaking, what we have here is a *cremation* urn.'

Nice one, Alan, I thought. Piss the guy off even more, why don't you?

Nikos kept his beady black eyes fixed on Alan for several heartbeats and then swivelled them back to me. 'You here to give me frickin' English lessons or deal some coke?'

This was obviously another rhetorical question because, without waiting for my answer, he picked up the urn and passed it back over his shoulder. The younger guy took it and removed the lid, frowning slightly as he peered inside. Then he licked the tip of his finger, dipped it into the urn and tasted. The frown deepened.

Nikos said something to him in Greek, the only word of which I caught was "tacky". I'd no idea whether he was referring to the choice of container or asking about the consistency of the coke, although it would have been a bit odd to drop in a single English word amongst all the Greek. Maybe it was the guy's name. Weird, but then I didn't know much about Greek names or Greece at all for that matter.

Tacky – it'll do as a name for now anyway – didn't

reply but took another pinch from the urn and rubbed it into his gums. He closed his eyes, most likely while he waited for whatever effect he was expecting. A bit of numbness, I suppose, like you get at the dentist's. Moments later, he opened his eyes again and in response to what sounded like a question from Nikos, simply shrugged and put the urn back on the desk.

I hadn't got a clue what the Greek was for "going off on one", but that was pretty much what Nikos did before yanking open one of the desk drawers and pulling out a small silver box. Lifting the lid, he took out a razor blade and then tipped a small pile of the urn's contents onto the desk. With impressive dexterity for a man with such podgy fingers, he chopped the powder into even finer particles and divided the pile into two thin lines. Next, he took a silver tube from the box and snorted each line in quick succession.

He sat back in his chair and brushed the residue from his moustache, staring up at the ceiling as if he was checking out a Michelangelo makeover.

My heart was pumping so fast, I could hear the blood rushing in my ears. It was like being an Oscar nominee or a contestant on one of those TV talent shows when the host opens the envelope and then takes forever to announce the winner. The big difference here, though, was that failing to win Nikos Spiropoulos's version of the Oscar or the Simon Cowell recording contract would result in more than just a few tears. My legs were beginning to feel like they wouldn't support me for very much longer, so I perched myself on one of the two chairs on my side of the desk.

Finally, Nikos eyeballs me, his moustache

contorting into an approximation of a grin. He says something in Greek, which I don't understand, of course, but there seems to be a far more amicable edge to his voice than before. The tension starts to seep from my body, my shoulders drop back to a more normal position, and I force a smile back at him.

He carefully replaces his snorting implements into the silver box, closes the lid and puts it back in the drawer. But instead of shutting the drawer, he takes out a—

Oh Jesus God almighty, a semi-automatic, and he's pointing it straight at my chest. At the same moment, Tacky whips out a gun from the waistband of his trousers, and I'm guessing the other two Greeks have done the same. Too late to even contemplate drawing my own weapon, and although I can't see them, I assume that Alan and Scratch are of a similar mind when it comes to pointless acts of suicidal bravado.

'This what you call English humour, yes?' says Nikos, picking up the urn with his free hand. 'Thought you could pull one over on Nikos Spiropoulos, eh?'

Then he slams the urn back onto the desk, and the yelling starts. 'You think I'm frickin' idiot? You think stupid Greek bastard buy any old shit?'

I've no idea what the fuck he's on about. Maybe the coke isn't quite the top notch quality Danny told me it was. Hardly my fault, but sure as hell it looks like I'm going to be the one to suffer for it.

'I don't understand the problem,' I say, 'but obviously if there's something wrong, we'll replace it.'

'What are you? John frickin' Lewis?' says Nikos, and he waves the barrel of the gun at my face. 'And how you gonna replace anything when your brains all over my frickin' floor?'

Christ, but doesn't he love his rhetorical questions, this guy. Rhetorical or not, I decide it's worth a shot at answering, if only to buy some time. 'The thing is, Mr Spiropoulos...' But I haven't got a Scooby what "the thing" is, so I just stand there with my gob half open like a concussed goldfish.

'Kosta?' says Nikos, looking past me at the bloke who's propping up the tower of bottle crates with his elbow. 'We'll start with Mr English Teacher, I think.'

I turn my head a fraction, not wanting to take my eyes off Nikos's gun for a second, and I watch as Kosta walks up behind Alan and shoves the muzzle of his semi-automatic into the back of his head, a few inches above the neck brace.

Say no to drugs? I wish to God I had. After all, I'm nowhere near posh enough to crook my little finger when I'm drinking a cup of tea, so what the hell else did I need them for?

13

Nikos cast his eyes downwards as if he was trying to see through the desktop to identify where the metallic "*clunk-click*" sound had come from. But I was damn sure he'd heard a semi-automatic being armed often enough to know exactly what it was without the benefit of X-ray vision. His eyes drifted back up and locked onto mine.

'What was it you were saying earlier about depriving people of their balls?' I said.

As far as I could tell without actually looking, I had the gun pointed directly at his gentleman's arrangements, even though the bullet would probably have had to pass through several rolls of overhanging blubber to get there. Still, Nikos had clearly got the message.

He rounded on the guy who was standing over by the door to the restaurant. The Freddie Mercury lookalike who'd let us in. 'You didn't *frisk* them?'

Freddie shrugged and dropped his gaze slightly but kept his gun aimed at Scratch.

'I forgot,' he mumbled.

'You frickin' *forgot*?' roared Nikos and then switched to Greek to launch into what was undoubtedly a tirade of expletive-ridden abuse, the younger guy making only the occasional half-hearted attempt to justify himself.

By the time Nikos had run out of steam, rivers of sweat were pouring down his face with globules of it beginning to drip from his moustache.

Time to press home our advantage.

'If you've quite finished,' I said, 'you can start by telling Kosta Coffee over there to drop his gun.'

There was a brief pause before Nikos gave Kosta the nod, and he obliged by removing his weapon from the back of Alan's head and placing it on the floor.

'And the rest,' I said.

Nikos was by far the last of the three others to lay down his gun, slowly lowering it onto the desktop while his eyes told me precisely how he felt about the situation. I reached across and picked it up, taking my own gun out from under the desk and aiming it at Nikos's chest. I checked to make sure that Alan and Scratch had drawn their weapons and were covering the other three, then kicked back my chair and stood up.

'Right,' I said and nodded towards a corner of the room that was furthest away from the fire exit. 'All of you over there and face down on the floor.'

Nikos was obviously struggling to lever his enormous bulk out of his chair, so Tacky stretched out a hand to help him. Nikos swore at him and brushed him away, finally managing to get to an upright position unaided. He passed within two feet of me on his way to the corner of the room, and the look he gave me was unmistakable.

'Yeah, yeah, I know. I'm a dead man,' I said, genuinely surprised at how confidently casual I sounded.

Truth be told, I was running on pure adrenalin by now, and the immediate priority was to get the hell out as quickly as possible – and preferably without any bullet holes in any of us. As for the likely and highly unpleasant consequences of severely pissing off a big time crook like Nick the Greek, there'd be plenty of time to shit myself later.

Once we'd got them all lying face down in the corner – Nikos needing the help of all three of the others on this occasion – I told them to clasp their hands behind their heads and then indicated the fire exit to Alan and Scratch with a wave of my gun.

'Shouldn't we tie them up first?' said Scratch.

'Probably,' I said, 'but I've no idea if there's anyone else hanging around in the restaurant, and I don't want to still be here if they decide to come and join the party. We'll take their guns, though, I think.'

Scratch kept his gun on the four prone Greeks while Alan collected up the semi-automatics from the floor and backed his way towards the fire exit. Over at the desk, I pocketed Nikos's pistol and picked up the cremation urn. I was going to need the evidence for the little chat I was planning to have with Danny at the earliest opportunity – if I lived that long, of course.

When Scratch joined Alan and I at the fire exit, I hit the crash bar and the door flew open.

'Yeah, you frickin' dead men all right. Every frickin' one o' you. But it ain't gonna be no quick and easy. First, I gonna rip—'

But whatever else Nikos was screaming at us was cut off as I slammed the metal door behind us. As I'd expected – or hoped – we were in the back alley that was used as a service road for the Acropolis and the other restaurants and shops on the high street, although it didn't seem to have had much of a "service" in quite some time. Overflowing industrial-sized rubbish bins and busted bin liners had spewed their contents in every direction, and there was an overwhelming stink of piss and rotting fish. I got Scratch to help me drag one of the bins in front of the fire door and roll it onto its side. It might only give us a few seconds' start, but that might just be enough to save our skins.

The Beamer was parked a dozen or so yards further along the alley than where we'd left it, and as we raced towards it, the sound of blaring pop music got louder and louder. To this was added the crash of metal on metal, and I glanced over my shoulder to see the three younger Greeks forcing their way out of the fire door and over the upturned rubbish bin. Still, we were almost at the car now, so there wasn't much they could do without their guns.

"*Kraakk*!"

Jesus Christ, where did that come from?

"*Kraakk*!" "*Kraakk*!"

Another two bullets whistled past us in quick succession, one of them slamming into the boot of the Beamer.

Bollocks. What an idiot. How could I possibly have believed that they'd only have four guns between them? Hell, scumbags like that probably had enough weapons to start a small war – or even a big one.

Scratch and Alan returned fire while I wrenched open the driver's door of the car. Toby was sitting behind the wheel, turning it this way and that and making engine noises, the music from the radio obviously too loud for him to have heard the gunshots.

'So you can drive then, can you?' I yelled.

'I'm sixteen, Unc. I haven't even got a—'

'Well, move over, and for Christ's sake keep your head down. Now!'

He wriggled over onto the passenger seat, and I turned to look back up the alley. The Greeks had taken cover behind three separate bins and were firing shot after shot. Scratch and Alan had the rear doors of the Beamer open, crouching behind them and keeping the Greeks pinned down. Bullets pinged off the car's bodywork and metal bins like we were stuck inside a pinball machine. The fact that this wasn't any sort of game, though, was instantly brought home when one of the rounds smashed through the rear window and lodged itself in the dashboard. A brief flash, and whatever Toby had been listening to came to an abrupt end.

'Fuck's sake, we need to go,' I said and slid in behind the steering wheel, wedging the cremation urn between my thighs.

Scratch and Alan dived into the back seat, and I fired up the engine. I glanced in the wing mirror as the three Greeks emerged from behind their bins and began running down the alley. Scratch and Alan had stopped shooting during the few seconds it had taken them to get into the car, so the Greeks must have thought we were out of ammo and decided it was safe to break cover. Big mistake.

As soon as they were in, Scratch smashed a hole in the already shattered glass of the rear window with the butt of his gun and carried on firing. With the second shot, the closest of the three clutched at his shoulder and went spiralling down onto the ground. One of the others skidded to a halt and bent over him, but the third kept coming, staying low and sprinting up behind us.

I floored the accelerator pedal. The engine roared, but the Beamer stayed put. Shit. Still in neutral.

I slammed the gear stick into first, but at the same moment, the muzzle of a gun appeared at my open window. No time to reach for my own weapon, and Scratch and Alan were too slow off the mark. No time even to blink as I stared into the black depths of the gun barrel and heard...

"*Klickk*."

Jesus Christ. Fucking empty.

The gun dropped a few inches, and Kosta Coffee's face appeared, gazing down at it in disbelief. I lashed out a fist and caught him with an uppercut just below the nose. A spurt of blood, and he catapulted backwards onto the floor.

I hit the throttle for a second time, and the car fishtailed as the tyres fought for traction.

Two more gunshots from behind, one of which sounded like it had caught one of the rear light clusters. Either Kosta had reloaded or the Greek Samaritan had got bored with tending to the sick and wounded and decided to rejoin the action. But whoever it was, it was a fair guess that they'd finally cottoned on to trying to shoot out the tyres. By now, though, we were almost at the end of the alley, and with little consideration for other road users, I slewed the Beamer out onto the main road, the back end only narrowly missing an oncoming bus.

I reined in the car to a more sedate pace and looked across at Toby, who had his head almost between his knees. 'You OK?'

'Yeah, I'm fine,' he said, sitting up with a massive grin lighting up his zit-speckled face. 'That was just *awesome*.'

Oh right. Awesome, was it? I was pretty certain his mum wouldn't agree if she ever found out the truth about Number One Son's first day on work experience.

I checked the rear-view mirror. 'Scratch? Alan? Anybody hurt?'

'Nah,' said Scratch. 'I'm good.'

Alan didn't answer. He'd taken off his neck brace and was examining it closely.

'Alan? What's up?'

'Gonna need a new one o' these probably,' he said. 'Bullet must've nicked it.'

'Never mind your poxy neck brace,' I said. 'What about my bloody car?'

'It's insured, isn't it?'

'Course it's insured. But what am I supposed to put on the claim form about all the fucking bullet holes? A serious infestation of metal worm?'

'And speaking of bullet holes in cars,' said Scratch. 'Don't you think it'd be a good idea to get it off the road before we get pulled over by some over-inquisitive bizzies?'

He had a point, of course. Two cop cars had already passed us in the opposite direction with full-on blues and twos, and in all likelihood heading for the alley behind the Acropolis Restaurant. Unlike in plenty of movies, the local constabulary presumably took rather a dim view of raging gun battles in the middle of the day – or any other time of day for that matter.

14

'How very odd,' said Danny when we finally managed to track him down the next morning.

Straight after the gunfight at the Acropolis corral, we'd tucked the Beamer away in a lockup I'd been renting and legged it round to the funeral parlour, only to be told by Sanjeev that his lord and master was out and wouldn't be back for the rest of the day. I'd tried calling him on his mobile several times, but he'd either had it switched off or he was somewhere out of signal range.

I'd packed Toby off back to his mum's with a dire warning about what I'd do to him if he breathed so much as a word about dope deals, gunfights or any of the other shit that wouldn't generally be considered to be part of the daily routine of working in a bank. Instead, I'd primed him with a few key words and phrases he could use in response to Melanie's inevitable "So, how did it go?" interrogation. "Filing" and "stuffing envelopes" were top of the list but with almost equal emphasis to be placed on "boring", "playing games on my smartphone" and "complete waste of time". My hope was that his mum would be so convinced by the waste of time element of the feedback that she wouldn't bother sending him back again for another day of pointless time frittering. But maybe getting him out from under her feet was of more importance to her than Toby gaining some work experience that was actually worthwhile, because there he'd been at the station, the same as the day before.

Once we'd got him settled in a caff round the corner from Danny's, Alan, Scratch and I had hammered on the door of the funeral parlour a few minutes before it was officially open, and Danny had greeted us with a cheesy grin and an 'All went well, I trust?'

After I'd explained in some detail how all had *not* gone well, he'd examined the contents of the cremation urn with a deepening frown of bewilderment.

'Very odd indeed,' he said again, replacing the lid of the urn and setting it down on the top of the reception desk.

'Odd?' I said. 'It's more than fucking odd, Danny. Whatever this shit is, it damn near got us all killed.'

'Yes, I can see why our Greek friend might have been a little peeved. You see, Max – and you'll have to forgive the self-aggrandisement here – but I do consider myself to be somewhat of an expert in this field, and I haven't one iota of a doubt that what you've just shown me is definitely *not* cocaine.'

'Yeah, I think that's been pretty well established by now.'

Danny tapped the lid of the urn. 'Common or garden cremains, I'd say.'

'Cre-what?'

'It's a widely held misconception that what's left after a cremation are the *ashes* of the dearly departed, whereas in fact all that remains – the "cremains", if you will – are fragments of bone and the occasional filling or overlooked item of jewellery. To talk about someone's "ashes", therefore, is a complete misnomer because what you actually end up with...' He tapped the top of the urn again. 'What you have here, for example, is finely pulverised bone matter.'

'Fascinating though that is, Danny – and as I keep telling you – this particular finely pulverised bone matter came very close to us all winding up in one of these bloody urns ourselves.'

I was aware that my voice had risen rapidly in volume until I was almost yelling at him by the time I got to the end of the sentence. Nor did it help my mood when Danny pointed out that we wouldn't all fit in the one urn and added a little chuckle that was just begging to be silenced with a well aimed punch in the face. I managed to restrain myself, however, and waited for what I hoped might be a sensible answer. Instead, I got something that took me totally by surprise.

'But surely,' said Danny, sitting back in his fancy office chair with a shocked expression that could almost have been genuine, '*surely* you can't think this was deliberate.'

Of the many theories I'd come up with since our near-death experience at the Acropolis Restaurant, this had certainly not been one of them. So why had Danny mentioned it? I was about to ask him, but he was clearly determined to defend himself against an accusation I'd never even made.

'Endanger the life of my oldest and dearest friend?

The very idea is utterly preposterous – especially when that oldest and dearest friend still owes me ten thousand pounds and isn't exactly going to be in the best possible position to repay it if he's pushing up the daisies.'

Fair point, I thought. Even if he wanted me dead for some reason, there was no way he'd pass up the ten grand I owed him.

'However,' he went on, giving the urn a shake like he was mixing a cocktail, 'and this is a very big "however", Max. The money you owe me is but small change compared to the eighty thousand quid's worth of coke – *my* coke – that has mysteriously gone missing.'

The slight narrowing of the eyes said it all, and I wasn't having any of it. 'I don't know what the fuck you're insinuating, Danny, but from the moment Sanjeev handed it over to us, the bloody urn's not been out of my sight for even a second, and if you're suggesting that—'

'Steady on, old chap. Steady on,' said Danny, his palms raised towards me. 'I'm not accusing you of anything. Not in the slightest. But since, as you say, this whole chain of unfortunate events began when young Sanjeev gave you the urn, perhaps he might be able to shed some light on the mystery of the disappearing nose candy.'

Sanjeev was polishing one of the display coffins near the back of the shop, and when Danny called out to him, he came scurrying over, wiping his hands on an old piece of cloth.

'Yes, boss?'

'Sanjeev, my boy,' said Danny, laying a paternal hand on his shoulder. 'Could you possibly explain why it is that my good friend Max here has an urn containing finely pulverised bone matter when he should in fact be in possession of an urn containing precisely two kilograms of finest cocaine?'

Sanjeev looked down at his feet and mumbled something about a mix-up.

Danny shifted his hand from the lad's shoulder and cupped it theatrically to his own ear.

'Can't hear you,' he said in a sing-song kind of voice.

'Look, I'm really sorry,' said Sanjeev, forcing himself to eyeball Danny and gabbling to get the words out, 'but there were three lots of people came in to collect urns all at the same time and the names on two of the bags were almost the same, so what must have happened was that I—'

Danny brought an abrupt end to the torrent of words by placing a finger against Sanjeev's lips. Then he turned to me. 'Do you still have the bag the urn was in?'

'Scratch might have it,' I said and opened the door of the funeral parlour to ask him.

Still not having overcome his phobia of all things death-related, he was mooching around on the pavement outside with Alan to keep him company.

'Yeah, it's in me pocket,' he said.

'Bring it in then.'

Scratch raised an eyebrow at me as he produced the plastic Ziploc bag from his jacket pocket, so I told him not to be such a wuss, and with a gentle shove from Alan, he stepped through the doorway.

Danny took the bag and scanned the label. '"Pemberton". Yes, now I see where the confusion must have arisen. You should have had the one marked "Pendleton". – My mother's maiden name, you know. Always use it for the merchandise. Makes it look... normal. Avoids suspicion if you know what I mean. – Sanjeev, be so good as to fetch me the Pemberton file, would you?'

'Oh, and Sanjeev?' he added before the lad had even turned his back.

'Yes, bo— *Ooff*!'

Danny had punched him hard in the stomach, and Sanjeev doubled over, clutching his guts.

'We'll have a bit of a... staff appraisal later, shall we?' said Danny, stooping slightly to give him a pat on the head.

Sanjeev cranked his upper body into a marginally more upright position, his lame excuse for a moustache and the rest of his features contorted in pain.

'Off you trot then,' said Danny, giving him a broad smile and, this time, a pat on the back.

Sanjeev staggered out into the storeroom behind the reception desk, still clutching his belly, and Danny flicked his smile in my direction. 'So, Max, when Gunga Din returns with the necessary information, I'm sure you won't have any trouble retrieving my—'

I didn't have to wait for the rest of the sentence to know what he was getting at.

'Me?' I said, jabbing a finger at my chest for a bit of extra emphasis.

The smile vanished from Danny's mug, and he tilted his head to one side. 'You have a problem with that?'

'This fuckup's got nothing to do with me.'

Next thing, Danny had got his arm round my shoulder and was almost whispering when he said,

'Oh, but I'm afraid it does, Max, old friend. You see, without the charlie I really don't know how you're going to pay me back the money you owe me.' Then he grabbed one of my hands and took hold of the little finger. 'You do see where I'm coming from with this, do you?'

I knew exactly where he was coming from, of course, so there wasn't a lot of point arguing the toss. I snatched my hand back just as Sanjeev re-emerged from the storeroom, still holding his stomach with one hand and a buff-coloured folder in the other. He was about to give it to Danny, but Danny jerked a thumb at me and said, 'Mr Dempsey's, I think, Sanjeev.'

I took the folder and headed for the door without even so much as a "Fuck you, Danny", and Scratch and Alan followed me out onto the street.

'And beware of Greeks bearing grudges,' Danny called out after us just before the door closed.

15

As soon as we were outside the funeral parlour, my very first thought was that I could have done with a drink to settle my severely frayed nerves, but taking my responsibilities seriously, I decided we should head back to the caff where we'd left Toby. That was the plan, anyway, but seconds after leaving Danny's, an all too familiar voice called out from behind us.

'Simon?'

I ignored her at first and quickened my step, but I knew that any attempt to escape was futile – especially when I realised that Scratch had stopped and I heard his chirpy 'Oh, hi, Carla. How's things?'

'Fine thanks, Michael. How are you? I haven't seen you in ages.'

Carla is about the only person on the planet that calls him by his real name. As far as I'm aware, she doesn't even know he *has* a nickname. And why would she when she doesn't even know I go by the name of Max Dempsey?

'Simon!'

Accepting the inevitable, I turned and walked back

with Alan creeping after me like he was trying to hide.

'Carla,' I said and made a vague attempt to inject a bit of enthusiasm into my voice when I added, 'What a surprise.'

She was holding three carrier bags, I noticed. Not the plastic supermarket types but the fancy cardboard ones you get from expensive boutiques.

'What were you doing in there?' she said with a nod back over her shoulder.

'There?' I said, knowing full well she must have spotted us coming out of Danny's but stalling for a couple of seconds to give me time to figure out an answer.

'In an undertaker's, yes.'

'Alan's mum,' I said, taking half a step to the side and depriving Alan of his human shield.

'Oh, hello, Alan,' said Carla. 'I didn't see you there.'

Alan gave her a smile that was so fleeting you'd have missed it if you'd blinked. 'Hello, Carla.'

'So what's this about your mum?'

'Er...'

'She's in here,' I said, grabbing the cremation urn from Alan and holding it out for Carla's inspection.

'Oh, I... Is she...?'

It was one of those very rare occasions that Carla was lost for words – or one word in particular. Dead? No, of course not. It's just that she's incredibly small and Alan likes to carry her around in a fucking cremation urn all day.

'She's dead, yes,' I said when I realised Alan was just staring back at her with his mouth half open.

Carla put her bags down and grasped his hand in both of hers. 'I'm so sorry, Alan. Was she very old?'

107

Alan's mum had died when he was a kid, and from the heavy creases on his forehead, he was clearly having trouble working out how old she'd be now, so I tried to bail him out.

'Not really. She was—'

'Thank you, Simon,' Carla interrupted, dropping her sincere condolences expression to shoot me a glare, 'but I rather think Alan has a much better idea of how old his mother was than you.'

'Forty-six,' said Alan.

Fuck's sake, Alan, that would make her younger than you are.

Judging by the frown that was beginning to develop, I could see that Carla was no better at the mental arithmetic than he was, so before the frown could get any deeper, I jumped in with, '*Nineteen* forty-six, he means. That's when she was born.'

'Ah,' said Carla, not looking too convinced. 'And was it very... sudden?'

'Oh yes,' said Alan. 'Very sudden indeed. Took me totally by surprise, it did.'

Carla nodded solemnly a couple of times and patted him on the wrist before snapping her attention back to me. 'So how come you're not at work?'

'I'm the manager, remember? I can take time off whenever I like.'

'And I didn't want to be on my own when I came to pick up my mum,' Alan added.

A bit late in the day, but he was finally beginning to get the hang of it.

'Oh God,' I said, making a show of checking my watch. 'Better be getting back or—'

'And where's Toby?'

'Er, back at the bank, doing some filing.' Otherwise

known as pratting about on his smartphone in a caff round the corner.

'Well, I hope you're not just using him as a general dogsbody and he's actually *learning* something.'

'Oh, he is. He is. He's definitely learning something.' I checked my watch again. 'Sorry, Carla, but I really have to—'

'Wait a minute,' she said as she rummaged in the depths of her Gucci shoulder bag. 'Since you seem to be going in that direction, you might as well... Ah, here it is.'

She pulled a slip of paper out of the bag and held it out to me. 'Dry cleaning receipt. One of your suit jackets you splattered dinner on.'

I took the receipt and stuffed it into my pocket.

'OK, I'll see you later,' I said and set off up the pavement before she could send me on any other errands.

'Bit of a coincidence, eh?' said Scratch when he and Alan caught up with me.

'One I could really have done without,' I said. 'And a fat lot of help you were, Alan. Forty-six, for Christ's sake?'

Alan shrugged. 'It's not my fault you haven't told her what you really do. In fact, I'm bloody amazed she's never twigged and still thinks you work in a bank.'

'Well, he does, kind of,' said Scratch. 'But it's more than just the one bank, isn't it... *Simon*?'

'Not funny, Scratch,' I said as the pair of them started to laugh. 'Not funny at all.'

16

Tess Pemberton's house was about a third of the way along a row of almost identical two-up-two-downs, each with its own postage stamp excuse for a front garden. Ms Pemberton, however, didn't seem to be at home. From what I could see as I bent almost double and peered through the letterbox, she wasn't the tidiest of people either. The hallway floor was partially covered with a liberal smattering of books, magazines, unopened mail, a couple of coats and a few other articles of clothing as well as several pairs of boots and shoes – except not in their pairs.

'Give it another go,' I said, and Alan rang the doorbell for about the fifteenth time.

There wasn't the faintest whisper of a sound or movement from inside the house.

'Nobody home,' said Scratch, stating the bleeding obvious.

'She could be dead, of course,' said Alan.

My lower back was starting to ache, so I let the metal flap of the letterbox slam shut and stood upright.

'Dead?' I said. 'Why would she be dead?'

Alan gave his theory less than a moment's thought. 'Everybody dies sometime, Max.'

'Yes, but why *her*? She can't be any more than mid thirties.'

'How d'you know that?'

'Because she was at Danny's collecting an urn at the same time as Scratch and me, and her granddad called her Tess, which happens to be the same name as in the folder Sanjeev gave us.'

'Yeah,' said Scratch. 'The girl with the dragon tattoo.'

'The girl with the—?'

'Yes, Alan,' I interrupted, 'but not the one you're thinking of.'

'Oh.'

Alan looked strangely disappointed and lifted his chin while he adjusted the position of his brand new, gleaming white neck brace.

'So now what do we do?' said Scratch. 'Bugger off and come back later?'

'Not a bit of it,' I said. 'In fact, her being out might well be a blessing in disguise, so why don't you go and see if there's a back way in?'

Scratch signalled his understanding with a click of his fingers and headed off towards one of the side alleys that presumably led to the back of the terrace. Rather pointlessly – although I didn't say so – Alan reprised his role as chief bell-pusher while I climbed onto the low wall of a flowerbed in front of the big bay window. I cupped my hands against the glass to cut out the reflection, but there wasn't much to see other than a small living room that, if anything, was even more untidy than the hallway.

'She's not in, dear.'

I very nearly lost my footing at the sound of the woman's voice but managed to avoid an embarrassing tumble with a bit of equally embarrassing arm flailing to keep my balance. The woman was standing about six feet to my right and was inserting a key into the door of the next house along. Her hair was snow white and heavily permed, and her face had more wrinkles than an elephant's nutsack. Eighty if she was a day.

'Not long missed her actually,' she said as she unlocked the door and pushed it open.

I stepped down from the wall of the flowerbed and gave her one of my honest-as-the-day-is-long smiles. 'Any idea when she'll be back?'

In response, I got an ear-piercing, high pitched shriek as she fiddled with the volume on her hearing aid.

'Sorry, dear, you'll have to speak up,' she said when the intense Metallica feedback eventually subsided. 'I'm a little deaf.'

I upped my own volume half a dozen notches and enunciated every word with exaggerated mouth movements in case she might be able to lipread. 'Do – you – know – when – she'll – be – back?'

'Went off in that van of hers. Her and her granddad.'

'Where to?'

There was a faint twinkle in the old woman's eyes as she patted at her hair without actually touching it. 'Oh, that's nice of you. Most men wouldn't even notice, you know.'

'Sorry?'

'Mind you, many moons ago when I was in my prime, so to speak, all the young men used to say how lovely my hair was. Of course, it wasn't this awful

112

white colour in those days. Dear me, no. In fact, it was—' She broke off at the sound of breaking glass in the not far distance. 'What was that?'

'What was what?'

'I thought I heard a noise.'

'I didn't hear anything,' I lied and turned to Alan for confirmation. 'Alan?'

Alan shook his head. 'Nope.'

The breaking glass must have meant that Scratch had got himself in at the back of the house. Obviously, I'd forgotten to add the word "quietly" when I'd given him his instructions. He'd be letting us in through the front door at any second. Time to get rid of Mrs Wrinkly.

'Well, it's been really nice chatting to you but—'

'Oh, that *is* odd,' she said, suddenly shifting her focus to Alan.

I thought for a moment she'd never seen a neck brace before, but then I realised her gaze was a couple of feet lower down and in the approximate area of the cremation urn Alan was holding.

'She had one exactly like that,' Mrs Wrinkly went on. 'Her poor old granny, God rest her soul. Mind you, she'll get terribly shaken up going all that way.'

'How do you mean "all that way"?'

'In that van of hers. All that bouncing around. Terribly shaken up, poor soul.'

This wasn't sounding good at all, and I don't mean the shaken up part of "all that way".

'Do you know where she went?' I said. 'Miss Pemberton.'

'Oh no, dear,' she said. 'I'm not Miss Pemberton. She lives next door.'

Christ, give me strength.

113

I tried again with the volume cranked up. 'Where – did – she – go?'

'Scotland,' snapped the old woman. 'I just told you. It was her granny's dying wish, apparently, to have her ashes scattered in the place she came from. She was Scottish, you see. The granny, that is, and not Miss Pemberton. She's English as far as I know, but I've never been a great one for recognising accents.'

At that precise moment, Scratch appeared at the bay window – but unfortunately the bay window of the old woman's house and not the one we were trying to get into. If she turned to go in through her front door, she'd spot him immediately, so I had to keep her talking until Scratch got himself the hell out of there. Besides, if she knew that they'd gone to Scotland, maybe she could give me something a bit more specific. If we were to stand any chance of tracking down Danny's coke, I needed to get as much out of her as I could.

'Any idea where in Scotland?' I said.

'The west, I think she said. Somewhere near... Ooh, where was it now?'

She looked down at the ground while she struggled to remember, which gave me the opportunity to glare at Scratch and mouth the words "What the fuck are you doing?".

He shrugged and pointed towards the dividing wall between where he was now and the house he should have been in but wasn't.

'Glen something or other, wasn't it?'

Mrs Wrinkly still had her eyes to the floor as she spoke, so I gave Scratch a sideways nod and mouthed at him that he should get out of the house – now!

"What?" he mouthed back, pulling a face that

114

indicated he hadn't understood my mouthing.

'Dumpees. That was the place. I remember thinking it was a funny sort of—'

The old woman cut herself off mid sentence as she looked up and caught me mouthing some choice words of advice at Scratch. She twisted her head in his direction but slowly enough that he had plenty of time to dodge back out of sight.

I needed to get her attention back in case Scratch was stupid enough – as he probably was – to show himself at the window again. 'She was in a van, you say.'

'That's right, dear. One of those camper things. A white one. And between you and me, I'm not sure if it'll make it all that way. Nearly as old as I am, it is.'

She chuckled like she was having a mild attack of asthma, and I flashed her a smile to acknowledge the joke.

'That was quite funny too,' she said, still chuckling. 'P - O - T.'

'Sorry?'

'I noticed it as they drove off.'

'P - O - T?'

'The whatchamacallit – registration number. Pot. Just like her old gran was in.'

The chuckle was just beginning to develop into a guffaw when she suddenly nipped it in the bud and said, 'Oh dear. You don't think that's like speaking ill of the dead, do you? Laughing, I mean.'

I really didn't have an opinion on the matter, but I did at least have part of the van's registration number. I asked if she happened to remember the rest of it, but she shook her head, seemingly too preoccupied with resolving her moral dilemma to be bothered with such trivialities.

'You all right, mate?'

Hearing Alan's voice, I turned to see that Scratch had returned from his breaking and entering and was sucking the blood from a cut on his hand.

Mrs Wrinkly had spotted him too. 'My, that's a nasty cut you've got there. Why don't you all come in for a nice cup of tea and I can put a bandage on it?'

It was unlikely we were going to get anything else useful from her, and the priority now was to try and catch up with the camper van before it got too far on its way to Bonnie bloody Scotland. And we also didn't want to be around when she discovered her broken window.

'That's very kind of you,' I said, 'but we're in a bit of a hurry, I'm afraid.'

Poor old biddy looked genuinely disappointed. 'Oh, that's a pity. I made some scones this morning and forgot to quarter the quantities, so there's far too many for me on my own.'

'Another time perhaps,' I said, getting the words out quick when I saw that Scratch and Alan had already begun to salivate.

'That would be lovely,' she said, brightening a little. 'And at least you know where I am now.'

'Of course. And thanks for your help.'

'My pleasure, dear.'

I set off towards the Beamer on the opposite side of the street, noticing with a twinge of satisfaction that my handiwork had done a pretty good job of patching up the bullet holes. The strips of black tape wouldn't have held up to closer inspection, but from this sort of distance the car didn't look quite so much like it had just been through a war zone. Sure, I knew people

116

who could have done a proper repair job on the quiet, but their discretion was the better part of a few hundred quid, which was a price I could ill afford. I did shell out for a new back window to keep the weather out, and I got the smashed rear light replaced because I didn't want to get pulled over by the cops. The knackered radio stayed knackered, partly because I hadn't got the cash for a new one, but mainly so that Toby couldn't use it to deafen the rest of us with the kind of shit music he'd probably describe as "awesome".

He was sitting on the back seat, farting about with his smartphone, as Scratch, Alan and I got into the car.

'What the fuck d'you think you were doing?' I said to Scratch the moment the doors were all shut.

'I made a mistake, all right?'

'Oh really?'

'There was this alley along the back, yeah? But there weren't any numbers for the houses, and I must've miscounted.'

'So you smashed in some poor old biddy's window,' Alan chipped in.

'It wasn't deliberate, for Christ's sake,' Scratch yelled, but then he dropped the volume and almost mumbled when he added, 'And anyway, I'll come back later when she's gone to bed and stick a few quid through the letterbox to pay for the damage.'

'What?' said Alan. 'And scare the crap out of her even more than you have already?'

'Well, what the fuck else do you want me to—?'

'I'm not sure that's gonna be possible anyway,' I cut in before the argument got out of hand. 'Not if we're halfway to Scotland by then.'

'Eh?'

While Alan began to fill Scratch in on what he'd missed, I started the engine and returned Mrs Wrinkly's cheery wave – but not quite as cheerily.

17

I couldn't remember what the law was about sixteen-year-olds in pubs, so we'd played safe and gone into a nearby caff instead. In any case, we couldn't afford to hang about, and I knew from long experience that once they were inside a pub, Scratch and Alan were almost impossible to shift. We did, however, need to come up with some kind of plan. Simply heading north in the vague hope of spotting the camper van wasn't going to cut it, so I'd bought a road atlas from the newsagent's next door, and having failed to find any such place as Dumpees in the index, I had it open at the page that showed a map of the whole country.

'After they get above Preston,' I said, tracing the route with my finger, 'it looks like there's only two roads they can take if they're heading for the west of Scotland. A6 or M6 motorway.'

'Sho what do we do?' said Alan through a mouthful of bacon sandwich. 'Tosh a coin?'

'We'll need a second motor, so between us we can cover both the roads at the same time.'

'Nick one, you mean?' said Scratch.

I shook my head. Nicking cars was a mug's game unless you only wanted one for an hour or two. Otherwise, what with all the technology the cops had these days, you were the proverbial sitting duck. And since neither Alan nor Scratch owned a car themselves and there was no way I could nip home and pick up the Honda without Carla knowing, there was only one option left.

'We'll have to hire one,' I said, hoping that at least one of my credit cards wasn't already maxed to the hilt. I snapped the atlas shut and drained the last dregs of my tepid coffee. 'We need to get a wriggle on if we've got that to sort out as well.'

'What about the lad?' said Alan with a nod in Toby's direction.

I was already on my feet, but I slumped back down again as the realisation hit me. Bollocks. Dropping Toby off at his mum's place was well out of our way and was going to waste time that we really didn't have, but what other choice had I got?

'We'll have to take him home first,' I said.

Toby's eyes popped, and he instantly suspended the slurping noises he'd been making for the last five minutes as he sucked milkshake foam from the bottom of his glass. 'No way, Unc. This is the best time I've had in, like, forever.'

'Listen, Toby,' I said in as calm a voice as I could muster. 'You're supposed to be doing work experience in a bank. How the hell do I explain to your mum that you probably won't be back tonight because you're on your way to bloody Scotland?'

'I dunno. Tell her it's a business trip or something.'

'Oh, sure.'

'Or just tell her I'm staying at yours tonight. Who's

to know?'

'Your Aunty Carla for a start. And what if your mum phones the house? See how you got on at the bank today or whatever?'

'She'll call my mobile.'

'No, I'm sorry, Toby. It's bad enough that you could have been killed in a back alley shootout. I'm not going to risk being—'

'You don't want Aunty Carla to find out what you really do for a living, do you?'

The kid's words hit me like a sledgehammer. That was the trouble with blackmailers – even teenage ones – they never let you forget quite how firmly they had you by the short and curlies. I glanced at Alan and Scratch for some moral support – moral indignation even – but all I got in return were a pair of shrugs that told me I was screwed. And they were right. I stared into Toby's eyes for several seconds, and he stared straight back at me without so much as a blink. No doubt about it, the kid wasn't bluffing.

I broke off from the staring match under the pretext of checking my watch and stood up again. 'Come on. We need to get a move on.'

'Awesome,' said Toby.

18

Watching the constant stream of traffic was making me seriously drowsy, and I'd have almost certainly nodded off if it hadn't been for the constant pinging and other irritating noises coming from Toby's smartphone. I would have told him to pack it in long ago, but I desperately needed to stay awake. Another bonus was that all the while he was conquering entire civilisations or zapping alien spaceships, we didn't need to speak.

It was getting on for two hours since I'd parked the Beamer on a bridge over the M6 with a clear view of the northbound carriageway, and my mood had got progressively worse. I was severely pissed off with pretty much everyone I'd had any contact with that day and not only my shit of a nephew for blackmailing me into taking him with us. There was Sanjeev and his fuckup over the cremation urns. Danny Bishop for making it *my* job to track down the one with the coke in. And last, but by no means least, Alan and Scratch for wasting valuable time by arguing the toss about which bloody car they were going to hire at the rental place.

'What d'you want a hatchback for?' Alan had said. 'It's not as if we're gonna be shifting a fridge or picking up a week's supply of your allergy meds from the chemist's.'

'It isn't because it's a bloody hatchback,' Scratch had said. 'It's because it'll be a damn sight quicker than that piece of crap you've got your eye on. And in any case, there's no way I'd be seen dead in a fucking Skoda.'

'You're just a car snob, Scratch. That's what you are. A bloody car snob. If you knew anything about cars at all, you'd know that Skoda was taken over by Volkswagen yonks ago.'

And so it had carried on until I couldn't stand it any more, and I went into the site office and signed them up for a two-litre Mondeo before they'd even realised I'd gone. As I'd predicted, they'd both moaned like hell at me for picking a Mondeo, but at least it had stopped them bickering with each other, and we'd finally managed to get going – them heading for the A6 and Toby and I for the motorway.

All the way, I'd been checking my mirror every other minute in case we'd picked up a tail. Just to make a shit awful day a whole lot worse, Danny had phoned me while we were at the car rental place and given me a piece of news I really didn't want to hear. According to him, Nick the Greek had some relative or other in the police, so it was a racing certainty that he'd be tapping them up for information on the Beamer's whereabouts. Gun battle or not, at least one of the three Greeks must have clocked the registration number, and I hadn't had time to switch the plates. Thanks a bunch, Danny-boy.

"*Kerphut!*"

There was what I guessed was supposed to be a massive explosion from Toby's smartphone, but it sounded more like an elephant farting.

'Shit,' he said. 'I was almost at the next level then.'

'Yeah,' I said without shifting my gaze from the motorway beneath us. 'Life really sucks like that sometimes.'

There was a brief pause, and I could sense that he'd turned towards me.

'You OK, Unc?' he said, and I could almost hear the frown of concern in his voice.

'Never better, Toby. Never better.'

Some kind of white van came into view round a slight curve in the motorway, and I grabbed the binoculars from on top of the dashboard.

Yet another false alarm.

'Scratch says it's all Alan's fault, all this mess we're in,' Toby said after several seconds of blissful silence.

'*We?*'

'Says it's because Alan got the wrong wall to drill into. Says it was the spiral staircase confused him.'

'Scratch talks too much.'

A couple of minutes of peace and quiet went by, but like Nature abhorring a vacuum, Toby obviously abhorred a silence.

'So how come Aunty Carla doesn't know what you really do?'

Christ, this kid's got more front than Brighton. First, he blackmails me, and now he's got the gall to remind me of it by bringing up the very thing he had over me. I ignored the question, but he clearly wasn't going to let it rest.

'Unc?'

'Long story,' I said in the certain knowledge that he wouldn't be satisfied until I'd answered him.

'So?' he said. 'We're not exactly in a hurry.'

I couldn't argue with that, although I could have just told him to shut up and mind his own business. Tempting, but maybe if I gave him at least part of the explanation, he might be a bit less keen to drop me in it with Carla in the future.

'It's just easier that way,' I said, sighing heavily in defeat. 'Did you ever hear the expression "What you don't know can't harm you"?'

'No.'

'Well, you have now.'

'I don't get it.'

'She'd worry all the time. Not so much about me but about what would happen to her and the kids if I got caught. And when your Aunty Carla worries... Well, put it this way. She'd be on my back even more than she is now.'

Silence again, apart from the hum of motorway traffic beneath us. Perhaps I'd done enough to satisfy his curiosity, or perhaps he was just working out his next question.

Apparently, it was the latter.

'Do you think maybe if you told her, she might think you were more... interesting?'

The pause before "interesting" made me smile. It was as if he'd tried to think of a more diplomatic way of putting it but given up and gone for the direct approach instead.

'Very possibly,' I said, although by this stage in our marriage I was long past caring whether Carla found me interesting or the dullest bloke in the world.

'Mum says Aunty Carla's always bitching to her about how boring—'

Saved by the bog standard ringtone of my bog standard mobile phone. True, I didn't give a toss what Carla thought of me, but I didn't particularly want the vivid detail.

I snatched up the phone and hit the answer button. 'Yeah?'

It was Alan. 'Any sign yet?'

'Yeah, they went past us about twenty minutes ago, but I decided to stay put and twiddle my thumbs for a bit to let them get ahead and make sure we had even less chance of finding them. Jesus, Alan, d'you not think I'd have told you?'

'OK, OK. It's just that it's been a couple of hours now and—'

'What are you, the speaking clock? I dunno. Perhaps they stopped off somewhere on the way.'

'Or what if they really had gone past before we got here?'

'I doubt it. The old biddy said the van was pretty clapped out, and they can't have had much of a start on us.'

Even less if he and Scratch hadn't spent quite so long fannying around at the car hire place.

'Yeah, I guess,' said Alan.

I spotted another white van heading towards us on the northbound carriageway, and I gestured to Toby to check it out with the binoculars. At the same moment, I heard a car door opening on the other end of the phone and then a strange yelping sound.

'What was that?'

'It's all right,' said Alan. 'Neck giving me a bit of gyp, that's all.'

126

'Yeah, martyr to your neck, aren't you?' It was Scratch's voice in the background. 'Here, take it, will you? And don't forget it's your round next time.'

'Christ almighty,' I said. 'You're not at a bloody pub, are you?'

'I wish,' said Alan. 'One of those mobile caff things in a lay-by.'

I watched Toby put the binoculars back on the top of the dashboard, and he shook his head at me. Another false alarm.

Over the phone there was the sound of a car door closing and then Scratch's voice again, a little louder this time. 'God, I fucking hate black tea.'

'Why didn't you get milk then?' said Alan.

'Lactose intolerant. Plays havoc with me guts, but the bloke in the caff didn't have any soya milk.'

Alan spluttered on what was presumably his own tea. 'Soya milk? Poxy canteen in a lay-by on the A6 and you ask for soya milk? Jesus, Scratch, sometimes I— Hold up. What's this?'

I pressed the phone closer to my ear and leaned forward.

'What?' I said. 'Is it them?'

My heart was starting to race as I waited for an answer.

'It's a camper van all right,' said Alan, 'but...'

The length of the pause was doing my blood pressure no good at all.

'Nope,' he said at last. 'Wrong registration number.'

I hung up the phone. 'Bollocks.'

All this waiting was doing my head in. And what if Alan was right and they'd already gone past before we got here? If they had, then the only option would be to

127

tear off up the motorway and the A6 and hope we caught up with them somewhere. But the way my luck had been going lately, I wouldn't have put bets on it. They might even have taken some other road altogether. The scenic route, whatever the hell that was. And if that was the case, we were totally screwed. The old woman had said that they were heading for some place in the west of Scotland called Dumpees, but according to the road atlas, it didn't bloody exist.

'But like I was saying,' said Toby, interrupting my miserable train of thought. 'If Aunty Carla knew you were a gangster instead of a—'

'For Christ's sake, Toby. I am *not* a bloody gangster, OK? I rob banks. End of story.'

'What's the difference?'

I couldn't be bothered to explain, and I wasn't even sure I could have done, so I sidestepped the question by pretending I'd spotted another van and picked up the binoculars.

'Unc?'

Even without the aid of binoculars, he could no doubt see that there was no van at all.

'What's the difference between a—?'

'Quiet, Toby. I'm trying to—'

Hang about. Now there really was a van. A white one. And...

I refocused the binoculars as it got steadily closer.

Yep. Definitely a camper.

Another slight adjustment of the focusing ring and—

'Bloody hell. I don't believe it.'

'Is that them?' said Toby, half leaning across me to get a better view through the side window.

'J-one-eight-eight-P-O-T. Certainly looks like it,' I said as the van passed underneath the bridge. 'The P-O-T bit's right anyway.'

'Awesome.'

I handed Toby my mobile. 'Here. Give Alan and Scratch a bell.'

He took the phone and called the number.

'Oh, and Toby,' I said as I started the engine. 'Do me a favour and stop saying "awesome" every five minutes, will you?'

19

Not that he was going to let on to anyone else, but Bernard was really rather enjoying this road trip. The van hadn't broken down yet, and Tess was actually a very good driver, so he'd only had to give her the occasional piece of advice. She was quite a dab hand at putting up a tent too, he thought, as he watched her banging in the last couple of pegs.

As soon as they'd arrived at the campsite and parked up, Tess had insisted on sleeping in the tent so he could have the van to himself. Naturally, he'd put up an argument, but they both knew this was purely for the sake of politeness, and he'd quickly capitulated.

'OK if I nip and have a shower now, Granddad?' said Tess when she'd zipped up the tent and walked back to where he was sitting on a camp chair next to the van.

'Of course,' he said. 'I might even have one myself once you've checked out the facilities and passed them fit for human habitation.'

Tess laughed and jumped into the van through the

open sliding door.

'Oh, and pop the kettle on while you're in there, would you?' Bernard called out after her. 'I'll get the washing-up done while you're away.'

He finished his beer and eyed the collection of plates, cutlery and glasses on the picnic table in front of him.

'Right then,' he said aloud. 'You lot aren't going to clean yourselves, are you?'

He started gathering them together as Tess stepped out of the van carrying a brightly coloured towel and a washbag.

'First sign of madness,' she said.

'What is?'

'Talking to yourself.'

'As a matter of fact, I happened to be addressing the dirty plates.'

'Which is, of course, a perfectly sane thing to do.'

'Just go and have your shower and leave me to get on with my work, will you?'

'Well, don't go talking to any strange saucepans while I'm gone then,' said Tess and set off towards the shower block.

'And make sure you wash behind your ears,' Bernard shouted, deliberately loud enough for any nearby campers to have heard.

Without turning or breaking stride, Tess gave him a wave with the back of her hand, and he smiled to himself as he watched her go. When she'd disappeared from view, he took the first pile of washing-up into the van and set it down on the draining board next to the sink. The kettle hadn't quite come to the boil yet, so he went and fetched the rest, leaving his beer mug and Tess's wine glass on the picnic table for later use.

The kettle had begun to whistle by the time he climbed back into the van, and he emptied it into the plastic washing-up bowl while adding cold water from the tap.

'So,' he said. 'Washing-up liquid.'

He stooped to open the floor-level cupboard next to the sink unit, but it was mostly filled with cans and packets of foodstuffs. Then he remembered having seen a bottle of Fairy Liquid in the cupboard above the sink where he'd stowed Dottie's cremation urn before they'd set off.

'Gotcha,' he said and took out the plastic bottle of green liquid.

But as he did so, the back of his hand brushed against the cremation urn, which rocked back and forth on its base and then toppled headlong out of the cupboard. Instinctively, Bernard thrust out the hand that wasn't holding the Fairy Liquid bottle to catch it but only succeeded in deflecting it onto the edge of the stainless steel sink with even more force than gravity alone would have generated. The deflection also altered the angle of impact in such a way that the lid of the urn flew off, and the urn itself bounced backwards into the washing-up bowl.

Paralysed with horror, Bernard watched helplessly as the urn quickly sank below the surface of the water, emitting a trickle of tiny bubbles before measuring its length on the bottom of the bowl. Moments later, the previously clear water nearest to the open mouth of the urn began to turn cloudy, instantly snapping Bernard out of his frozen stupor, and he snatched the urn out of the bowl.

'Damn and bugger,' he said and peered into the neck of the urn.

It was difficult to see clearly, so he tipped a small amount of the urn's contents onto the palm of his hand. He gazed in disgust at the soggy off-white paste for several seconds and then rinsed it off in the washing-up bowl.

Slumping down on the back seat of the van, he grasped the urn in both hands and addressed it directly. 'I'm sorry, Dottie. I don't know which bit of you that was, but I hope it wasn't too important. Probably not much more than the tip of a little finger with a bit of luck.'

He wasn't convinced she would have appreciated his little joke, and he didn't feel much like smiling himself either. On the contrary, he was struggling to fight back the tears.

'Oh, for goodness' sake, pull yourself together, Bernard,' he said with a hearty sniff. 'You need to think, man. But more than that, you need to *do* something before Tess gets back. Can you imagine how upset she'd be if she knew?'

Rousing himself to action, he held the urn up to his ear and shook it gently in the faint hope that at least some of the ashes had escaped the drenching. As he'd feared, however, all he could hear was a slight glooping sound.

Even so, the beginnings of a plan were starting to form in his mind, and he levered himself upright and picked up the fine-meshed sieve that Tess had used earlier for draining the peas. Holding it above the sink, he emptied the contents of the urn into the sieve and watched as a thin stream of whitish liquid dribbled through the mesh and turned the water in the washing-up bowl even cloudier than it was already. He raised the sieve to just beneath his nose to bring it into sharper focus and noticed that on top of the otherwise glutinous mess there was a layer of dry powder that the water hadn't reached. Carefully scraping this off with a dessert spoon, he transferred the powder into an empty coffee mug on the worktop.

Next, he took a Tupperware box from the floor-level cupboard and removed the lid. It was empty, although according to the scrawled handwriting on the label, it once contained sugar.

'This'll do nicely,' said Bernard and almost completely filled the box with the gloop from the sieve.

He sprinkled the dry powder from the coffee mug over the entire surface and replaced the lid before returning the box to the cupboard.

'Sorry, old girl,' he said as he closed the door. 'I'll try and sort you out later. Hopefully you might have dried out a bit by then.'

His back was starting to ache from all the bending and straightening, and he would dearly have loved a five minute sit-down, but there was no time to lose. He still had the now empty cremation urn to deal with, but if Tess was washing her hair, he might just get the job done before she reappeared.

He tore off a couple of sheets of kitchen roll and did his best to dry the inside of the urn, although his hand was far too big to get much further than a few inches into the neck. Then, taking a box of washing powder from the cupboard above the sink, he filled the urn to approximately the right level, put the lid back on and gave it a shake.

'That's better,' he said, satisfied that at least it *sounded* like there were ashes inside.

But his satisfaction was short-lived. The sieve

looked as if he'd been using it to strain wallpaper paste. Quickly rinsing it under the tap, he was at a complete loss as to how he was going to explain a bowlful of milky-coloured liquid if Tess walked in on him in the next few seconds. Not only that, but he hadn't even made a start on the washing up. Tipping the bowl down the plughole wasn't an option as this would almost certainly clog up the drainage pipe. And in any case, that was no way to treat even a fraction of his wife's remains.

There's only one thing for it, he thought, and taking care not to spill any of its contents, he lifted the washing-up bowl out of the sink and stood for a moment in the open doorway of the van. The sun had already set, but the campsite lights hadn't yet been switched on, so he tilted his head from side to side as he squinted through the gloom in the direction of the shower block. There was no sign of Tess, but just as he was about to step out of the van, a young couple appeared on the periphery of his vision.

'Hello,' said the woman.

'Nice evening,' said the man.

'Yes, it is, isn't it?' said Bernard. 'I'm just emptying the washing-up bowl.'

He'd no idea why he'd felt the need to explain himself to two total strangers, although guilt undoubtedly played a large part. That and the mounting apprehension that Tess might be about to catch him in the act.

The young man and the young woman both smiled at him, and each gave a slight nod which Bernard interpreted as mildly patronising in the "bless him, the silly old codger" sense. Perhaps this was why they continued on their way without making any further attempt at conversation. Probably terrified he was going to bore them rigid by launching into a string of interminable stories of the "when I were a lad" variety.

But whatever the reason, Bernard was no longer under observation as he carried the washing-up bowl over to a large, circular flowerbed about twenty feet from the back of the van. Somewhat surprisingly for a campsite, it had been well tended and was generously stocked with a wide range of flowers and shrubs. He briefly surveyed the bed for an appropriate spot until he caught a particularly fragrant scent on the evening air.

'Perfect,' he said to himself. 'Roses were always your favourite, weren't they, Dottie?'

Picking out the rosebush that he decided was the most attractive, and despite his fear that Tess could come back at any moment, he exercised due reverence in taking his time to empty the washing-up bowl at the base of the bush and stood watching until the last of the cloudy liquid had seeped into the earth.

'Sorry to mess you about like this, love, but I hope you understand. You always said I was a clumsy old bugger, didn't you? I remember once when I'd dropped one of your favourite china cups and it smashed into a hundred pieces, and you told me I was like a bull in a china shop. So I tried to make a joke of it and pretended you'd said I was *likeable* in a china shop, but that made you even crosser. Still, you did see the funny side of it in the end, and we both had a jolly good laugh about it.'

'Talking to rosebushes now, are you?'

Bernard's heart skipped a couple of beats, and he slowly turned to see Tess standing about six feet behind him with the brightly coloured towel wrapped around her head, turban style.

'Rosebush have anything interesting to say?' she said with a hint of a grin.

'You didn't... hear anything, did you?'

Tess shook her head. 'Not from the rosebush, no. Just you saying about both of you having a good laugh about something. I didn't know roses *could* laugh – or even had a sense of humour. What was it? Some joke about pruning or fertiliser maybe?'

'Oh no, I'm afraid it's far too risqué to repeat in front of a young lady of such a delicate disposition as yourself.'

'Young lady, eh? Well, I don't remember ever being called *that* before.'

Bernard had begun to relax and was enjoying the banter with his granddaughter, grateful also that she hadn't asked him to explain what he was doing out here in the semi-darkness with an empty washing-up bowl.

'Come along,' he said and set off back towards the van. 'There's work still to be done.'

'Work? What sort of work?' said Tess, slowing her natural pace to walk beside him.

'Washing up, of course.'

'My God, Granddad. What have you been doing all this time? Oh yes, I know. Talking to rosebushes.'

Bernard was well aware that the reprimand was purely in fun, but he realised that some form of explanation was necessary. 'Call of nature, if you must know.'

'In the flowerbed? With a washing-up bowl?'

'No, you're quite wrong. It was Colonel Mustard with the lead piping in the library.'

'Ha, ha,' said Tess. 'Although on second thoughts, I

think I'd rather you spared me the unpleasant details. I am a "young lady" after all.'

Bernard laughed and stood aside when they reached the van. 'Ladies first then,' he said with an exaggerated flourish of his arm.

Tess stuck her tongue out at him and stepped inside. Bernard followed and was refilling the kettle at the sink when there was a knock on the side of the van. Immediately afterwards, two men appeared at the open doorway. Both were casually but smartly dressed, and the shorter of the two was wearing a neck brace.

'Sorry to bother you,' said the taller of the two, 'but we're looking for a Tess Pemberton.'

20

At the speed the van had been travelling at, it hadn't been difficult to keep it in sight, and it was only a little over half an hour before Tess and her granddad had pulled off the road and parked up at a campsite near the coast. The downside was that I'd then had to wait for Alan and Scratch, who'd somehow managed to get themselves lost even though the A6 ran almost straight past the campsite entrance. By the time they'd arrived, Tess and the old boy were already tucking in to an early evening meal, so being of a considerate disposition – and because I was just so bloody relieved to have finally caught up with them – I'd decided to leave them to it until they'd done. But as soon as they'd finished, Tess had headed off towards the shower block and Granddad had disappeared inside the van for a while before reappearing and emptying a washing-up bowl into a flowerbed. Probably better to wait till they were both together, I'd thought, so we'd sat tight for a while longer before making our move.

It was hardly a big surprise that Tess and Granddad Pemberton had taken some persuading that they'd got the wrong ashes, but then I'd shown them the label on the Ziploc bag. Granddad had said something about how he'd thought they'd just misspelled Pemberton as Pendleton when they'd collected their urn, so from then on, it had been a done deal. Even so, the old man had seemed quite shifty – almost guilty-looking – when he'd handed over their urn. I'd no idea what that was about, but he was knocking on a bit, so maybe it was just a touch of the dementias or something. Tess, on the other hand, had got quite emotional and was positively gushing in her gratitude.

'How terrible it would have been if we'd scattered someone else's ashes instead of Granny's,' she'd said as she wiped away a tear.

'Yes indeed,' I'd said, 'and Alan's mum had never been north of Hendon in her life, so what she'd have thought about ending up in Dumpees is anybody's guess.'

'Dumpees?' Tess had said with a heavy question mark.

'Isn't that where you're headed?'

'Dum-*freece*. D-U-M-F-R-I-E-S. Near there anyway. A hill called Blackrigg Law. It's where my granny used to spend a lot of her time when she was growing up.'

'Ah.'

So that explained why Dumpees hadn't been listed in the road atlas's index.

Something else that wasn't a big surprise was that they'd both wanted to know how we'd found them. And because this *hadn't* come as a big surprise, I had my answer already prepared. This amounted to a sly wink, tapping the side of my nose and shooting them some crap about having the right contacts. For good measure, I even added the old line about having to kill them if I gave them any more details. They'd seemed to swallow this, and if it hadn't been for Alan's snigger, they'd probably have guessed I was in the Secret Service or somesuch. The name's Dempsey. Max Dempsey.

Explanations and the urn swapping ceremony successfully concluded, we'd dropped the hire car off at a local branch of the rental company, having unanimously agreed that we were all too knackered to think about heading all the way home. And now that we'd finally got hold of Danny's coke, I'd decided we could afford to treat ourselves and splash out on a hotel for the night. The nearest Travelodge was full, so we'd checked into a motel outside Lancaster. Daring to believe that my money worries might soon be over, I'd even gone crazy and booked two rooms instead of all crowding into one. For now, though, we'd all assembled in my and Toby's room to check out the urn that Tess and her granddad had given us and make sure that we really had got the right one this time.

I'd put it on the little desk-cum-dressing table at the side of the room and was sitting staring at it while I attempted to get my heart rate down from ridiculously rapid to acceptably energetic. Scratch was hovering at my shoulder with Alan perched on the end of one of the twin beds a few feet away. Toby was stretched out on the other and seemingly taking minimal interest in the proceedings.

'And now for the moment of truth,' I said, and I picked up the urn and gradually eased off the lid.

Never having used the stuff myself, I was certainly no expert, but there was something about the contents of the urn that didn't look quite right. A second later,

Scratch confirmed what I suspected might be wrong with it.

'Are there supposed to be little blue bits in it?'

'I dunno,' I said. 'I've never had coke in my life.'

'Me neither,' said Scratch.

Even though I was pretty sure of the answer, I thought it was worth a shot, so I twisted round in the chair and said, 'How about you, Alan? You ever had coke before?'

He shook his head and then winced from the pain in his neck. 'Only out of a can,' he said through gritted teeth.

I raised the urn to a couple of inches below my nose and sniffed gingerly. There was no way I was going to risk inhaling any of this shit.

'Well?' said Scratch.

'Bit weird,' I said and took another whiff. 'It's a bit like... sort of cheap perfume.'

'That don't sound right.'

'No, it doesn't.'

'So is it coke or not?' said Alan.

'How the fuck should I know?' I said, putting the urn back on the desk. 'But I tell you this. There's not a snowball's chance in hell that we're gonna try and palm this off unless we're absolutely bloody certain that it's the real McCoy this time.'

'What d'you mean, "palm it off"? I thought we were supposed to just find the stuff and then give it back to Danny.'

'Christ's sake, Alan, what's that gonna achieve? Back to square one, that's what, with me still owing him ten grand and him still not letting me off it until we've sold his gear for him.'

'Well, we ain't gonna be able to flog it to Nick the

142

Greek, that's for sure,' said Scratch.

I closed my eyes and silently counted to five. 'Yes, I do realise that, thank you, Scratch. We'll just have to find another buyer, that's all.'

'Oh, that's all, is it?' Alan snorted. 'So how exactly do you propose that we—?'

'I've had coke.'

It was the first time Toby had spoken a word since we'd walked into the room and he'd flopped himself down onto the bed.

The three of us turned towards him. He was lying on his side, propped up on an elbow and with an ever-so-pleased-with-himself grin smeared across his face.

'You what?' I said.

The grin faded slightly. 'It was only a little bit. At a party.'

'Jesus, Toby, you're sixteen years old.'

The grin vanished entirely. 'So? There's plenty of kids younger than me who—'

'Enough!' I shouted. 'I don't wanna hear it, OK?'

Truth be told, I didn't want to hear any more because it would have had me thinking about what my own kids got up to. But that's what a responsible parent is supposed to do, isn't it? Keep an eye on their kids to make sure they're not getting into something they shouldn't be getting into? Christ, my own brother had almost died from that sort of shit, so I should be making bloody certain that Brad and Emma weren't heading in the same direction. All in all, I'd been pretty crap as a dad lately – for a lot longer than that if I'm honest – but neither of them made it easy. Then again, though, I don't imagine there's more than a handful of teenagers on the planet who give a toss about making their parents' lives easy.

143

So lost was I in this bout of self-recrimination that I hadn't noticed Toby sidling over to the desk and picking up the cremation urn.

'I can test it for you if you like,' he said.

'No you bloody won't,' I said and grabbed the urn from him.

'Oh, come on, Unc. I'm only trying to—'

'No!'

Toby scowled and then slouched his way back to the bed.

'Doesn't look much like the coke I had,' he said. 'Maybe it's been cut with something.'

'Doubt it,' said Scratch. 'Danny told us it was pure.'

'Yeah, well,' said Alan. 'I think we all know about Danny's less than intimate relationship with the truth.'

This was getting us nowhere. One of us was going to have to try it and see if they got any effect.

'Don't look at me,' said Scratch. 'I've got enough allergies as it is. What if it's... you know... same as the last lot?'

Another snort from Alan – but not the kind I was looking for. 'So you're allergic to human ashes now, are you?'

'Course it's not ashes,' I said. 'How can it be?'

'I'm just saying, that's all,' said Scratch and then began counting off some of his allergies on his fingers. 'I've got enough trouble with nuts, milk, cheese, eggs, wheat, shellfish. Christ, I'm comin' out in a rash just thinking about it.'

As if we hadn't got the point already, he started vigorously scratching various different parts of his body.

I'd had more than enough of messing about by now, so I took a twenty pound note out of my wallet and rolled it into a tight tube.

'Here,' I said, holding it out to Alan and fixing him with a stare that told him in no uncertain terms that I wasn't having any argument.

It didn't work.

'Why me?' he said. 'Why can't you do it?'

'I need to keep a clear head' wasn't the best of reasons, I admit, and Alan didn't buy it either, so I shifted down a couple of gears to a more softly-softly approach.

'Come on, Alan, mate,' I said, hanging an arm round his shoulder. 'You don't have to take that much.'

His eyes darted back and forth between the rolled-up note, the cremation urn and my face a few times before he finally snatched the note out of my hand. 'Well, OK then, but it better not be somebody's bloody ashes.'

'It isn't,' I said. 'I already told you.'

Alan tutted and dragged the urn closer to the edge of the desk. Gently inserting the banknote into his nostril, he bent forward, but just as the other end of the note was within an inch of its objective, he suddenly straightened up again.

'Now what?' I snapped, forgetting that I was still supposed to be in softly-softly mode.

'Just gimme a minute, will you?' he snapped back and then took several short, sharp breaths like he was back in his weightlifting days and about to attempt a world record lift.

Eventually psyched up to his apparent satisfaction, he bent forward again, but instead of a recognisable snort, all I heard was a slight sniff. He started to lift his head up from the urn, but I was ready for him.

'Bit more than that,' I said, my hand exerting enough downward pressure on his upper back to keep him where he was.

I didn't even hear so much as a sniff this time, and I was about to offer a few words of encouragement when Scratch marched up behind him, thrust his hand between Alan's legs and none too gently grabbed hold of his balls. The sharp intake of breath was damn near enough to send the twenty quid note rocketing to the back of his brain.

Mission accomplished, Scratch released his grip, and Alan shot upright, coughing and spluttering, and whipped the note out of his nostril.

'You fucking wanker!' he yelled, rubbing frantically at his nose with the back of his hand.

Admittedly, the fact that Scratch, Toby and I were all pissing ourselves laughing by now wasn't much help in calming him down, but after a good few seconds, the coughing and spluttering gradually subsided.

'What the fuck did you do that for?' he said, alternating between opening his eyes as wide as they'd go and blinking away the tears that were streaming down his cheeks.

'Getting any effect yet?' said Scratch, scarcely able to get the words out through his laughter.

Alan spun round and hurled himself at him. 'I'll bloody 'ave you, you— Aagh, Jesus, it's—'

No sooner had his hands made contact with Scratch's throat than they flew back to his own face, and he shrieked in pain. For a moment, I thought the sudden movement had put his neck out again, but then he raced off into the bathroom, and immediately afterwards there was the sound of running water and a lot of splashing.

The laughter in the room didn't end quite as abruptly as Alan's attack on Scratch, but it certainly diminished considerably in volume. This was reduced still further to little more than the odd snigger when Alan yelled, 'Fuck me, there's foam comin' out of me nose.'

And when he came back out of the bathroom a moment later and we saw for ourselves that there was indeed a strange white foam erupting from his nose, a stunned and total silence descended.

21

It wasn't anywhere near as serious as it had looked, even though Alan had been convinced that his nose was disintegrating from the inside out and would eventually drop off completely. He'd calmed down once the foam had finally stopped oozing and his eyes had stopped watering, but he'd still been mightily pissed off with Scratch for the goolie-grabbing incident. But after Scratch's profuse and repeated apologies – genuine or not – the tension between them had begun to ease. Then Alan had announced that he was ravenously hungry, so I'd packed the pair of them off to fetch a takeaway in the hope they'd have the peace treaty properly signed and sealed by the time they got back.

Now, although I don't know a lot about drugs, I've heard that some of them give people the munchies, but I very much doubt that Alan's sudden craving for food had anything to do with snorting washing powder – which the stuff in the urn almost certainly was. It definitely wasn't coke, so what the fuck had happened to that? Had this Tess woman and her granddad sussed what was in the urn that Sanjeev had given them and kept it for themselves? They were hardly the sort, though, were they? But how could you tell? Granddad had seemed pretty shifty when we'd done the swap, and besides, what about all those stockbrokers and City types who apparently shoved a small fortune's worth of coke up their snotlockers every day of the week but didn't usually come across like the walking dead in pinstripes?

Too many questions, and the only way we were likely to get any answers was to pay another little visit to Ms Pemberton and her granddad. The campsite was only about twenty minutes away, but we needed to get moving as soon as Alan and Scratch got back. It wasn't that late in the evening yet, although the old man probably hit the sack early with his Bournvita, and far be it from me to want to interrupt his beauty sleep. And speaking of Alan and Scratch, where the fuck were they?

Toby must have read my mind. 'They're taking their time, aren't they? I'm starving.'

The kid was stretched out on the bed, watching some crap on the TV while I was sitting on the chair by the desk, also staring at the telly screen but taking nothing in.

'They've only been gone an hour,' I said, playing it cool. I didn't want to let on until the last minute that I'd be leaving him here with Alan while Scratch and I went back to the campsite. Otherwise, he'd be arguing the toss about wanting to come too. 'More than likely they've stopped off for a couple of beers.'

Toby grunted and muttered something about lucky bastards at the same moment as my mobile phone started ringing. Who was it this time? Danny or Carla?

I checked the display. Carla. That made it Carla eleven and Danny eight in the last hour alone.

Danny was obviously champing at the bit to find out if we'd got his coke back, but I hadn't answered any of his calls since he'd told me that Nikos might be on my tail. What was I going to tell him if I had? "Well, Danny, the good news is that we've tracked down the urn. The bad news is that it's full of bloody soap powder."

As for Carla, she'd just be wanting to give me earache for not letting her know that I'd be late home from work, and with the added information that my dinner had gone in the bin ages ago. She'd already left half a dozen voice messages, presumably to that effect, but I hadn't listened to any of them. The more recent ones would probably have been even more frantic. "Where the hell is Toby?" "Melanie's beside herself with worry." Not unreasonable, of course, but—

And that's when the thought occurred to me that I hadn't heard Toby's phone ring for hours.

'Toby?' I said, feeling the panic starting to rise from somewhere in the region of my lower intestine.

'Yeah?'

'You spoken to your mum yet?'

'No, my phone ran out of charge.'

'Jesus, Toby. The only reason I let you come on this…' I'd no idea what to call what it was we were "on" other than a wild bloody goose chase, so instead of calling it anything at all, I lobbed my mobile over at him and told him to ring her on that.

He caught it one-handed and scowled at it like he'd fished it out of a festival toilet. 'Why don't you get yourself a decent phone, Unc? This thing looks like it should be in a museum.'

'Just phone her, will you?'

'She in your contacts list?'

'No, she isn't in my contacts list. How often do you think I call her, for Christ's sake?'

He started pressing buttons as if the next one might be linked to some explosive device that would cause the phone to blow up in his face.

Brilliant. Toby's mum must surely have called Carla by now, so on top of everything else, I was going to get it seriously in the neck from both of them for leading the kid astray. Abducting him, even. I couldn't exactly tell Carla that he'd blackmailed me into taking him with us because then she'd want to know what it was that he was blackmailing me *with*. But right at that moment, I hadn't the foggiest how I was going to come up with some bullshit explanation that didn't involve having to come clean about my real day job. Christ on a bike. And there was me thinking there was no way today could possibly get any worse.

'Engaged,' said Toby, dropping the phone onto the bed.

'Well, leave a bloody message then and keep trying.'

He picked up the phone again and gave me one of those teenage pouts and half a shrug. 'So what do I say?'

It was actually a good question. If he'd called his mum earlier like I'd told him to, he was supposed to have told her he was staying the night at my place, so she'd have had no reason to ring Carla and find out the truth. Missed the boat on that one now, I reckoned. 'I don't know,' I said. 'Tell her you—'

But just as my brain went into floundering

overdrive, the mobile rang in his hand.

'That's probably her phoning back,' he said, and before I could say "Check who it is first", he hit the answer button. 'Oh, hello, Aunty Carla. I thought it was Mum calling me back.'

Oh. Fuck.

Even at this distance and with the phone up against Toby's ear, I could hear Carla jabbering on nineteen to the dozen, and the noise got even louder as he jumped down off the bed and came towards me. Although there didn't seem to be any space to get a word in, he said, 'Perhaps it'd be better if Uncle Simon explained it himself' and thrust the mobile at me.

I mouthed a "thank you" with heavy sarcasm and held the phone about a foot from my ear.

'... on earth do you think you're doing... about to call the police... Toby's mum's beside herself with...' and so on and so on, blah blah blah.

At the volume she was shrieking, it was impossible to block out all of what she was saying, but I did my best and put the phone on the desk, turned it upside down and watched it vibrate itself up against the wall. I knew, of course, that Carla would eventually have to pause for breath and start demanding answers, and I needed to come up with some kind of story that would at least quieten her down if not shut her up completely. But it had been a very long and very shitty day, and my brain was firing on less than half a cylinder. All I could think of was to make some interference-type sounds over the phone and make out that the signal was crap.

Since this was about the best I was likely to come up with off the top of my head, I reached for the phone, but as I did so, there was a knock at the door.

Probably Alan and Scratch back from the pub – hopefully with a takeaway that wasn't stone cold by now. I nodded to Toby to go and let them in and picked up the mobile, coincidentally at the very moment that Carla *did* take a breath.

'Sorry, Carla – *kerrreeshooweeh* – bad line and – *sheeeeshaaashooo* – hardly hear – *kerroooshwoooosh…*'

While I was speaking – or rather doing what I reckoned was a not-bad-at-all impression of a rubbish connection – I kept half an eye on Toby as he went over to the door and turned the handle. But from barely the crack of an opening, the door came crashing inwards, and Toby leapt back, only just managing to stay on his feet. A split second later, two familiar figures barged into the room, each with a semi-automatic stretched out in front of them.

'I think I'd better call you back,' I said into the phone, the signal having apparently and miraculously zoomed up to five bars all of a sudden.

Then I hung up.

22

Nick the Greek stood framed in the doorway – or rather, *wedged* in the doorway until he was able to force his vast bulk into the room. Pavarotti-style, he was mopping the sweat from his face with what looked like an already sodden white handkerchief. He was breathing heavily, partly from the effort of getting himself through the doorway and presumably also from the effort involved in climbing the steps up to the outside walkway that led to our room.

'So, here you—' he started but broke off immediately to launch into a phlegm-ridden coughing fit that would have had him bent double if his enormous gut hadn't made it a physical impossibility.

With a bit of luck, the bastard would choke to death on the spot, although that wasn't necessarily going to get me out of this particular hole. Kosta Coffee and Tacky would no doubt have jumped at the chance to carry on their dad's business, and Kosta's trigger finger was already looking decidedly itchy as he kept his gun pointed steadily at my chest. His eagerness to inflict serious and probably fatal damage on me was very likely fuelled by my having been the cause of the strip of white tape across the bridge of his nose and the heavy dark rings under both eyes.

I was still sitting at the desk-cum-dressing table, and Toby had retreated to the top end of his bed, his back pressed against the wall and hugging his knees like a hypothermic Oliver Twist. For all his "awesome" this and "awesome" that, the kid was obviously shitting himself.

'So, here you are at last.'

Uh-oh. Fatboy Nick had apparently got his breath back again.

'Yes indeed,' I said. 'And *here* you are too.'

Flippancy probably wasn't the best approach in the circumstances as I could tell from the narrowing of Nikos's eyes, but what had I got to lose? – Oh, wait a minute. I remember now. My balls. Yes, that was it. One or both was what he'd told me, depending on how seriously I'd pissed him off, although from the look on his face, it was a fairly certain bet that this was going to be the full double whammy.

Unblinking, he held my gaze for a few more seconds before his microscopic brain told him to check out the rest of the room. His droopy moustache crimped into the beginnings of a smirk when he spotted Toby on the bed.

'Well, well,' he said. 'I see you have a liking for the young boys, eh?'

'He's my nephew.'

'Ah, yes. Good idea. Keep it in the family.'

He turned back to me and tapped the side of his nose with a podgy finger. Given the opportunity, I'd have done a whole lot more than tap it at that particular moment.

155

'Uncle Niko?'

The voice seemed to be coming from Nikos's direction, but unless he was an accomplished ventriloquist in his spare time, I was sure I'd have seen his lips move despite the droopy moustache.

'What?'

Definitely saw his lips move that time.

'Can I come in? It's cold out here.'

Nikos, who hadn't moved from his position just inside the open doorway, muttered something that sounded like Greek. Then he took a couple of shuffling steps further into the room.

The ventriloquist's dummy edged past his puppet master and plonked a large canvas holdall onto the floor with a clunking metallic sound. Some kind of toolbag, I guessed.

'You so frickin' cold, Dimitri, why you not close the frickin' door?'

Nikos didn't even look at the guy when he spoke. Clearly not his favourite nephew.

'Sure, Uncle Niko. Sure I will,' said Dimitri and went to close the door.

Maybe Nikos wasn't his favourite uncle either, but Dimitri was either shit scared of him or a committed brown-noser. Possibly both.

He was in his late twenties and snappily dressed in expensive leather slip-ons, cream chinos and a matching open-neck shirt. Good-looking if you liked the swarthy type with the slicked back black hair, heavy eyebrows and razor-straight nose. The family resemblance with Kosta and Tacky was instantly recognisable. Or was it just that all Greek blokes looked like that? I hadn't had a lot of first-hand experience apart from this bunch of arseholes.

Nikos's handkerchief was fighting a losing battle with the sweat-mopping job, so he stuffed it into his pocket and lumbered over to the second bed – the one that Toby wasn't on – and eased himself onto it, one bum cheek at a time. Placing his hands on his tree trunk thighs, wrists outwards, he leaned forward slightly and eyeballed me from about five feet away.

'So,' he said. 'You and me gonna have a little chat, yeah?'

Even from that distance, the stink of sweat was almost overpowering and wasn't doing my osmophobia any good at all. On the other hand, that was nothing compared to the likely outcome of the "little chat" we were about to have.

'Lucky for you, you din kill 'im,' he went on.

'Kill who?'

Nikos's sudden and unexpected guffaw nearly knocked me off my chair. '"Kill *who*?" he says. You hear that, boys? "Kill *who*?".'

He shot a glance at Kosta Coffee and then Tacky to check whether they'd found my question as hilariously funny as he did, but they simply grinned back at him with what looked like little more than filial duty.

Nikos's guffawing ended as abruptly as if his laughter circuit had blown a fuse, and he instantly reverted to scary gangster mode.

'My son, Vasilis, you shitfrick. No-one shoot my boy and not pay the price. Like I say, is lucky for you you din kill 'im.'

Oh Christ. The one that Scratch had hit in the alleyway. I'd almost forgotten.

'But they were shooting at *us*,' I said, heavy on the indignation. 'What were we supposed to do?'

'And then there's the matter of you try to screw me

over some shit I don't know what is, but sure as frick ain't no frickin' coke.'

OK, I had to put my hands up to that one, but pleading mitigating circumstances was definitely worth a stab. 'That was a genuine mistake, yeah? If I'd known it wasn't coke, I'd never have—'

'Enough of your bullshit!' roared Nikos, cutting me off in my lawyerly prime. And then he turned to Kosta with a sideways nod at yours truly.

He barked something at him in Greek, which in turn led to Kosta doing his own nodding thing at the Dimitri guy. 'Bring me the bag.'

Dimitri looked delighted to be directly involved in whatever unpleasantness was going to happen next, and he picked up the canvas holdall and deposited it at Kosta's feet.

'Keep him covered,' said Kosta, handing Dimitri his gun and stooping to unzip the bag.

The grin on Dimitri's face widened like he was about to cream his pants, and he aimed the gun at my head, two-handed and with his feet spread apart as if he was some over-zealous cop in an American TV show.

If he was trying to impress his Uncle Nikos, it was an epic fail.

'What the frick you doing, Dimitri? This ain't no Hawaii Fifty, for frick's sake.'

Dimitri's grin slipped down a gear, and he shuffled his feet together and switched to a single-handed grip on the gun.

Meanwhile, Kosta had extracted a couple of lengths of rope from the holdall and had begun to tie my wrists together behind the back of the chair.

I glanced over at Toby, who was still hunched up on

the bed and looking even more terrified than before. I thought about saying something reassuring to him, but there wasn't much that came to mind. Our only hope was that the cavalry would arrive at any minute in the unlikely form of Alan and Scratch bursting into the room with their guns blazing and preferably sober.

'Fat chance of that, old son.'

It was the voice in my head come back to haunt me. I hadn't heard a peep out of it since it had tried to persuade me to shove Toby under a train, or maybe I'd managed to blank it out for all that time.

'As I see it,' the voice went on, 'your only chance is to try and *talk* your way out of it.'

'Oh yes? And what do you suggest I talk *about* exactly? How it's all been a terrible misunderstanding and I promise not to shoot any of his kids again or stitch him up over a coke deal as long as he doesn't deprive me of my bollocks?'

'No need to be facetious. I'm only trying to help.'

'Well why don't you try suggesting something useful then?'

'OK. For a start, you haven't even *mentioned* the other urn. The one you got from Tess whatsherface and her granddad.'

I shot a quick glance at the urn on the desk beside me. 'Oh yeah, that's genius, that is. The guy's about to perform a bollockectomy on me because I gave him a cremation urn full of some old granny's ashes instead of coke, and now you're telling me to give him another one that's full of fucking soap powder.'

'All I'm saying is that it'll buy you some time in the admittedly unlikely event that Scratch and Alan might actually come to your rescue. And when all's said and done, what else can he do to you? You've only got the two testicles as far as I'm aware.'

If the voice had been standing in front of me instead of only existing inside my head, I would have given it a withering glare and possibly even punched it in the face. But even the punch in the face would have been out of the question because, by now, my hands and feet were securely tied.

His task completed, Kosta Coffee then picked up the canvas holdall and set it down on the bed beside his dad and master. Nikos had a good old rummage through the contents as if he was looking for his car keys inside a giant and overstuffed handbag.

'Ah yes. This to start with, I think,' he said eventually and triumphantly produced what looked very much like a portable blowtorch.

This turned out to be *exactly* what it was when Kosta took it from him, and I heard the hiss of gas and the click of a cigarette lighter, then watched the flame being adjusted to what I imagined was maximum agony level.

Jesus Christ. Maybe the voice had a point after all.

'The thing is,' I blurted, 'there's some different stuff in this urn here.'

Nikos's gaze followed my nod to the urn on the desk. 'Ah, yes… urn. Not jar. Urn. For the ashes. You know, in Greece, we never burn the dead bodies.'

'Is that right?' I said, hoping to prolong any conversation that might be on offer.

'No. Only the live ones.'

Once again, Nikos roared with laughter at his own joke whilst pointing at the mini flamethrower in Kosta's hand. And as before, the hilarity ended as abruptly as it had begun.

'You think I born yesterday?' he yelled at me from

too close quarters. 'Frickin' urn is exact same like last time.'

'It's not, I promise you. The other urn was—'

But before I could get any further, he jerked his triple chin round to address the room in general and added a few extra decibels. 'What the frick is that goddamn frickin' noise?'

'Sounds like a car alarm, Papa,' said Tacky.

Maybe it was the blood pumping in my ears that had drowned it out, but I hadn't been aware of the racket from outside the room until that moment.

'Holy mother of God,' said Nikos, reducing his volume by a couple of notches. 'Dimitri, go check it's not *my* car.'

The beginnings of a "Why me?" expression began to form on Dimitri's face, but he presumably thought better of it and set off towards the door.

'And leave the frickin' gun,' Nikos shouted after him.

There was an audible sigh and a very definite pout as Dimitri handed his semi-automatic to Tacky, and then he was gone.

'Papa, I don't know how much gas there is in this thing,' said Kosta, brandishing the still flaming blowtorch.

'Ah yes, we must strike while the iron is hot, as you English say.'

Only about a three on the guffaw scale this time but all of it directed at me.

'But first the trousers, I think,' Nikos added, beckoning Tacky with a tilt of his head. 'They look expensive. Such a waste to damage them.'

Tacky thrust his own gun and the one Dimitri had given him into his waistband, but before he'd taken

161

more than two steps, the door flew open.

'It *is* your car, Uncle Niko,' panted Dimitri. 'Someone's trying to break into it.'

'Holy Christ, boy,' said Nikos, reintroducing his handkerchief to the sea of sweat on his forehead. 'Just go and frickin' deal with it then.'

'I'll need a gun, though.'

Nikos momentarily suspended the brow mopping operation. 'You serious? Some frickin' kid and you gonna blow 'em away?'

'No, but—'

'They get away with my frickin' car, you get the same as this *maláka*, OK?'

Nikos pointed in the general direction of my wedding tackle, and after less than a moment's hesitation, Dimitri slouched back out of the door and slammed it behind him.

'What I do to deserve this prick in the family?' said Nikos to nobody in particular. 'My sister, I tell her no good would come from marrying a crazy-arse bum from Crete, and now look what happen.'

There was a bit of chat back and forth between Nikos and his two sons, but I was hardly listening. There wasn't much point anyway because it was all in Greek. Instead, I let my mind wander over the slim possibility that the car alarm might have something to do with Alan and Scratch and some kind of rescue attempt. But I snapped back into the reality of the situation when Tacky stooped in front of me and started to undo the top button of my trousers.

'Hang on, hang on,' I said. 'What about this other urn? The coke?'

Nikos frowned like he was finally giving the idea some serious thought, the creases on his forehead

162

almost silver in the reflected light from the sweat.

By the time he'd finished thinking and frowning, my trousers were round my ankles.

'For God's sake, try it, Tacky,' he said at last. 'Anything to shut him up.'

It occurred to me that there were plenty of other ways of doing that – a gag being one of the least painful, for instance – but pointing this out would have been entirely counterproductive.

Tacky reached past me and picked up the urn from the desk-cum-dressing table. He removed the lid and peered inside.

'It's got blue bits in it.'

'I told you it was different to the other stuff,' I said, 'and I really don't know if it's coke or not, so why not give it a snort and see what you think? I mean, where's the harm in that?'

I knew precisely what "the harm" would be, of course, and it certainly wasn't going to endear me to Tacky or any other member of the Spiropoulos family here present, but keeping my scrotum intact for even a few extra minutes was by far my number one priority right now.

Tacky cocked an eyebrow at Nikos for some fatherly advice on how to proceed, and in return he got a "Get the frick on with it, you pussy" in Greek – or something like that. Daddy Nikos was getting distinctly grumpy. Maybe it was the fact that he hadn't eaten anything in the last fifteen minutes or so, or maybe he was just anxious to get the torturing part of the evening's entertainment started. Either way, Tacky tipped some of the urn's contents onto the back of his hand and took a couple of generous inhalations.

23

In an almost exact repeat of Alan's experience earlier, Tacky was now in the bathroom, liberally splashing his face with water.

'Not cocaine, I think,' said Nikos in a calm, measured kind of tone that made him sound even more like a psycho than when he was yelling his head off.

I could hardly argue the point, but it was worth a try.

'I told you I didn't know if it was coke,' I said. 'The people we got it from must have swapped it. Given us the wrong stuff by mistake maybe. But I can get it for you. The actual coke, I mean.'

Nikos ignored me, or perhaps he was simply distracted by Tacky's reappearance in the bathroom doorway, traces of foam still dribbling from his nostrils and his eyes blood red and streaming.

'Christ, this stuff stings,' he said, rubbing his eyes with the heels of his hands.

'Mama always said we should keep our noses clean,' Kosta chuckled.

Tacky told him to fuck off, and Nikos slapped his

meaty paws down onto his even more meaty thighs.

'Enough of this,' he said. 'My stomach she tells me is late for her dinner.'

A vague flap of his hand was all the encouragement Kosta needed, and he strode towards me with what I considered to be unnecessary haste. He stood over me and adjusted the flame on the blowtorch, his leer of a grin leaving me in no doubt that he was about to take great pleasure in his work. All I could hope for was that the bloody gas ran out first, although God knows what other little toys they had in their toolbag that might cause even more agony than having my bollocks torched. I couldn't imagine quite what they might be, but then again, I wasn't a fucking psychopath with a PhD in the gratuitous inflicting of pain like these bastards.

'Wait,' said Daddy Psychopath just as Kosta was preparing to take aim. 'I almost forgot. Underpants first, Tacky.'

'Eh?' Either Tacky didn't understand what his old man was asking him to do or he knew perfectly well and wasn't at all keen on the idea.

'Take – off – his – frickin' – underpants,' said Nikos, enunciating every word and then turned his attention back to me. 'You see, this is point where most people they shit themselves. It make terrible mess of your Kevin Kleins.'

Oh yeah, and as if the blowtorch wasn't going to destroy them completely. The only good news was that Tacky hadn't moved so much as a muscle to expose my nether regions.

Nikos had spotted it too. 'For frick's sake, Tacky, I thought I told you to—'

He was interrupted by the ringing of a mobile

phone. Mine, to be precise, and I wasn't going to waste what was likely to be the very last straw I could clutch at. 'That's probably them now.'

'Them? Them who?' said Nikos, although if he was genuinely interested in the answer, he was disguising it well.

'My supplier,' I said. 'They've probably realised there's been a mix-up with the coke, and they're calling to make some arrangement to put things right.'

'Bullshit.'

'No, seriously. I'd stake my life on it.'

'Or your balls?'

I gave him as much of a shrug as I could manage with my hands tied behind my back. 'If you like.'

'Yes, I do like. I like very much indeed,' said Nikos, and after a few seconds of twiddling with one end of his droopy moustache, barked at Tacky to, 'See who the frick it is, and do something useful for once in your life.'

For his part, Tacky seemed more than happy to be relieved of his underpants duty, however temporarily, and he snatched up my mobile from the desk-cum-dressing table. More than likely, it would turn out to be Danny or Carla again, but there was still a very remote possibility that it might be—

'Someone called Alan,' said Tacky, gazing at the display on my mobile as if he'd been expecting a call from Santa Claus instead.

Let the bugles sound. The bloody cavalry at last.

'That's him,' I said, trying not to shout. 'My supplier.'

Nikos narrowed his eyes at me while his little grey cells tried to figure out whether I was lying or not. Apparently, his remaining twelve good cells and true

166

failed to reach a verdict, so he held out his hand for Tacky to pass him the phone.

He hit the answer button, which, given the thickness of his fingers and the smallness of the buttons, was no mean feat in itself, and he held the phone up to his face. 'Yes?'

'Max?'

I was close enough to Nikos to be able to hear what Alan was saying at the other end of the line.

'No, not Max. Max is... a little tied up at the moment.'

Christ, this guy should be on the stage. He'd go down a storm as long as the audience was packed full of Nikos clones, since he was the only one who seemed to find his jokes the least bit funny.

'Oh, right,' said Alan. 'So you must be the fat Greek twat who's got more sweat on him than a Sumo wrestler in a Turkish bath.'

Good one, Alan. Very subtle. I just hope to God you've got something up your sleeve to back that up with.

Nikos muttered something in Greek and then, 'What do you want?'

'I want to talk to Max.'

'I just told you. Max is—'

'Yeah, yeah, so what if I was to tell you I have something that belongs to you?'

Nikos suddenly sat forward as far as his belly would allow. 'You do?'

'Certainly.'

'So where are you?'

'In the car park, right outside where you are now.'

'But this is excellent. Bring the stuff in to me now, and we can—'

167

'Don't think so, fat boy. Much better we have our little chat out here in the open. And make sure you come on your own. I see anyone else, I won't be responsible for the consequences.'

'Consequences? What consequences?'

But judging by the bleeping noise from the phone, Alan had already hung up.

I hadn't got the slightest idea what Alan was playing at, and I hoped to hell he knew what he was doing. There was no way he could have got hold of the coke, so what was it that he'd got that belonged to Nikos? A straightforward bluff was going to achieve doodly squat, unless... Oh yeah, that might work a treat.

I allowed myself a flicker of a smile as I watched Nikos plant his hands on either side of him on the bed and kind of bounce two or three times in an effort to force himself upright.

'Frick's sake,' he grunted after a couple more failed attempts, 'one of you come and help me up here.'

In fact, it took both Tacky *and* Kosta Coffee to get him onto his feet and then a load more grunting and groaning as he squeezed himself out through the door and onto the walkway. From where I was sitting, I had a clear view of him as he placed his hands on the metal guard rail and looked down into the car park.

There was a pause, and all I could hear was the blare of the car alarm and Nikos shouting 'What?'

Another pause and still the racket of the car alarm.

'I can't hear a frickin' word you say,' yelled Nikos and then turned back into the room. 'Tacky, you got the car key?'

Tacky fished in his various pockets but without success.

'What's happening, Papa?' said Kosta.

'They got Dimitri sat on front of my car with a gun at his head.'

This was sounding promising.

'Who's "they"?'

'Two of *his* boys, far as I can see,' said Nikos, jabbing a finger in my direction.

'So they don't have the coke?'

'It don't look like it, no. – Tacky, the key's on the frickin' bed.'

Tacky's gaze followed his father's nod to the foot of Toby's bed, then he scuttled over and handed him the little lump of black plastic. A moment later, there was a bleeping sound and the car alarm instantly quit its blaring.

'So tell me again,' shouted Nikos, only marginally quieter than before. 'What the frick is it you want?'

'Let Max and the boy go, and you can have him.'

It was Alan's voice. Distant but still clearly audible.

'Why?'

'Why what?'

'Why I want him back?'

'Christ, I dunno. He's one of yours, isn't he?'

'My sister's boy, yes.'

'You want us to shoot him or what?'

'Please yourself. Kid's a pain in the arse. You got the merchandise?'

'No, we fucking haven't. And I'll say it again 'cos maybe you didn't understand me the first time. Let Max and Toby go or your nephew gets it. Capiche?'

'Fine. Just don't damage the paintwork on my car, OK?'

With that, Nikos battled his way back into the room and flopped himself down onto the bed again.

169

I had to admit that, as a rescue attempt, Alan and Scratch's plan hadn't turned out terribly well.

'Now then,' said Nikos. 'Enough of pissing about. If we don't get this done and eat soon, I gonna die of frickin' starvation. Kosta?'

As before, Kosta readjusted the flame on the blowtorch.

'What about the underpants?' he said.

'Screw the frickin' underpants. Just do it.'

Seemingly satisfied with the blowtorch's flame, Kosta brought it steadily closer to its intended target. I squeezed my eyes tight shut, and I felt my teeth involuntarily clamp together. The temperature in my groin rocketed rapidly from a not unpleasant warmth to seriously hot to Jesus Christ almighty and the unmistakable aroma of singeing cotton.

24

I take it all back. Nephew Toby is a fantastic kid, and I won't hear a word spoken against him. OK, so he did blackmail me and landed me in all kinds of shit with Carla, but from now on I'll always love him as the saviour of my balls – and my knob as well, come to think of it, as the blowtorch would presumably not have been able to differentiate.

There I was, tied to the chair and about to have my uglies char-grilled when all of a sudden Toby shouts out, 'Wait! I've got an idea.'

I slid open both eyelids to see that Toby was no longer clutching his knees to his chest but was sitting bolt upright on the edge of the bed. Now, even though I wouldn't have expected Nick the Greek or his poxy progeny to take a scrap of notice of a sixteen-year-old kid, Kosta Coffee instantly backed off with the blowtorch – not by much, it has to be said, but enough to give my meat and two veg a very welcome cooling off period.

During my mercifully brief time in their company, I'd become aware that the brothers Spiropoulos would scarcely even breathe without their daddy's say-so, and this was no exception. Still half-stooping, Kosta swivelled his head round to gawp at Nikos while he awaited further instruction. On this occasion, however, it proved to be the wrong response.

'What the frick you stop for?' said Nikos.

'Er… the kid?' said Kosta.

'Oh, so you take orders from kids now, do you?'

'No, but—'

'I'm serious,' Toby interrupted. 'It's the only way you can guarantee to get your coke. Frying my uncle's balls isn't going to get you anything except… well, fried balls, I guess.'

The lad ought to be a lawyer when he grows up. Convincing Nikos was no mean feat, but Toby managed it eventually, putting forward a case that was impossible to find fault with. Well, his mum and Carla would have done, of course, and before I get accused of not giving a toss about my own nephew's health and wellbeing, I wasn't exactly over the moon about the idea myself. Agreeing to leave Toby in the hands of a nutjob gangster was not a decision to be taken lightly, but the kid had been insistent that it was the only way out of my current predicament. All I had to do was track down Nikos's precious coke, and Toby would be returned to me without so much as a hair out of place. It had sounded straightforward enough in theory, but in practice? Actually getting hold of the coke could well be a damn sight easier said than done.

As soon as Nikos had agreed the deal, he'd started complaining about his life-threatening hunger pains again and squeezed himself out of the room, leaving a couple of barked instructions in his wake. Dutiful as always, Tacky had untied me from the chair while

Kosta – scowling with brokenhearted disappointment – extinguished the blowtorch and returned it to its fellow pain inflicters in the canvas holdall. Toby had got down off the bed, and as the two brothers had led him away, he'd turned and winked at me over his shoulder.

'Don't worry, Unc. I'll be fine,' he'd said, and I'd smiled weakly back at him, trying to exude as much confidence as I could muster even though I was scared shitless of what would happen if I failed to come up with my end of the bargain.

Still wearing only my Calvin Kleins, I'd followed them out onto the walkway and looked down into the car park below. Alan and Scratch were perched on the front of a black Mercedes – presumably Nikos's – with Dimitri sandwiched between them and looking decidedly groggy. I shouted down to them that I'd done a deal with Nikos and to let Dimitri go. Not surprisingly, they'd started firing questions up at me, but then they'd spotted Nikos lumbering towards them with Kosta, Tacky and Toby in tow, and they'd lapsed into a bewildered silence before sliding themselves off the bonnet of the Merc. Dimitri stayed where he was, scarcely able to support himself, until Nikos sent him sprawling onto the tarmac with a full power backhander to the side of the face.

Alan and Scratch had stepped away from the car and watched as Nikos clambered into the back seat with predictable difficulty and Kosta dragged his cousin to his feet and bundled him into the passenger seat. With Tacky at the wheel and Toby wedged between Nikos and Kosta in the back, the Merc had sped off to whatever eatery Nikos was going to stuff his face at.

Back in the motel room and fully dressed again, I'd then had to explain everything to Alan and Scratch. To put it mildly, they hadn't been too impressed with the plan, but at least they'd stopped short of calling me a heartless bastard who cared more about preserving my genitals than I did about my own nephew – well, not to my face anyway.

Alan and I had been all for heading straight back to the campsite for the coke until Scratch had pointed out that it was already well past midnight, that we were all totally knackered, and that we'd function a lot better after a few hours' kip.

'As long as we get there early enough in the morning before they set off, I don't see why we need to rush over there in the middle of the night and scare the pants off 'em.'

For once, Scratch's logic had seemed to be impeccable, so he and Alan had headed off to their own room while I'd climbed into bed and buried myself under the duvet without even bothering to get undressed again. What with the Toby situation and all the other shit that was battering at my brain cells, I was pretty certain that sleep wasn't going to come easy, if at all. As it turned out, though, I must have nodded off the moment my head hit the pillow because the next thing I was aware of was the bright daylight streaming through a gap in the curtains, immediately followed by the terrible sensation that there'd been a massive fuckup. This was confirmed when I glanced at my watch.

Half past nine? How the hell did it get to half past fucking nine?

I was sure I'd set the alarm on my phone for half five, but when I snatched it up from the bedside table,

I saw straight away that I'd set it for 5.30 in the afternoon instead of 5.30 in the morning. I've never been a fan of the twenty-four hour clock and always had my mobile on the twelve-hour setting. Piss and bollocks.

Clearly, Alan and Scratch hadn't set an alarm at all – or they'd slept through it – because when I hammered on their door less than a minute later, it was several seconds before a bleary-eyed Alan opened it and treated me to an up close and personal view of his tonsils with an enormous yawn.

'Shit, I guess we're screwed then,' he'd said helpfully when I told him what time it was. 'If they're anything like yer average camper, they'll have been up and away an hour or so ago at least.'

And so it had proved to be. On the off-chance that Ms Pemberton and her granddad might not be "yer average camper" and been enjoying a leisurely breakfast before hitting the road, we'd raced over to the campsite only to find an empty space where their van had been the evening before.

So here we were now, heading north on the M6 and silently praying to whoever might be listening that sooner or later we'd catch sight of the camper van. But it was a silence that was beginning to get on my nerves. It had been half an hour or more since we'd exhausted the hotly disputed topic of whose fault it was that we'd overslept, and from then on, nobody had uttered so much as a cough. Maybe it was my paranoia or my guilty conscience, but I'd also been getting the distinct impression that Alan and Scratch were still narked at me for allowing Toby to be taken as a hostage. Like as not, it wasn't going to make a whole lot of difference – and I certainly wasn't expecting absolution – but I had to at least make *some* attempt at clearing the air.

'Listen,' I said. 'I don't like it any more than you do. He's my nephew, for Christ's sake, but what else was I supposed to do?'

I was in the back seat with Scratch driving and Alan in the passenger seat, and I easily caught the glance that passed between them.

'Didn't say a word,' said Scratch, eyeballing me in the rear-view mirror.

'Precisely my point,' I said. 'I mean, it's all very well for you two to sit there in judgement, but what would you have done in that situation?'

'Nobody's judging you, Max,' said Alan. 'It was the kid's idea after all, and I don't see you had much choice. It was either that or…'

He left the sentence hanging, but Scratch completed it for him. 'Incinerated goolies.'

'Christ almighty,' I said. 'Carla and her sister will have my balls anyway just for bringing Toby along. What do you reckon they'll do when they find out I've left him as a hostage with a bunch of psychopathic Greek drug dealers?'

'Could be worse,' said Scratch. 'I've heard those Russians are a right—'

'Shut up, Scratch.'

'Look,' said Alan, the voice of reason. 'All we've gotta do is get hold of the real coke, and Nick the Greek'll let him go.'

'Simple as that, eh? We don't even know if the happy campers have actually got the stuff.'

'They must have. Sanjeev gave them the urn with the coke in. We got the urn back. No coke. So they must have switched it.'

176

'Why?'

'How should I know?' The voice of reason was getting tetchy. 'Maybe when they sussed what it was, they decided to sell it themselves.'

'Oh yeah, 'cos they really looked like big league dope peddlers to me. What did you think, Scratch?'

Scratch got as far as 'Well, I—' when Alan cut in with, 'OK, smartarse, so where else is it gonna be?'

He was right, of course. If the Pemberton woman and her granddad didn't have it, where the hell else could it be?

I stared out of the side window as the scenery raced past at well over the legal speed limit. My body was telling me it was desperately in need of more sleep, but my brain wasn't having any of it. Even so, it was an uphill battle to stop my eyes from closing, but whenever they did, it wasn't for very long. I had Danny, Carla and my mobile phone to thank for that.

And right on cue, there it was again. I checked the display. Carla.

I clicked the red button, and a temporary peace returned.

25

Carla put the phone back in its cradle on the kitchen wall. No point leaving a message. She'd left a dozen already, and the bastard still hadn't called her back. So what in God's name was he doing, and where the hell was he? More to the point, where the hell was Toby?

Melanie had been calling her about every ten minutes. Not surprisingly, she was doing her nut.

'Maybe they've been in some terrible car accident,' she'd said on the last occasion, only narrowly managing to control her sobbing. 'Perhaps I should start phoning round all the hospitals.'

'Simon didn't take the car. It's still in the driveway,' Carla had told her. 'He was meeting Toby at the railway station, the same as yesterday.'

'Train crash then.'

'I doubt it. I've had the news on all the time, and there's been no mention of anything like that. In any case, every time I try and phone Simon, it doesn't ring for long enough, so he's obviously physically able enough to reject my calls.'

'But what if he's OK and Toby isn't? What if

something awful's happened to Toby, and Simon can't bring himself to tell us?'

It wasn't an unreasonable assumption, of course. Simon had always been a great one for burying his head in the sand whenever a situation arose that he didn't want to face up to. Carla couldn't remember a single time that he'd yelled at the kids. It had always been her that had had to lay down the law, but at least that had earned her a modicum of respect. Emma and Brad might well have thought of her as a bit of a dragon, but that was a damn sight better than being an ineffectual prat, which she was fairly sure was their opinion of Simon.

She glanced at the clock on the wall. It was one of those fancy designer jobs that was more for decoration than being much use to tell the time by, so it took her a moment to figure out that it was still a little too early for wine even by her standards.

'Coffee then,' she said aloud and began to fill the kettle.

But no sooner had she returned the kettle to its base and flicked the switch than the opening notes of *Love is a Stranger* announced that there was an incoming call on her smartphone.

At bloody last, she thought, but the flicker of hope was instantly dashed when she saw who was calling. It was always good to hear from Dimitri, of course, but a cosy little chitchat with her lover wasn't going to help her find out where Toby was and to know for sure that he wasn't lying face down in some gutter in a pool of his own blood.

'Hello? Dimitri?'

'What's up, Carla, my angel? You don't sound very happy it's me.'

'Sorry, no, I was expecting... someone else.'

'Hey, don't tell me you've found yourself another lover.'

Carla could hear the smirk in his voice, but she was in no mood for kidding around.

'Where are you?' she said.

'I, my darling, am in...' There was a brief pause as if he was expecting a drum roll, and then he continued with a rough approximation of a posh English accent, '... the Excelsior Hotel, Lancashire.'

'Lancashire?'

'Correct.'

'Which town, though?'

'I just told you.'

'Lancashire's a county. Do you mean Lancaster?'

'Er... yeah, that's it. Lancaster. Anyway, babes, you just wouldn't believe this place. Five star with all the trimmings. I mean, how cool is that, man?'

Carla had lost count of the number of times she'd asked him not to call her "man", and she wasn't overly keen on "babes" either, but had finally admitted defeat.

'So what are you doing in Lancaster?' she said.

'It's kinda complicated,' said Dimitri. 'Uncle Nikos is here, though, and Kosta and Tacky. Or at least they *were* here, but they've gone out to get something to eat. Left me in charge, they did.'

She could almost see him preening like a kid who'd just told his parents he'd come top of the class.

She'd known he'd been going on some sort of trip with his uncle and two of his cousins, but he'd been irritatingly vague and mysterious when she'd quizzed him about it. She'd never met any of his family, although she'd heard enough about Uncle Nikos to know that he was bordering on psycho. Whatever he'd left Dimitri in charge of was likely to be something she really didn't want to know about, but she felt compelled to ask the question anyway.

'Left you in charge? In charge of what? A hotel room?'

'Like I said, it's complicated. But, hey, have a look at your screen and check *this* out.'

Carla did as she was told and stared at the screen on her phone as he gave her an audiovisual tour of the room. It was hardly any different from any of the handful of other five star hotels she'd been in, but she resisted the temptation to tell him so and made the occasional noises of approval to demonstrate how impressed she was. One thing that struck her as slightly odd, however, was that he seemed to deliberately skirt around the second bed in the room without showing it in all its silk-sheeted glory as he did with the other one. Presumably the two beds were exactly the same and he didn't want to bore her with the repetition. Not that she could have been any more bored than she was already, and she would have been relieved when the tour was finally over if it hadn't been for the sudden shift of focus and the totally unexpected image that now appeared on her screen.

'And what about this little beauty?' said Dimitri.

Carla's mouth dropped open as she stared in horror at the gun he was holding up to the camera. 'Christ almighty, Dimitri. What the hell are you doing with that?'

'Cool, huh?'

'No, not cool. Not cool at all. Is it real?'

'Course it's real. Wouldn't be much point if—'

'So what are you *doing* with it?'

'Can't really tell you that, babes. Let's just say there's a bit of a hostage situation going down right now.'

'Hosta—? Oh God, don't tell me you've kidnapped somebody.'

'Hey, don't worry about it. He gives me any trouble and... blam!'

Carla watched as the camera panned shakily upwards, following the gun until it seemed to be pointing at something – or some*one* – in another part of the room. Possibly in the direction of the bed that Dimitri hadn't shown her earlier.

'Are you completely bloody insane?'

'Nah, kid's a pussy,' said Dimitri.

'Kid? You've kidnapped a *kid*?'

'Wanna peek at him?'

'No, I don't want a bloody peek.'

The image on her screen began to rotate rapidly around the room, but before whoever the "kid" was came into view, Carla clamped the phone to her ear. She had no wish to see Dimitri's hostage and what sort of state he might be in.

'Come on, pussy-boy,' Dimitri was saying. 'Big smile for the nice lady.'

'Get that thing out of my face, you fucking bellend.'

The voice over the phone was a young boy's. Teenage probably. Carla thought she might even have heard it before somewhere but couldn't place it.

'You speak to me like that again,' said Dimitri, 'and I'll put a bullet in your fucking head.'

'I don't think you've fully grasped the concept of hostage taking, have you? And what do you think your Uncle Nikos is going to say when...'

But Carla didn't need to hear any more. She snatched the phone away from her ear and stared at the screen to confirm that the impossible was really happening.

'What the...?'

No more words came to mind, her brain fully occupied in keeping her upright as her hand sought the stability of the granite worktop. She took several deep breaths as she battled to regain the power of speech. Her head was awash with a thousand questions, but they'd have to remain unanswered for the time being. Right now, her nephew's safety was by far the most urgent priority.

'If you—' she began, but broke off when her voice came out as little more than a high pitched squeak.

She cleared her throat and tried again. 'Listen to me, Dimitri. If you harm so much as a hair on that kid's head, so help me I will personally break every single bone in your body, then cut out your heart and eat it for breakfast.'

In an instant, the image on Carla's phone switched from Toby's face and back to Dimitri again, his dark features several shades lighter than normal.

'Why?' he said. 'What's the problem, babes?'

'The problem, "babes", is that the lad that you happen to be holding at gunpoint also happens to be my fucking nephew.'

By the time she'd finished speaking, the phone was an inch away from her mouth and her voice had risen in volume to an almost deafening screech.

She checked the screen again. Dimitri's lower lip was clamped between his teeth, and his complexion was far closer to Arctic Circle than Mediterranean. His limited capacity for rational thought was clearly struggling to get to grips with what he'd just heard.

'So, if this kid is your nephew, who's Max Dempsey?'

'Who?'

'Max Dempsey. The kid's uncle. Your husband's name is Simon, so is he your brother or what?'

'What the hell are you talking about? I've never even *heard* of a Max Dempsey.'

During the next few minutes, Carla listened with mounting impatience and a rapidly escalating sense of horror to Dimitri's faltering explanation until she'd gleaned enough to realise that immediate action was called for.

'Shut up and listen,' she said, cutting him off mid sentence. 'The first thing you do is you get Toby out of there right now – and I mean *right now* – and as soon as you're clear of the place, you call me again, OK? I'll check out train times and tell you where and when to meet me.'

'But I can't do that,' Dimitri protested. 'Uncle Nikos will—'

'At this precise moment in time,' Carla interrupted, 'I couldn't give a monkey's whether your Uncle Nikos cuts off your dick and makes a souvlaki out of it. What I'm telling you is I'll do a damn sight worse if you don't get my nephew out of there by the time I count to ten. And if that's not enough of an incentive, how about this? – "No, officer, I've no idea why he's got a sixteen-year-old boy tied to his bed in a hotel room".'

26

Bernard hated shopping of any description. Buying shoes was one of the worst. Dottie had always insisted he had a new pair about every six months or so, even though there was nothing wrong with the dozens of pairs he already owned. She never bought shoes for herself at anything like that kind of regularity and only at all if it was for some special occasion or other.

Shoe shops had always brought out the inner teenager in Bernard in the sense that the moment he stepped over the threshold of a Clarks or a Russell and Bromley's, he would slouch, shuffle and pout like a grounded thirteen-year-old. From then on, any question that was addressed to him – either by Dottie or the shop assistant – was met with a barely audible cross between a grunt and a mutter.

'They're half a size bigger than the other pair. Any better?'

'Ugh mmph.'

'I'm sorry?'

'Ugh mmph' but with a shade more stress on the "mmph".

The only *good* thing about shoe shops was that you could actually sit down for most of the time you were in one, which was why Bernard hated supermarkets even more than he detested shoe shops.

'Keep up, Granddad,' Tess called back over her shoulder. 'It's like shopping with a ten-year-old.'

Bernard was lagging about five yards behind, his forearms resting on the handlebar of the still almost empty shopping trolley, his head bowed and his ears trying to block out the constant "*squeak squeak squeak*" of the wheels and the appalling supermarket muzak. Tess had stopped to let him catch up, so he didn't bother to increase his speed.

'Damn thing doesn't even run straight,' he said when he drew level with her. 'Keeps veering off to the left all the time. Spot of oil on the wheels wouldn't go amiss either.'

'Not a fan of retail therapy then?'

Bernard stared at her. He really hadn't got the slightest idea what she was talking about.

A smile drifted across Tess's face. 'Don't worry. We'll be at the booze section soon. But first things first. Do you want to stick with Weetabix or do you want something else for a change?'

'I'll stick with Weetabix. You know where you are with a couple of Weetabix. I mean, look at some of this other nonsense. If I wanted chocolate for breakfast, I'd buy a bar of Cadbury's Dairy Milk, and as for the so-called "healthy" stuff, most of it looks like the sweepings off the floor of a carpenter's workshop – and that's even when they've jazzed it up in the picture on the box to try and make it look appetising.'

As Tess reached up for a twelve-pack of Weetabix,

it triggered a mental note in Bernard's brain.

'Sugar,' he said.

'Why, what's up?'

'No, I don't mean sugar as in the irritatingly twee way that people say "Oh sugar" when they really mean "Oh shit". You should know me better than that.'

Tess raised an eyebrow. 'Uh-huh?'

'We need to *buy* sugar.'

'What for?'

'Well, it's general use is to add sweetness to a range of—'

'But we've got loads already. There's plenty left in that Tupperware box. – Mind you, though, most of it did seem quite damp when I gave half a cup of it to a woman on the campsite this morning.'

'You did *what*?'

'Gave her half a cup of sugar. While you were having a shower. She'd run out and asked if she could borrow some.'

'Seriously?'

'Yes, of course. Why wouldn't I?'

Bernard closed his eyes and hid his face behind his hands.

'Granddad? Are you all right?'

She took hold of one of his wrists and eased his hand downwards.

He blinked at her and swallowed hard. 'Um,' he said. 'Bit of a confession, I'm afraid.'

* * *

Bernard was grateful for the hammering of the rain on the roof of the van and the constant swishing of the windscreen wipers. Otherwise, the silence would have been unbearable. Tess had every right to be angry, of course, but this was the first time she'd ever really lost her temper with him, and it left him feeling thoroughly miserable.

Despite Tess's increasingly vociferous demands that he shouldn't keep her in suspense a moment longer, he'd insisted on keeping his confession to himself until they were out of the supermarket and back inside the privacy of the van. If she was going to start shouting at him – which he'd fully expected she would – far better that it didn't turn into a diverting floorshow for a bunch of bored shoppers. The only downside was that the inevitable yelling seemed to be amplified by several more decibels within the close confines of the van than it would have been in the far more open environment of the supermarket.

Her initial blank astonishment when he'd told her of his accident with the cremation urn and the washing-up bowl had quickly given way to an outburst of unrestrained fury. Not about the accident itself. That could have happened to anybody, she'd said. But she was livid with him for not *telling* her at the time, even though the sodden ashes later turned out not to be her granny's at all. However, and somewhat surprisingly to Bernard, she'd reserved the crescendo of her anger for his admission to giving a complete stranger an urn full of BioDazzle Ultra when he'd been expecting the last remains of his dearly beloved mum.

'Why the fuck didn't you give them the real ashes?'

Bernard had never heard her use the F-word before, but this had hardly been the moment to point out that it wasn't very ladylike.

'I don't really know,' he'd said. 'I was a bit...

embarrassed, I suppose.'

'Embarrassed?'

'They were in a Tupperware box for a start, and they were still a bit soggy. I thought they were your gran's, and I hadn't had time to dry them out yet.'

'Well, if you think that was embarrassing, wait till you hand over the real thing and tell them that what you'd given them before was an urnful of soap powder.'

'And how are we going to do that? All we've got is a name. No address, no phone number, no nothing.'

'We've got the undertaker's number, though, haven't we? So we get the details from him.'

And after she'd spent several minutes calming herself down to the extent that she could speak with a reasonable degree of coherence, that's exactly what Tess had done. Or tried to anyway. Bishop had been quite cagey at first, droning on about the importance of client confidentiality, but he'd relented in the end and agreed that Mr Pendleton would much prefer to have his mother's true remains rather than a pound or so of washing powder. Not that he'd been prepared to give Tess any details directly. Instead, he'd taken her mobile number and promised to pass it on to Mr Pendleton, who could then get in touch with her if he so wished.

Bernard had been relieved at how much Tess's mood had seemed to lighten after the phone call, and he'd decided to seize the opportunity to try and reduce the tension between them with the injection of a little humour. Unfortunately, though, making a joke out of the woman on the campsite who'd asked to borrow half a cup of sugar and gone away with half a cup of someone's ashes had only served to reignite Tess's fury, and they hadn't spoken since.

If anything, the rain was coming down even harder now, and Bernard wondered how Tess could see anything of the road ahead, even with the windscreen wipers battering away at full speed. He hesitated for a moment, fearing that anything he said would result in his head being bitten off, but he finally summoned up the courage and cleared his throat.

'Do you think it might be an idea to get off the road for a while till this rain eases up?'

Tess didn't reply and continued to squint fixedly through the driving rain at what she could still see of the road in front of her. Ten minutes later, however, she steered the van into the first services she came across and switched off the engine.

27

At least the pissing rain had started to ease up, which was more than I could say for my lousy mood. If anything, I'd become even more doubtful that we'd catch up with the Pemberton woman and her granddad. And even if we did, what were the chances we'd get to them before they'd scattered two kilos of cocaine over some bloody Scottish hilltop – or whatever the hell else they were planning to do with it if they'd figured out what it really was?

I'd managed to screen out most of the doom and gloom input from the voice in my head for most of the journey so far, but still the occasional blast of negativity had broken through my defences. The ever increasing bickering between Alan and Scratch had been much harder to ignore, however, and it was driving me crazy.

'So how far is this Dumpees place then?' said Scratch as he dropped the speed of the windscreen wipers to a notch below manic.

'Dumpees?' said Alan. 'What the fuck is Dumpees?'

'It's where the old lady said they were going to scatter the ashes of the other old lady. The dead one.'

'It's not Dumpees, you tit. It's Dum-*freece*.'

'You sure about that? I could have sworn she said Dumpees.'

'Yes, she did say Dumpees, but only because she's about as daft as you are. And if you'd been paying attention, you might remember that's why Max couldn't find any such place as Dumpees in the bloody road atlas.'

'Yeah?'

'Yeah.'

Scratch thought about this for a moment and then said, 'So how'd you find out it was Dum-*freece* and not Dum-*pees*?'

'Christ, Scratch, what parallel fucking universe are you on? The Pemberton bird and the old fella told us last night when we swapped the urns.'

'OK, but if you hadn't always got your thumb up your bum and your brain in neutral, *you* might remember that I wasn't actually there at the time.'

'Yeah, but we told you afterwards, though.'

Scratch shook his head with exaggerated emphasis. 'No you didn't.'

'Yes we did. And we also told you the exact place where they said they were going to scatter the ashes.'

Another theatrical shake of the head from Scratch. 'Nope.'

'Top of some hill called… What was it?… Blackrigg Law.'

'Never heard of it.'

'Max?' said Alan, wincing from the pain in his neck as he turned his head a little too quickly. 'Did we or did we not—?'

'I really don't recall,' I said. 'And do you think we could have a bit of hush for a while because the pair of you are giving me a bloody headache.'

Alan opened his mouth to say something, thought better of it and – more carefully this time – turned his head back to face the front.

Peace reigned for a merciful ten minutes or so until Scratch broke it with, 'There's a services just up ahead. Anybody fancy a quick bite? I'm starving.'

I was about to explain that we didn't have time if we were to stand any chance of catching up with our runaway coke snatchers when Alan cut in before me.

'What, and hang around for God knows how long till you find something you can eat that doesn't spark off one of your hundreds of bleedin' allergies?'

'Oh, that's rich, that is,' said Scratch. 'Coming from someone who has to give us a minute by minute update on "Ooh, my neck hurts" and "Ooh, my neck isn't half giving me gyp today".'

As an impersonation of Alan's whiny "Mummy, I've got a pain in my tummy" voice, it was a pretty good one, but I wasn't feeling a lot like laughing.

'We haven't got time, Scratch,' I said. 'Just keep going, yeah?'

Scratch grunted and then gazed wistfully at the services as we passed. So wistfully, in fact, that he totally missed the blur of white that shot out in front of us from the exit.

Fortunately, Alan was paying rather more attention to the road ahead. 'Jesus, Scratch! Brake!'

Scratch hammered on the brakes and just avoided rear-ending the van by about four feet.

The van? This was no ordinary white van, but a strangely familiar white *camper* van.

Alan yelled at Scratch to quit flashing his headlights and blasting the horn and leaned forward in his seat.

'J-one-eight-eight-P-O-T,' he said, reading the number plate out loud. 'Fuck me, it's them all right.'

Maybe there was a God after all. Or maybe it was just way past time that we caught a break.

I told Scratch to drop back and keep about thirty yards between us and the van. Then I sat back and treated myself to a sigh of relief. Not that we were in the clear quite yet, of course. Not by a long chalk. There were still plenty of obstacles in our way before we could hand over the coke to Nick the Greek and get Toby released. Who was to say that the fat bastard would stick to the deal anyway? And what if the old guy and his granddaughter didn't have the coke at all? If they *did* have it, how the hell were we going to get it back off them? Oh yes, and one more thing. Even if we got hold of the coke, how were we going to explain to Danny that we'd handed it over to Nikos free of charge?

I decided that the sigh of relief had been grossly premature, and I instantly retracted it.

At the same moment, it suddenly occurred to me that nobody had tried to ring me for a good hour or so, and the torrent of calls from Carla and Danny had stopped at round about the same time. I should have been glad to have finally got some peace from the pair of them, but instead, I found it strangely unsettling. It could have been a complete coincidence that they'd both simultaneously given up on me after so many attempts, of course, but as someone much wiser than me once said, 'Coincidence is for people who are too stupid to figure out the connections.' Or something like that.

28

'Hardly what you'd call a car chase, is it?' said Scratch when we'd been tailing the van for a little more than ten minutes and it turned off the motorway, heading west towards Dumfries.

'No,' said Alan, 'because a car chase generally requires that the person being chased *knows* that they're being chased. It is also customary to be travelling at speeds somewhat in excess of...' He leaned across to check the speedometer. 'Forty-two miles per hour.'

Scratch ignored the sarcasm, and there was a lengthy pause before he spoke again. 'This is doing my head in, this is. Why don't we just run 'em off the road and have done with it?'

'We wait,' I said, secretly pleased at how firm and commanding I sounded.

'What, till I die of boredom?'

'Oh, hark at Steve McQueen here,' said Alan, and Scratch punched him hard in the upper arm.

I didn't have to put up with their bickering for much longer, thankfully, because a few minutes later, the van pulled off the road and into a lay-by. It was about fifty yards long, and the van didn't stop until it reached the far end. I told Scratch to pull up at the nearest end, and we watched as the driver's door of the van flew open and Tess Pemberton jumped out. Clearly in a hurry, she trotted into the woods that butted up against the lay-by and disappeared.

'Bit desperate for a pee by the look of her,' said Alan.

'I don't know how you do it, Holmes, I really don't,' said Scratch.

'Right,' I said, 'let's get this done while it's only the old guy.'

I reached under the passenger seat and pulled out three black balaclavas – the sort that only had holes for the eyes and mouth – and handed one each to Alan and Scratch. Then I got Scratch to ease the Beamer slowly along the lay-by until it was almost bumper-to-bumper behind the van. With the engine still running, Scratch and I got out while Alan slid himself over into the driver's seat. Semi-automatics at the ready, the two of us crept up to the side of the van.

OK, so guns and balaclavas were maybe a bit on the heavy-handed side, but if there was even the slightest possibility that these people knew what they'd got, they might not be too eager to hand it over.

I gave Scratch the nod, and he grabbed hold of the handle on the sliding door and yanked it open.

Granddad was standing with his back to us, and it sounded like he was filling a saucepan or something at the sink.

'Thought we might as well have a brew now we've stopped,' he said.

'That's very kind of you,' I said, 'but we're actually

in a bit of a hurry.'

The old man spun round, kettle in hand, and his mouth dropped open at the sight of the balaclavas and the guns.

'So,' I went on, 'if you'll just hand it over, we'll be on our way, and nobody needs to get hurt.'

He closed his mouth and looked down at the kettle.

'No, not the fucking kettle,' I said. 'You know what I'm talking about.'

'I'm sorry,' he said, recovering his composure surprisingly quickly, 'but I've absolutely no idea what the "it" is you're referring to. Perhaps if you could be a little more specific?'

The geezer was way too calm for my liking, and I was rapidly losing patience. Not only that, but I wanted to get the job done and out of there before the granddaughter got back. For all I knew, she might be a black belt in jujitsu or somesuch.

'OK, OK, that's it,' I said. 'Out of the van, Granddad, and make it snappy.'

I beckoned him out with my gun, and after he unhooked his walking stick from the edge of the sink, he took almost as long getting out of the van as it takes Usain Bolt to run two hundred metres.

Once he was finally at ground level, I kept him covered while Scratch jumped into the van and started rummaging through the cupboards. Opening the one directly over the sink, he took out a china cremation urn that looked much the same as the one we'd handed over the day before.

'Hey, careful with that,' said the old man. 'My wife's in there.'

Scratch ignored him, removed the lid of the urn and peered inside.

197

'Well?' I said.

'Dunno,' said Scratch. 'There's no blue bits, though.'

Most likely it was the real ashes we'd given them yesterday, but it was best to make certain, so I told Scratch to give it a taste.

The old man started to object, but Scratch got there before him. 'Not in a million years, mate. I told you that the last time.'

Before I could argue the point any further, Scratch said he'd put the urn back in the cupboard for now while he searched the rest of the van for any other likely suspects.

'Well, for Christ's sake hurry up then,' I said, but the words were hardly out of my mouth when the back of his hand brushed against a packet of washing powder that was next to where he'd replaced the urn, and it came tumbling out of the cupboard.

There was a flurry of activity as Scratch fumbled to grab hold of it, and even though he eventually succeeded, most of the contents from the packet had spilled down his front and onto his hands.

'Shit and bollocks,' he said in a relatively unfazed oh-well-these-things-happen kind of tone, but as he reached up to put the box back in the cupboard, he glanced at the label, and his tone escalated into one of blind panic. 'Oh, Jesus Christ, no!'

'What is it?' I said.

Scratch dropped the box like he'd suddenly realised it was highly radioactive. 'BioDazzle bloody Ultra, that's what. Brings me out in a right vicious rash, this stuff.'

Then he turns on the sink tap full blast and starts frantically rinsing the soap powder from his hands.

Even from where I'm standing, I can see the foam rising up out of the washing-up bowl and oozing over the rim onto the floor. The next thing I know, there's a crunching pain to my right wrist, and every nerve ending in my arm is screaming in protest all the way up to my shoulder.

Distracted as I had been by Scratch's pissing about with the soap powder, Granddad had seized the opportunity to whack me one with his walking stick. If his intention had been to get me to drop my gun, his aim had been spot on.

As I'm bending to pick it up off the ground, I notice that Scratch must have heard the commotion because he makes a grab for his own gun, which he'd left on the worktop while he'd been searching the cupboards. But his hands are so wet and slippery from the soap suds that the gun instantly slithers out of his grasp and bounces across the floor.

Meanwhile, my fingers are within a couple of inches of *my* gun when…

'Aaagh! Jesus!'

The second blow from Grandpa's stick catches me across the back of the head, and although it's not quite enough to lay me out cold, it's more than enough to lay me out face down in the dirt.

'*Leave* it,' he says like he's training a fucking dog.

I lift my already throbbing head far enough to see that Scratch is reaching for his gun on the floor of the van, and the old man is pointing my semi-automatic at him. Scratch freezes mid stoop and looks at the old man like he's weighing up the odds against him actually pulling the trigger. Apparently, he decides they're not that great, and he straightens slowly, his hands at shoulder level, palms outwards in surrender.

199

A flicker of movement at the edge of my vision. I swivel my eyes towards it, and there's Alan, gun in hand, but he only gets as far as 'All right, Pops—' when "*thwack!*", and down he goes.

Shit, and there's me been fretting over whether the granddaughter might be a black belt in some martial art or other when all she needed was a bloody great tree branch to do just as much damage as anything Bruce Lee himself could have dished out.

The branch having successfully completed its mission, she tosses it aside and picks up Alan's gun, which is the old man's cue to order Scratch out of the van, hands behind his head.

'You too. Up you get. Hands behind your head,' he says, and I'm guessing from the none too gentle prod in the ribs from his walking stick that he's talking to me.

It's not the easiest thing in the world getting up from face down on the ground with your hands behind your head, especially when it's throbbing like a bastard, but I manage it eventually.

Then he tells us to walk backwards over to the Beamer, and we both nearly trip over Alan, who's still spark out on the floor.

'Now one of you toss me the keys,' says little Miss Pemberton, so Scratch opens the door of the car, reaches in for the lump of black plastic gadgetry and lobs it over to her.

She catches it one-handed, and in almost the same fluid movement, hurls it into the woods like she's going for Olympic gold in the javelin.

That's when the voice in my head starts up again. 'An old geezer and a girl? You could take 'em easy.'

'Yeah, well, it may have escaped your notice, but

this particular old geezer and girl both have guns, and they're pointing straight at us.'

'What? You seriously think they're gonna use 'em?'

Although I didn't think it was likely, I wasn't prepared to take the risk. After all, Granddad and "the girl" had already pole-axed me and Alan with a walking stick and a tree branch, so who knew *what* they might be capable of?

It was too late to launch a frontal assault now anyway because Tess had started the van's engine while her granddad kept us covered, and then he too had climbed into the van and slammed the sliding door shut.

I watched the van disappear off up the road with the Titanic of all sinking feelings.

Alan had begun to stir, and he rubbed at the back of his head. 'What the fuck…?'

I couldn't have put it better myself.

29

Once they were well clear of the lay-by, Tess eased off on the accelerator, and Bernard – not without some difficulty – clambered through from the back of the van to the passenger seat.

'You OK, Tess?'

'Yeah, I'm fine. More in shock than anything. How about you?'

Bernard slowly nodded his head a couple of times while he assessed his own condition. 'About the same as you, I'd say.'

'Do you think we should call the police?'

Bernard considered the question for several seconds until Tess grew impatient for an answer and glanced across at him. 'Granddad?'

'No, I don't think so,' he said. 'Best not to get involved.'

'Involved? We've just been held up at gunpoint by three men in balaclavas. We could have been killed. I don't think you can get much more involved than that.'

'But that's my point. Guns. Balaclavas. They're

obviously desperate men, Tess. Gangsters. And I've seen enough TV shows to know that those sort don't take at all kindly to their victims calling the police in.'

'I think you'll find that's usually when there's been a kidnapping.'

'Either way, do you really want to take the risk?'

Tess didn't respond, so Bernard followed up with another question that he believed to be highly pertinent to the matter at hand.

'Did they seem familiar to you at all?'

'Three men in balaclavas? Hardly.'

'How about the shorter, stockier one? The one that you clobbered. Did you notice he was wearing a neck brace?'

Tess turned her head to look at him and for rather longer than any driving instructor would have considered safe. The blast of a horn from an oncoming car snapped her eyes front again, and she quickly corrected the rightward drift of the van.

'The same people who came to swap the urns last night?' she said when she'd regained control of the van as well as her heartbeat.

'Bit of a coincidence, wouldn't you think?'

'Hang on, though. What exactly did they say when they showed up just now, when I was in the woods?'

'Something about handing it over and they'd be on their way.'

'It?'

Bernard's knees were throbbing after the recent exertion, and he shifted uncomfortably in his seat. 'They didn't specify.'

'But if they *were* the same people, the undertaker was supposed to phone them and tell them about the mix-up over the ashes. So, if he did, how come all the

203

guns and balaclavas?'

'And if he didn't tell them?'

'Well, why wouldn't he?'

Bernard shrugged. 'Damned if I know.'

'And how did they manage to find us?'

'They didn't seem to have any trouble the first time.'

'Christ, this is driving me crazy.' Tess took one hand off the steering wheel and clasped it to her forehead. 'So, OK, they find out that the urn we gave them is full of BioDazzle Ultra and not the ashes they were expecting, but even so, an armed holdup seems a bit excessive if that's all they're after, unless...'

'Unless?' Bernard prompted.

'Unless it wasn't the ashes at all. Something else that we've got that they're so desperate to get their hands on.'

'Such as?'

'You thought that what you tipped into the sugar box was Granny's ashes, right? But it turned out not to be *her* ashes but someone else's instead.'

'Yes, although—'

'So what if it wasn't?'

'Wasn't what?'

'Somebody's ashes at all.'

'What else could it be?'

'Well, what with the guns and all that, it has to be *something* dodgy. Drugs would be my guess. Heroin or cocaine or something. I mean, why else are three men in balaclavas going to threaten us at gunpoint? For a couple of pounds of Tate and Lyle? – Jesus, Granddad, what have you done?'

Bernard could see Tess's knuckles glow white from the intensity of her grip on the steering wheel, and she lapsed into what he could only describe as "quietly fuming". He let her be for a couple of minutes before summoning up the courage to speak again.

'I think it might be an idea if we pull over somewhere and check it out. The sugar box. Preferably somewhere out of sight of the main road.'

Tess grunted, but whether this was a grunt of agreement or a grunt of anger, he really couldn't be sure.

30

In a predictably futile attempt to cheer Alan up, I'd pointed out that at least the rapidly developing headache from the branch-whacking would take his mind off the almost permanent pain in his neck. His response had fallen a long way short of gratitude for my up-cheering efforts and was, I thought, unnecessarily abusive. Since then, he'd been sitting on the ground with his back against the side of the Beamer and moaning and groaning like a hippo with gout.

Meanwhile, Scratch had been floundering around amongst the trees and bushes in the wood as he searched for the little lump of black plastic that would get us back on the road again. He hadn't exactly volunteered for the job, of course, and had protested long and loud about his badly swollen and crimson-blotched hands which, according to him, were so hot that they were likely to spontaneously combust at any moment. In the end, he'd reluctantly conceded that Alan was in no condition to go foraging about in the woods and that I was the only one who knew how to hot-wire a car, so I'd need to stay and work on that in case he didn't find the key.

In fact, it was total bollocks that I'd ever hot-wired a car in my life, but Scratch wasn't to know that. And in any case, from what little I knew about it, it was virtually impossible to hot-wire a modern top-of-the-range motor like the BMW without some techno-gadget for messing with the onboard computer, and I didn't happen to have one.

Even so, time was marching on, and I was beginning to wonder if it might be worth sacrificing a perfectly good pair of shoes and possibly an almost new pair of trousers to add another set of eyes to the search.

'You found it yet, Scratch?' I shouted.

'Yeah, course I have. Just thought I'd fanny about in the bushes a bit longer with my hands throbbing like shit 'cos I'm having such a great time.'

'For Christ's sake, Max.' It was the voice in my ahead again. 'Do you wanna be here all day, or are you gonna go and help him? So what if you scuff a pair of shoes and get a bit of a tear in your trousers? It'll be a gazillion times worse if you don't catch up with little Miss Pemberton and her granddad before they've tossed two kilos of top grade nose candy to the four winds.'

I wasn't convinced that that was what they were likely to do. For one thing, I was as sure as I could be that the urn we'd given them last night had nothing in it but ashes, and I knew for a fact that the one they'd given us was full of soap powder. So, if they'd realised what the coke was and kept it in something else, why would they scatter that as well?

'Who knows?' said the voice. 'Maybe out of some

sense of moral outrage? It's entirely up to you, Max, but if I were you – which essentially I am – I wouldn't be taking any chances.'

The voice was right. This was no time to be obsessing about shoes. We needed to catch up with them sharpish.

'Where the fuck are you going?' said Alan before I'd taken more than a couple of steps towards the edge of the wood.

'To help Scratch look for the key,' I said. 'We'll be here all day if I don't.'

Alan groaned his loudest groan so far. 'I need to get to a hospital fast. Feels like I might have brain damage.'

I resisted the obvious response and said that getting him to the hospital was the very reason I was going to help Scratch to try and speed things up.

'Feels like my head's gonna explode at any minute,' he said. 'We've still got a couple of guns. Why don't we just hijack the next car that comes along?'

'Oh, sure,' I said. 'And add another major crime to what they could do us for already. They'll throw away the bloody key, the rate we're going.'

It wasn't the best choice of words in the circumstances, but Alan was in no state to pick up on the irony.

'Well, flag one down then,' he said. 'Tell 'em we've broken down and it's a matter of life and death that you get me to a hospital pronto.'

Despite what I'd told him a minute ago, getting Alan to a hospital didn't rank too highly right now, although it would have been at the top of the list if I'd believed for one second that his life really was in danger. But what if we *did* get a car to stop? What

208

then? Maybe they could drop us some place where we could hire a car and get after the camper van again.

It was starting to sound like our best option, and after listening to a few more seconds of Scratch's rummaging in the undergrowth, I stepped to the side of the road.

There was no shortage of vehicles heading west, but not a single one of them showed any sign of slowing down, never mind stopping. And I swear to God, a few of them even seemed to speed up as they passed. Maybe some of them spotted the car was a BMW and made an instant decision that there was no way they were going to help out the rich, arrogant prick who owned one of *them*. Probably even pissed themselves laughing to see a conked-out Beamer as well.

After ten minutes of frantic arm waving like I was repeating the same semaphore letter over and over again, my shoulders were starting to ache, so a short break was in order. I glanced behind me, but, as expected, there was no sign of Scratch triumphantly brandishing a little lump of black plastic.

The back of my head was still pretty sore from where the old geezer had whacked me with his walking stick, and I reached up to give it a bit of a massage. But instead of the anticipated hair, there was the altogether different texture of some kind of acrylic/polyester fibre.

I wrenched the balaclava off and glared at it.

Bollocks.

'Yeah,' Alan called out. 'Might have more luck without that on.'

'You *knew*?'

Alan shrugged, which I took to mean a "yes", so I stomped over to him and flung the balaclava at his face. 'Well, why the fuck didn't you tell me before?'

Another shrug. 'Dunno. Thought it might have been deliberate.'

'Deliberate? Are you *completely* bloody insane? – Oh yeah, I know what I'll do. Stand at the side of the road waving my arms around like a fucking lunatic and dressed as a fucking bank robber. They'll be queueing up to give us a lift.'

'Leave it out, Max. I've probably got concussion or something.'

To be fair – even though I wasn't feeling particularly magnanimous at the time – it was as much my fault as it was Alan's, so I let it drop and turned my attention to Scratch instead.

'Any joy yet, Scratch?'

When I got the same sort of sarcastic response as before, I decided to try a different tactic. One which might seem rather more socially acceptable. Taking up position at the start of the lay-by to give a car plenty of time to pull in, I stuck out my thumb.

It was clearly a far better strategy than the previous one because the fourth car that came along swung off the road at speed and screeched to a halt about thirty yards further up the lay-by. I put my head down and legged it. Bright yellow hatchback of the VW Golf variety or somesuch. Booming exhaust and booming drum and bass sounds to match from inside the car. As I got closer, I could make out two people in the front and one in the back. Bit of a squeeze to get me, Alan and Scratch in as well, but we'd manage it somehow.

Five yards from the car and my lungs about to burst, I hear an even louder boom from the exhaust, the brake lights go out, and there's a fleeting smell of burning rubber as the tyres struggle for traction. Then the rapidly disappearing face of the wanker in the back seat, grinning like a demented chimpanzee and flicking me the finger.

I bent over, hands on my thighs, while I fought to get my breath back, and although I'm very rarely driven to acts of violence, I seriously wished I'd had a bazooka with me.

Composure and oxygen levels partially restored, I strolled back to the start of the lay-by, and out went the thumb again.

Holy Christ, I couldn't believe it. The gods, or whoever controls these things, were finally smiling on me instead of wetting themselves laughing. The very first car was a big black Mercedes and, like the canarymobile before, pulled into the lay-by at speed and slammed on its brakes. No way was I going to get caught out a second time, so I walked towards it at little more than a leisurely pace. Two seconds later, the hazard lights came on and the Merc began slowly reversing. There was something disturbingly familiar about it, but there had to be more than one big black Mercedes in the world, so maybe my luck really was changing after all.

The car stopped a few feet in front of me, and I walked round to the driver's door. All the windows were tinted – well, not just tinted but totally black – so I couldn't see inside at all. There was a longish, uneasy pause, and I was contemplating a politely gentle tap on the glass when there was a soft, whirring sound to my left, and the rear side window slid downwards. I took a sideways step and brought my face down level with the now fully open window.

'Car trouble, Mr Dempsey?'

31

A blast of cold air hit me smack in the gob. The aircon inside the car must have been on full blast, but even so, the sweat was seeping out of every pore of Nick the Greek's balloon of a face.

I opened my mouth to speak, but that was as far as I got. There were far too many questions somersaulting around in my head, each one demanding that I asked it first. Any form of coherent speech was utterly impossible.

Nikos filled the silence. 'You wanna get yourself a better car. Like this baby. She never break up.'

Despite the need to clear up some rather more pressing matters, this was a slur against my Beamer that couldn't go unchallenged.

'I haven't broken *down*,' I said, pointedly correcting his English. 'I've just lost the key, that's all.'

'You a careless man, Mr Dempsey. Two times you lose my coke and now your car key.'

He tutted theatrically a few times and then told me to get in the car. I wasn't keen, of course, and not only because this would drastically reduce any chance of survival to sitting duck level, but also because the stink of stale sweat was already pretty unbearable even from *outside* the car. But then I heard the "*clunk-click*" of a semi-automatic being armed, and I straightened up to see that Kosta Coffee had got out of the front passenger door and was aiming his gun at my head. This somewhat detracted from the element of choice, so I walked round the back of the Merc and climbed in next to Nikos. Well, I say "next to", but when Kosta slammed the door shut behind me, I pressed myself up against it to keep as far away from the reeking fat bastard as possible. Not that it made much difference since his ample arse occupied almost half of the spacious back seat.

'So where you running to this time?' said Nikos the moment my relatively trim buttocks hit the beige leather upholstery.

'Running?' I really had no idea what he was talking about or if it was simply a mistranslation from the Greek.

'Yes, "running" – before your frickin' car break up.'

Some people just don't *want* to learn, do they?

'I really don't know what you mean,' I said because I still didn't have any more information to go on. 'Why would we be running?'

Nikos gave one of his psycho laughs. The kind that lacked the slightest hint of genuine amusement and was cut off in its prime as abruptly as a blown light bulb. 'You a funny man, eh? You think you frickin' clever too, eh? Now you got your nephew back, you stick up the two fingers and you say, "Screw you and your coke, Niko".'

'My nephew? Toby?'

213

'Yeah, very frickin' clever. You wait till me and my boys go out of hotel and you sneak in and rescue the kid.'

'*Toby*?' I repeated but with even more emphasis. Had the guy totally lost the plot or what?

'And what you do with *my* nephew?' he went on. 'You shoot the useless prick in the head and leave him in a frickin' ditch someplace? Is OK with me.'

Christ on a bike, this was getting ridiculous. What was up with the man? Sampling too much of his own product probably.

'We didn't even know what hotel you were in,' I said, 'so how the fuck were we supposed to sneak in and rescue him?'

Another psycho laugh, and then he tells me I'm a "frickin' liar". But if Nikos was serious about not still having Toby – and it certainly seemed that way – then where the hell was he? As if I wouldn't be in enough trouble already with Carla and her sister for taking him along on this jaunt and then allowing him to be held as a hostage by a bunch of Greek gangsters, what if *Toby* was the one who was lying dead in a ditch somewhere? And it wasn't only the shitstorm I was going to get from Carla and Melanie either. I was really fond of the kid, and I'd never forgive myself if he wound up dead. Or maybe the Dimitri guy had decided to make a few quid for himself on the side and sold him into some kind of— Jesus, it didn't bear thinking about.

I was vaguely aware that Nikos had been chuntering on at me for the last couple of minutes or so, but I hadn't heard a word until, '… so I sick of your frickin' games, and I kill you now. Out of my life forever.'

OK, time to concentrate.

'The thing is,' I began and launched into what I considered to be a perfectly reasoned argument as to why killing me wouldn't be such a great idea.

I kept at it all the while Kosta and Tacky were marching me into the woods at gunpoint, and on this occasion I was grateful for Nikos's massive bulk. Not surprisingly, he was eager to witness the execution himself, but because he was struggling to keep up, we frequently had to stop and wait for him. This gained me the extra few minutes I needed to persuade him of my honest intentions vis-à-vis his coke.

It was a close run thing, though, as I was already on my knees among the mud and dead leaves with the muzzle of a gun rammed up against the back of my head when he recovered his breath long enough to wheeze out the words, 'One last frickin' time, Dempsey. You hear me? One last frickin' time. And if I no get my frickin' coke, I kill not just you but all your frickin' family.'

* * *

Luxury top-of-the-range Merc or not, it wasn't the most comfortable of rides once Alan had joined us on the back seat. I'd been a bit canny, though, and managed to wangle it so that he was wedged in the middle between me and Nikos like my very own human shield against the stink of the fat man's sweat. I'd got out of the car when Tacky had stopped to pick Alan up, and I'd whispered to him to keep schtum about Scratch. There'd been no chance of keeping Alan out of this as the Greeks had already spotted him, conspicuous as he was in his neck brace and slumped on the ground by the Beamer. Scratch, on the other hand, was presumably still searching for the key in the wood, and besides sparing him from the clutches of Nikos Spiropoulos and sons, I'd decided he'd be more use on the outside. We'd been pretty short on miracles lately, but in the unlikely event that one *did* happen and Scratch found the key, he could follow us. He knew exactly where we'd be heading, and if everything went pear-shaped – as was highly likely – there was at least a faint possibility he'd be able to come to the rescue. It was a theory anyway.

From the very moment that Tacky had pulled the Merc out of the lay-by, Alan had started on again about needing to get to a hospital, but it was hardly a great surprise that Nikos was having none of it.

'If you don't shut your noise right now,' he'd said, 'you ain't gonna need no frickin' hospital, you gonna need a frickin' priest.'

Apart from some fairly frequent groaning and grunting, I didn't hear a peep out of Alan for the rest of the journey. Nikos, however, was firing questions at me like a KGB interrogator. He wanted to know the whole story from when they'd untied me from the chair in the motel room right up until they'd caught up with us at the lay-by.

Naturally, I didn't go into too much detail about the failed holdup. In fact, I left that part out altogether and told him that we'd been following the van when the Beamer had developed some kind of mechanical fault. It was one thing to admit that I'd lied about losing the key and to let him have his told-you-so moment of glory about the car breaking down, but admit to a bunch of psycho gangsters that we'd been done over by a woman and her coffin dodger of a granddad? No chance.

But I had questions of my own, and right up there at the top of the list was, 'What the fuck's happened to Toby?'

'I got no frickin' idea,' he said, being uncharacteristically straight for once. 'All I know is me and my boys leave my shithead nephew and the kid in the hotel room when we go out for food, and when we get back, they both gone. Poof!'

The last word was accompanied by a sudden raising of the palms, and I guessed it was meant to convey something about disappearing in a puff of smoke.

'But I tell you this,' he continued. 'I gonna catch up with that frickin' Dimitri sooner or later, and when I do…'

He didn't bother to finish the sentence, and instead, he drew one of his sausage fingers sharply across his throat, even though this was hidden beneath his impressive number of chins. Somehow I doubted that his nephew's death would be quite so quick and painless.

Perhaps the thought of all the potential for blood, gore and excruciating agony was too much for even Nikos's warped imagination because he suddenly changed the subject.

'So,' he said, plastering a weird grin across his fat chops, 'I speck you wanna know how it was we find you.'

Danny had already told me about some relative of Nikos's being a cop, but it was obviously something he was itching to gloat about, so I let him have his second moment of glory.

'I have contact in police,' he said, and tapping the side of his nose, added, 'Technology, eh?'

It was clear that I was supposed to be impressed.

217

'I'm impressed,' I said and threw in a couple of "wow, I'm impressed" kind of nods for good measure.

Apparently satisfied with my response, Nikos's grin widened still further, and he puffed out his chest with pride, which made Alan groan and grunt even louder from the increase in pressure against his ribs.

After that, Nikos announced that he needed to sleep, so everyone was to 'Shut the frick up or else.'

Less than a beat of a pause later, he was snoring like a donkey with adenoid problems, but aside from that and Alan's groaning and grunting, the rest of the trip passed off in relative silence. Until, that is, Kosta Coffee started alternating between squinting at the sat nav and leaning forward to peer through the windscreen.

'I think that might be the hill up ahead,' he said, and not for the first time in the last few days, there was a distinctly unpleasant sensation somewhere deep inside my bowel department.

32

It looked somehow unnatural, this hill, as if it had been artificially constructed or like a much bigger version of one of those grassed-over slagheaps you see in coal mining areas. From what I could tell as we drove towards it, it was almost perfectly circular at the base, and its smooth green sides rose fairly gently to a height of about four or five hundred feet.

Following Kosta Coffee's instructions, Tacky steered the Mercedes off the main road and onto a single lane track which ran close to the foot of the hill. After a couple of hundred yards, there was a parking area on our left, and Tacky turned into it.

'I don't see no frickin' camping van,' said Nikos, stating the blatantly bleeding obvious since the car park was empty of any vehicle whatsoever.

'Maybe they've stopped off somewhere and we've got ahead of them,' I said, hoping to Christ that Tess and her granddad hadn't been and gone already. 'Or maybe there's another parking place on the other side of the hill.'

After a few more colourful threats from Nikos on

the subject of what he was going to do to me if he didn't get his coke, he told Tacky to carry on driving round the hill. As it turned out, there wasn't any other parking area or even any vehicle parked on the side of the track, and we'd covered the whole circumference of the hill until we'd got back to where we'd started.

Nikos was of the opinion that we should drive back to the parking area and wait, but I pointed out that there was one thing guaranteed to scare these people off, and that was the sight of a dirty great black Mercedes with blacked-out windows. Anything that looked more like a gangstermobile I could scarcely imagine. And in any case, they might park up somewhere else and not even go near the parking area.

I didn't actually *say* the bit about the gangstermobile, but Nikos seemed to get my drift. 'So what you suggest we do instead, Mr Smartguy?'

'Leave the car somewhere out of sight and wait for them at the top of the hill.'

Nikos fixed me with his beady black eyes and pulled out his handkerchief to mop at the cascade of sweat that began to pour from his brow despite the frigid conditions inside the car. 'Top – of – the – hill?'

'Uh-huh.'

'And how we get up there, you think?'

'We walk,' I said and did a little walking mime with my fingers.

Nikos didn't respond immediately but gazed out of the side window at the summit of the hill for several seconds before letting out an almighty sigh. 'You frickin' crazy? You tryin' to frickin' kill me?'

'It's OK, Papa,' said Kosta. 'You can stay in the car if you like. Me and Tacky can handle it ourselves.'

'You two? You two couldn't handle your own dicks

without a frickin' map.'

And so it was that once the car had been partially concealed behind some trees at the side of the track, I set off up the hill with Alan, Tacky, Kosta and Nikos in single file behind me. Since Nikos's dire warning, Alan had thankfully said not a word about hospitals, brain bleeds and CAT scans, and even his grunting and groaning had dwindled to the bare minimum. Nikos, on the other hand, started huffing and puffing and moaning and groaning before we'd gone more than half a dozen yards. I mean, I'm no Edmund Hillary myself, and although this wasn't exactly the proverbial walk in the park, the slope was pretty gentle and the going easy enough for the average three-year-old toddler.

Predictably, though, we had to stop every two or three minutes for Nikos to catch up and get his breath back and dry himself off with his handkerchief. Each time, I used the opportunity to scan the surrounding area, firstly for any sign of a black BMW and secondly a white camper van. The higher we got, the further I could see, but every road through the rolling green and purple landscape was entirely free of traffic.

After the latest rest break, I led the snail's pace conga on a slightly more diagonal route up the hillside so I could get a better view of the parking area, but this too was empty. Nikos had obviously spotted this as well because the next time we stopped, he pointed down the hill and, in between gasps for breath, said, 'Ain't no… frickin' van… I can… see.'

'Oh, full marks for observation,' I muttered but nowhere near loud enough for the fat fuck to hear it.

'What you say?'

'I said "No, that would appear to be the case".'

221

As he glared back at me, presumably trying to figure out whether that was really what I'd said, I had a momentary fantasy of giving him ever such a gentle prod in the chest with my finger, which was about all it would have taken to knock the great tub of lard off balance and send him roly-polying all the way back down to the bottom of the hill. Sadly, though, a fantasy was all it was ever going to be since Kosta Coffee and Tacky both had their guns drawn, and I was pretty certain they wouldn't have hesitated to use them in such circumstances.

'When the frick… this van… it coming then?'

Breathless or not, Nikos was clearly building up to deliver another one of his threat-filled rants, so I told him we hadn't exactly made an appointment and set off up the hill again. I picked up the pace a little this time, and Alan fell into step with me.

'So what do we do if the van doesn't show up?' he said. 'Nick the Greek's not gonna want to wait up here forever.'

'Dunno, mate,' I said because I really didn't, but then I told him why I'd decided to leave Scratch behind at the lay-by in the hope that he might find the key to the Beamer and get after us.

Alan looked as doubtful as I felt. 'You think?'

I answered with a half-hearted shrug, and after that, we walked on in silence until we reached the top of the hill.

There was no peak as such but a large, almost circular plateau that sloped gently upwards from where we were standing. It was as if the whole top of the hill had been sliced off at an angle of not much more than about ten degrees. Here and there were sections of broken-down stone walls that had long since outlived their usefulness. At the highest point of the slope, and furthest away from us, stood a roofless and equally tumbledown stone building that was too small for a cottage but had maybe once served as some kind of shepherd's shelter.

Having surveyed the area, I took another look down at the car park just as a white camper van drove into it. I was almost certain it was *the* white camper van, but it was too far away to see who was inside, let alone read the number plate. I allowed myself a moment of relief, but this was instantly cut short by the voice in my head casting serious doubt that Tess and her granddad still had Nikos's coke. And even if they had, our last attempt to get it off them had ended in total disaster. But, I reasoned, the Spiropoulos brothers were probably a damn sight better than us when it came to armed robbery, so that part of the operation was unlikely to present any problems.

'So then what?' said the voice. 'You think Nick the Greek is just going to forgive and forget all the shit you've put him through even when he's got the stuff in his fat sweaty paws? If you ask me, it's more than likely he'll—'

'Well, I didn't ask you, so do us all a favour and shut the fuck up.'

'I didn't say a word,' said Alan.

'What?'

'You just told me to shut the fuck up.'

'No, not you. Sorry, I…' There was no way I was going to tell Alan I heard voices in my head, so I changed the subject. 'You see the van?'

'Certainly looks like them,' he said, following my gaze.

'Is that…?'

They were the only two words that Nikos had breath for as he finally joined us on the edge of the plateau with Kosta and Tacky taking an arm each to support him.

'I think so, yeah,' I said, failing to sound as positive as I'd intended.

'You th—?' Nikos couldn't even get the second word out this time as he was suddenly stricken with a severe and lengthy fit of coughing.

'So who's that then?' said Kosta, half-heartedly patting his father on the back with one hand while waving his gun in the direction of the parking area with the other.

I watched as a large silver saloon pulled up on the far side of the car park from the van, and the passenger door and both rear doors opened in unison. Probably a taxi, judging by the sign on the roof that I could just make out but without actually being able to read it.

'Taxi, by the look of it,' I said.

'Yes, I can see that for myself,' Kosta snapped, apparently having much better eyesight than I did, 'but who are those three?'

'How the hell should I know,' I snapped back, peering down at the blonde woman and the youngish looking blokes who'd got out of the cab. 'Tourists probably. Come to admire the view from up here.'

Kosta tutted, but I realised that the more that total strangers joined us up here, the better. The more of an audience there was, the less likely Nikos was going to blow our heads off. Or was that just wishful thinking?

Once again, I scoured the landscape in every direction for a black Beamer, but there was still no sign of Scratch.

'So why the top of a frickin' mountain in frickin'

Scotland anyway?' said Nikos, wheezing heavily but now able to speak without having to gasp for breath between every word.

'It's complicated,' I said.

I hadn't expected this would satisfy him as an explanation, but perhaps he was too knackered to press me on it because all he said was, 'I need to sit.'

'Oh, what a shame,' said Alan. 'How thoughtless of us not to have brought the deckchairs and the picnic set.'

Nikos raised an eyebrow. 'Deckchair? What is deckchair?'

'Ignore him, Papa,' said Tacky. 'He's taking the piss.'

'Oh yeah?' said Nikos, his eyebrow dropping back to join its mate as he narrowed his eyes. 'Maybe you won't feel so much like taking piss when I…'

And off he went again on one of his long and unpleasantly vivid descriptions of the pain and suffering he was longing to inflict.

'There's a big pile of stones over there where we can probably find somewhere for you to sit down,' said Kosta when Nikos had finished, and he pointed to a section of wall that was only partially collapsed about thirty yards up the slope and a little to our right.

Despite the short distance and only a slight incline, Nikos's lumbering pace meant that it still took us the best part of five minutes to reach the wall, and when we got there, Tacky picked out a reasonably flat slab on the far side that was almost large enough for his father's enormous arse. Once he and Kosta had helped him down onto it, they both ducked down behind the wall and ordered Alan and I to do the same. Assuming that Tess and her granddad took the well worn track which zigzagged up from the parking area, we'd see them as soon as they appeared over the rim of the plateau without being spotted ourselves. As an alternative to simply waiting for them out in the open it seemed unnecessarily melodramatic, but there was little point in arguing, so Alan and I did as we were told.

When we were all in position with Kosta and Tacky on either side of us, their guns at the ready like a couple of cowboys bracing themselves for the Apaches to attack, the four of us peered over the top of the wall and waited.

33

There was quite a long wait before the Apache horde finally arrived in the shape of Tess and Grandpa Pemberton, and they paused as soon as they reached the edge of the plateau. The old man looked almost as done in as Nikos had been after the climb, and he handed something to Tess before bending forward at the waist and supporting himself on his walking stick.

'Is that them?' Kosta whispered.

I nodded. 'Uh-huh.'

'A girl and some old bloke with a stick?'

I could tell that the smirk was beginning to sprout without even looking at him.

'Well, rather more than a girl, I'd say.'

'And they're your suppliers, are they?'

I cleared my throat and was about to say something about appearances being deceptive when Nikos cut in with, 'For frick's sake, is it them or not?'

He was still sitting on his slab beside the wall and couldn't see anything that was happening.

'So *he* says,' said Tacky, the "he" being me, of course, and the tone heavily sceptical.

'And what about my coke?' said Nikos. 'They got it or not?'

'Dunno, Papa,' said Kosta. 'The girl looks like she's carrying something – two things, I think – but I can't tell what they are from this distance.'

Granddad had straightened up by now and was holding his finger up in the air, turning it this way and that, presumably to check the wind direction so they didn't end up covered in the ashes of their dearly departed – or much worse still from my point of view, Nikos's coke. Then they both started pointing in various different directions across the plateau as they apparently tried to decide where the best spot would be for the scattering ceremony. There was no cairn or, as far as I could see, anywhere else that seemed particularly appropriate, but all of a sudden, Granddad pointed at a small section of dilapidated wall near the centre of the plateau, and they set off towards it.

Instinctively, Alan, Kosta, Tacky and I ducked down out of sight, which instantly struck me as pretty ridiculous. Why were we hiding at all? The whole purpose of this little exercise was to get the coke off these people, so why not just get the job over and done with?

I raised my head to look over the top of the wall again, but this time there was a damned good reason for dropping back out of sight, so I did. Within half a second, I'd spotted not only that Tess and the old man were slowly making their way up the slope but also that the three tourists from the taxi had made their appearance over the edge of the plateau. Except they weren't tourists at all.

'Jesus,' I said as I slumped to the ground with my back against the wall, my brain whirring frantically, trying to make any kind of sense out of what I'd just seen.

There was an immediate barrage of the "What is it?" variety, but I could scarcely bring myself to speak.

'C – C – Carla,' I stuttered eventually.

'Carla?' said Alan.

'Carla?' said Kosta.

'What the frick is Carla?' said Nikos.

'She's here,' I said. 'She's on the f – fucking hill. Her and – and – T – Toby.'

'What?' said Alan. 'That's crazy.'

'Toby must've told her about the hill,' I said, finally getting my breathing under some semblance of control. 'Oh, bollocks, and probably all the other stuff as well.'

Alan popped his head up to have a look for himself. 'And there's that Greek lad with them. Dimwit or whatever his name is.'

Nikos stirred his arse on the stone slab. 'Who you say?'

It was Kosta's turn to peer over the top of the wall. 'Fuck me. It's Dimitri.'

'Dimitri?' said Nikos, floundering around on the slab like a tortoise that had been flipped over onto its shell. 'Somebody help me up, for frick's sake. I gonna kill the little bastard.'

It took both Kosta and Tacky to get Papa onto his feet, and as soon as he was upright, he staggered round the end of the wall and waddled off across the plateau. Tacky and Kosta exchanged a fleeting glance and a shrug before Kosta waved his gun at Alan and me and told us to get moving. So, off we went, following in Nikos's footsteps, which, for him, were relatively quick. This was no doubt partly due to his having to walk across the slope rather than up it, but probably had a lot more to do with his eagerness to get to Dimitri.

For some reason, Carla, Toby and Dimitri were also heading for the broken down piece of wall in the middle of the plateau, and the moment they got there, Nikos marched straight up to his nephew and delivered a brain rattling slap to the side of his head. Dimitri let out a yelp and only just managed to stay on his feet by about one degree short of his tipping point.

'You frickin' little shit!' Nikos roared. 'Why you never do what I frickin' tell you, you useless frickin' prick?'

Possibly for the sake of symmetry, he then used his left hand to aim a blow at the other side of Dimitri's head, but the lad was a fraction too quick for him and ducked out of the way just in time.

The torrent of high octane abuse that Nikos launched at the guy was so loud I couldn't even hear what Carla was screaming at me.

'Did you hear what I said?' she said, hands on hips and the blustery wind destroying what was probably a recent and expensive hairdo.

'No, actually, I didn't,' I said, preparing myself for a similar ear-bashing – both literal and metaphorical – that Nikos had dished out to his nephew.

'I said, "What the bloody hell's been going on?" And more to the point, what about Toby? From what I've been hearing you could have got him *killed*, for God's sake.'

As if I hadn't got the message already, she put her hand on the small of Toby's back and nudged him towards me.

'It's a long story,' I said, 'and I really can't deal

with this right now.'

'Oh, you can't, can't you? Well, let me tell *you* something then. Let me tell you how I've been—'

'BE QUIET, ALL OF YOU!'

There was an immediate silence, and even Nikos quit his ranting at Dimitri as we all turned as one to Tess's granddad, his face almost crimson from the effort of bellowing.

'Now, I've no idea what this is all about or who most of you people are,' he said, his tone softening dramatically once he knew he had our attention, 'but my granddaughter and I have come a very long way, purely for the purpose of fulfilling the last wish of my recently departed wife. Not that this is any business of any of you, but this was to have her last remains scattered on the top of this very hill, which is something that deserves the appropriate degree of dignity and respect, and above all else, a little bit of peace and quiet!'

For the last few words of his speech, his volume had rocketed back up to bellowing level, but it seemed to have the desired effect, and during the stunned hush that followed, he held out his hand to Tess. As if reading his mind, she passed him the greeny beige cremation urn but, I noticed, kept hold of a small plastic box that she was carrying.

'So then,' the old man continued in little more than a whisper, 'if you'd all kindly bugger off, we can get on with what we came here to do.'

'Is not gonna happen, old man,' said Nikos. 'Is not your dead wife in that… urn. Is my frickin' coke.'

'Coke?'

'Cocaine,' said Tess. 'I thought it must be something like that.' She looked down at the plastic

231

box in her hand, which rather gave the game away.

So why had they brought it up here along with the real ashes? Since they'd clearly suspected it was coke, maybe they'd realised it was too valuable to leave unattended in the van or maybe – as I'd feared – they'd been planning to scatter it out of some sense of moral duty. But whatever the reason, I decided it was time to step in and keep everybody happy. That way, Nikos could walk away with his precious charlie, leaving all of us alive and Tess and her granddad to carry out their ashes scattering ceremony in peace. That was the plan anyway.

'It's not in the urn,' I said. 'It's in that plastic box she's holding.'

Nikos grunted. 'Yeah, 'cos I'm gonna believe anything *you* say.'

I started to protest, arguing that he might as well check out the plastic box first, but he was having none of it. Maybe it was because he thought I was bluffing him for some reason or maybe it was just to spite me. Either way, he told Granddad to hand over the urn, but the old man point blank refused and clutched it to his chest.

Nikos said something gangsterish about doing things the hard way and then barked a few words at Kosta in Greek. It wasn't hard to get the gist, though, because Kosta walked straight up to Tess's granddad with his gun stretched out in front of him and aiming it directly at his face.

'Do yourself a favour, Grandpa,' he said, holding out his other hand for the urn. 'Just give it here, and nobody needs to get hurt.'

'It?' said the old man. 'That's my Dottie you're talking about, so show a little respect, eh?'

Before he'd finished speaking, his Excalibur of a walking stick came crashing down onto Kosta's gun hand, giving me a touch of the déjà vu's. Unlike me, however, Kosta managed to keep hold of his gun, and his yelp was more out of surprise than pain. That came next, though, and was a whole lot more than a yelp when Tess brought her knee up very hard and very accurately between his legs.

Kosta doubled over, and Tess grabbed his wrist in a teeth-gritted attempt to make him drop the weapon while Granddad laid into him with his trusty walking stick. The rest of us looked on in stunned silence until "*Kraakk*!". A single shot rang out, and Kosta collapsed onto the ground, rolling from side to side and clutching at the self-inflicted hole in his right foot. No yelping this time but an impressively full-blooded howl.

As a bit of good old British understatement would have it, Nikos isn't at all happy about this, and he yells at Tacky to, 'Frickin' kill them! Both of them! Now!'

Tacky, who until now has been keeping Alan and me covered, swings his gun round in Tess and her granddad's direction. But before he can squeeze the trigger, there's another shot – much more distant this time and sounding more like a rifle than a handgun. Tacky staggers backwards, a hand clasped over the rapidly spreading red stain near the left shoulder of his white shirt. The gun slips from his fingers, and he stands open-mouthed for a good five seconds before his legs give way and he crumples to the ground.

I scan the plateau for any sign of the shooter, but there's no-one apart from our own merry little band at the centre. Then, out of the corner of my eye, I see Dimitri pull a semi-automatic from the waistband of his chinos, and he's taken two or three quick strides towards Tess and her granddad when Toby snatches up a hefty looking rock and smashes it down hard on the back of the young Greek's head. He's out cold before he even hits the floor.

Three down, one to go, I'm thinking, and I swivel round to check on Nikos. He's got his hand inside his jacket, and it's on its way out again when "*Kraakk!*". Another rifle shot, rapidly followed by two more, and each one sends Nikos tottering back for a foot or two until the force of gravity kicks in, and his massive bulk crashes to the earth.

'Up there,' says Alan, and I turn through a hundred and eighty degrees to see where he's pointing. The derelict shepherd's hut near the top of the slope. The perfect sniper's spot with an uninterrupted view of the entire plateau.

All around me there's shouting and shrieking and groaning and moaning, but I'm oblivious to all of it. The horror-stricken and the wounded can wait. For now, I can't take my eyes off the hut, and I'm starting to wonder which of us might be the next victim when there's movement inside what's left of the doorway. A second later and a figure – two figures – step out into the daylight.

Jesus Christ. What the fuck are *they* doing here?

34

As they strolled at a leisurely pace down the slope towards us, I could see that Danny was clutching a rifle in both hands, holding it diagonally across his chest like a soldier on parade but without the goose-step. By his side, a smiling Sanjeev, a pistol swinging loosely at his hip.

While I waited for their arrival – and an explanation – I glanced around our little group. Not a lot of movement but plenty of groaning from the prostrate Tacky and Kosta, and amazingly, it appeared that Nikos wasn't quite ready to shuffle off his mortal coil even though he'd been hit three times. Maybe it was because the bullets had had so much blubber to get through, they hadn't managed to reach any of his vital organs.

Tess and her granddad were hugging each other – and the cremation urn – and staring ashen-faced (no pun intended) at the carnage all around them.

For a change, Alan wasn't doing any moaning or groaning at all, so presumably the suspected brain bleed had failed to materialise. He was standing a few feet to my left, fiddling with his neck brace and with his eyes fixed on the approaching Danny and Sanjeev.

Toby was looming over the fallen Dimitri with the rock still in his hand and a smug grin on his face. The kind of expression I imagine David must have worn when he'd just pole-axed Goliath.

As for Carla, she was kneeling on the ground, cradling Dimitri's head in her lap and ever so gently stroking his brow. She was very definitely not the Florence Nightingale type, so what the hell was she doing playing nurse to a complete bloody stranger? Unless... No, surely not. Her latest shag buddy? Jesus Christ almighty, she was damn near old enough to be his mother.

She must have felt my eyes on her because she tilted her head up to glare at me.

'My God, Simon, but you've got some explaining to do,' she said, forcing the words out between tightly clenched teeth.

'I could say the same to you,' I said with a nod at the stricken Dimitri.

All I got in response was a heavy scowl – and was that a slight reddening of the cheeks? It was hard to tell because she immediately went back to her nursing duties and her already mussed-up hair fell forward over her face like a curtain.

'Good afternoon, everyone, and how are we all this fine day?'

The cheeriness in Danny's voice couldn't have been less appropriate in the circumstances, but then again, since it was him and Sanjeev who'd been doing all the shooting, I could only assume he was congratulating himself over the result. I had plenty of questions for him, of course, but the first one that sprang to mind was: 'How the hell did *you* get here?'

'Train and taxi, old boy, although I expect what you *really* want to ask is how did I know where to find you in this delightful but somewhat remote spot of the Caledonian countryside.'

'That'll do for starters,' I said.

'Briefly then…'

For a change, I thought.

'… it was shortly after the thoroughly charming Ms Pemberton here engaged my professional services apropos the sad demise of her beloved grandmama that she happened to impart to me the precise location where the deceased wished her cremains to be conveyed. And when I learned via a telephone call from Ms Pemberton that you had still not retrieved my "merchandise" from her – coupled with your apparent unwillingness to respond to my repeated attempts at communication – I guessed – correctly, as it transpires – that there was a very strong possibility that the denouement of this affair might well occur at this very spot. My suspicions were further corroborated when I became aware that our Mr Spiropoulos had indeed been following you, as I'd predicted, and would therefore also be in attendance. This was thanks in no small part to a clever little gadget that Sanjeev fitted to the underside of his swanky Mercedes when I first realised that the bastard was planning to betray my prophetically fragile trust. It was something of a rush to get here in time, I have to say, and yet I did have another particular reason for being here in addition to my not unreasonable desire to safeguard my interests. But more of that anon. For now, I have a more pressing matter to attend to. In fact, a matter of life and death, you might say.'

And without leaving me even the slightest opportunity to question him further, he breezed past the rest of us and stopped a couple of feet short of the beached whale that was a seriously wounded Nick the Greek.

'Dear oh dear,' he said, stooping over him and tutting. 'That doesn't look good at all, dear chap. Not good at all, I'm afraid.'

He prodded one of the bullet holes with the muzzle of his rifle, and Nikos let out a roar of agony that was instantly cut short by a bout of coughing and spluttering, the blood spattering over his already crimson stained shirt like a monochrome Jackson Pollock painting.

'Curse of the modern age, you know, obesity,' said Danny. 'Kills more people every year than… Well, you'll forgive me if I can't quite remember the precise statistics just now, but take it from me, being a grossly overweight lardarse is far more likely to prematurely snuff out one's candle than almost any other cause known to medical science. Still, looking on the bright side, it's not every day that we can prove the quacks wrong, is it? And that, my elephantine Hellenic friend, is precisely what you'll be doing in a few short moments from now.'

All the while Danny was speaking, Nikos gulped at the air and struggled to fight back the rising tide of blood in his throat as he battled to form words of his own.

'Sorry, old chap. Didn't quite catch that,' said Danny when he'd come to the end of his speech, and he stooped a little lower with a hand cupped to his ear. 'You'll have to speak up.'

Nikos's eyes popped wide with the effort of taking

in enough air without choking, and he falteringly croaked out what I guessed were some choice words of abuse in Greek.

'No, no, no. This won't do at all,' said Danny, easily overtalking him. 'In English, I think. I mean to say, we wouldn't want your last words on this Earth to be misinterpreted, now would we?'

Still in a stooping position, and without taking his eyes off Nikos, Danny held out the rifle at arm's length and slightly behind him.

'Swapsies, please, Sanjeev,' he said, and Sanjeev took the rifle from him and substituted the semi-automatic in its place.

Then, in one continuous movement, Danny arced the gun round in front of him and put a neat round hole in the middle of Nikos's forehead.

'In the midst of life, blah, blah,' he said as he made a rough sign of the cross and spun round to face the rest of us.

There was a few moments' pause while he looked at each of us in turn – or at any rate, those of us that were still on our feet.

'Oh, why all so shocked?' he said with the merest of shrugs. 'They shoot horses, don't they? And besides, you should all be grateful to me for ridding this world of a very, very evil man indeed.'

'That's as may be, Danny,' I said, finally summoning up the brain power to speak, 'but don't you think you might have rather shot yourself in the foot there?'

There was a groan from Kosta's direction, but I ignored it.

Danny chuckled. 'Interesting choice of metaphor, Max, but you might need to enlighten me.'

'The coke?' I said, almost whispering the words even though it was hardly a big secret any more to most of the people there.

'Coke?'

God almighty, what was wrong with the man?

'Cocaine,' I said. '*Your* cocaine. But you've just gone and killed the guy who was gonna buy it.'

No point letting on at this stage that I'd done a deal to *give* the stuff away.

Danny raised an eyebrow. I'd no idea why the stupid prick was still playing dumb, but I added the part about selling the coke so I could pay him back the ten grand I owed him, and the penny finally seemed to drop.

'Ah yes, of course,' he said. 'And you have the merchandise here, do you?'

'Yeah, it's in that plastic box,' I said, hoping to hell that it was and pointing to the Tupperware container that lay on the ground where Tess had dropped it during her struggle with Kosta Coffee.

'But I gave it to you in a cremation urn. What's it doing in a—? Oh, never mind,' he interrupted himself and held out his gun-free hand. 'If you'd be so kind.'

For some reason, I glanced at Tess and her granddad as if I was seeking their permission, but they just stared blankly at me like they were in some kind of trance, so I picked up the box and gave it to Danny.

'This is it then, is it?' he said. 'My finest Colombian marching powder. Not sugar, like it says on the label?'

I nodded with as much confidence as I could muster, and Danny passed his gun to Sanjeev before prising off the lid of the box. Licking the tip of his little finger, he dipped it in and tasted, then pursed his lips and waggled his head from side to side as if he was struggling to make up his mind.

I crossed my fingers behind my back and mentally crossed every other part of my anatomy that was crossable. OK, so I hadn't got a buyer any more, but if this stuff was the genuine article, at least I wouldn't owe Danny a couple of kilos of coke on top of the ten grand.

'Hmm,' he said at last. 'I'm not sure our Greek chum here would have been terribly interested in buying a couple of kilos of human cremains, Max. And certainly not for the *second* time. I mean, it's not even as if he knew the dearly departed in question.'

35

Danny replaced the lid on the Tupperware box and handed it to Sanjeev, who gave him back the semi-automatic in return.

'But that's impossible,' I said, aware that the pitch of my voice had risen by an octave or so. 'There were only ever two cremation urns, so this has gotta be the coke because we've got one of them and it's full of washing powder, and they've got the other with the real ashes in.'

I wafted a hand in the general direction of Tess and her granddad but without actually looking at them. I was far too intent on watching Danny for the first visible signs of a reaction.

I didn't have to wait long as the initial glimmering of a smile spread slowly across his face, and then he roared with laughter.

Thank fuck, I thought. The bastard's having me on. Yeah, good one, Danny-boy. There's me on the edge of a nervous breakdown, and you're pissing yourself laughing. Still, no real harm done, I guess. He's got his precious coke back, so all's right with the world.

I forced a grin back at him to indicate how much I appreciated his little joke, but this made him laugh even harder.

'Oh dear, oh dear,' he said through the guffawing. 'You really don't get it, do you?'

Well, I thought I *had* "got it", but this was beginning to sound worryingly ominous.

'Sorry, Danny,' I said, just about managing to retain the grin. 'You've lost me there.'

'Oh, come now, Max,' he said, his laughter gradually subsiding. 'You don't seriously imagine that I'd trust a dipshit like you with such a large amount of my pharmaceuticals, do you?'

Uh-oh. Some serious alarm bells kicked off in my head.

'No doubt this will come as something of a shock to you,' Danny went on, 'but there never *was* any coke. At least, not in the urn I gave to you. I even kept up the pretence a few minutes ago when I was a tad economical with the truth about being here to safeguard my interests concerning my valuable merchandise. All part of my little game, you see? My cunning plan. And it all went rather splendidly, I think… Well, up to a point.'

'Jesus, Danny. What the fuck are you talking about?'

Danny's laughter had utterly evaporated by now, but there was still the trace of a smile on his ugly mug.

'You know, they say you should never ever explain a joke, and I really am rather pushed for time,' he said, glancing at his watch, 'but in the circumstances, and given that you're an old chum, I suppose I could give you the potted version at least. You see, when your little bank job went tits up, as the somewhat tawdry expression puts it, you handed me the perfect opportunity to, as it were, kill two birds with one stone. The late, unlamented Mr Spiropoulos here thought he could dispense with my services, and I'd heard a rumour that he was even trying to find out who my suppliers were so he could deal direct with them himself. This, of course, would have been severely detrimental to my business and could not be tolerated. So, when it transpired that you were unable to pay me the money you owed me, I immediately conceived of a little deception which might very well have resulted in the demise of not only my troublesome Greek but your own good self into the bargain. At the very least, I would have expected one of you to have saved me the bother of—'

'Me? You wanted *me* dead? For the sake of a poxy ten grand?'

'All in good time, Max. All in good time,' said Danny, flapping a hand to wave me to silence. 'You see, I knew that our Greek friend would not be at all happy about you trying to sell him something that was... well, very obviously not cocaine, and that he would remonstrate with you most assiduously. Very probably with fatal consequences on either or both sides. This was to have occurred during your little tête-à-tête at the Acropolis Restaurant but,' he sighed theatrically, 'unfortunately, I had not factored into my plan the extraordinary incompetence of both parties concerned, nor Sanjeev's mind-boggling ineptitude in giving you the wrong urn, and this is why we find ourselves today on this rather fine but somewhat chilly Scottish hilltop. I'm afraid I couldn't resist the entertainment value of coming here to watch the pair of you "slugging it out", so to speak, but I have to say, my long trip north has brought me little but disappointment in that regard. It was damned uncomfortable in that ruin up there, and I got so tired of all the dithering about that I decided to take matters into my own hands.'

'And speaking of long trips north,' said Tess's granddad, whose very existence I'd almost forgotten, 'I've no idea what this is all about, but my granddaughter and I—'

Danny didn't even flick so much as a glance in the old man's direction, his unblinking eyes remaining fixed on mine when he said, 'Sanjeev, if Grandpa opens his pie hole one more time, kill him. Same goes for the rest of them.'

There were several assorted gasps, and over Danny's shoulder I saw Sanjeev lift the rifle to his hip and slowly arc the barrel back and forth a couple of times to take in all of us that weren't already dead or wounded.

'Now, where was I?' said Danny, failing to mask his annoyance at the interruption.

'You were going to tell me why you wanted me dead.'

'Ah yes, of course.' He was only about three feet in front of me at the time, but he took a step forward and lowered his head slightly. 'Have a sniff of my hair.'

Jesus, this was getting more and more surreal by the second. 'You what?'

'Go on,' he said, tapping at his scalp. 'Have a good whiff.'

I stared at the waves of thick, grey-streaked brown hair for several seconds, wondering what the hell this had to do with his wanting to kill me, but decided to humour him anyway. I took a tentative sniff from a distance of at least six inches.

'Anything?' said Danny.

'I dunno,' I said, not having detected anything particularly out of the ordinary. 'Some kind of shampoo maybe?'

'Not disinfectant then? Toilet cleaner, for instance?'

'Don't think so, no.'

'How strange,' said Danny, straightening up and eyeballing me again. 'You see, even after all these years, I still seem to catch a whiff of it every now and then. Oddly enough, it's often when I'm in your company, Max. Or should I say Simon? And while we're on the subject of names, the name "Pisshead" ring any bells?'

'Danny, I have absolutely no fucking idea what you're—'

The interruption this time was from a lightning flash memory that was all too vivid as it played itself out. Shrieks of laughter from half a dozen or more pre-pubescent male voices. Half a dozen boys jostling for a better view. Dark blue jackets. Paler blue braid round the lapels. Identical ties, randomly skewed. Another boy. Not laughing. His back to me. On his hands and knees. Held there by two pairs of hands. He's struggling to lift his head, but another pair of hands forces it back down into the toilet bowl. The cistern flushing. The sound of rushing water. The laughter reaches a crescendo. Then chanting. 'Pisshead!' 'Pisshead!' 'Pisshead!' Over and over again.

I want to be sick.

'Ah, I see you remember now,' said Danny with a peculiar kind of smirk.

'Jesus, Danny. That was thirty-odd years ago.'

'Twice, sometimes three times a term for a whole year. And it wasn't just the toilet either. There was—'

'Look, I'm sorry, OK? Is that what you want to hear? But if you remember, it was never actually me who—'

'You know,' said Danny with a hint of the sombre undertaker tone creeping back into his voice, 'in my line of business you hear a lot about "closure". The final laying to rest of a loved one. That sort of thing. Well, this is mine, if you like. My closure. After all these long years of grieving, I can finally get closure.'

'Closure? Are you serious? Listen, if you want this "closure" so much, why me? Why not any of the other kids? The ones who actually *did* that kind of shit to you. I was only ever a fucking spectator.'

'So you don't recall me informing you of the tragic and unpleasantly gruesome deaths of our old school chums, Kevin Parry and Christopher Delaney?'

'That was *you*?'

'Ah yes, and even more recently, a certain Gordon "Chopper" Harris. I suppose that would make me *officially* a serial killer. I think there has to be more than two to merit that particular designation, don't you? There were a couple of others on my list, of course, but one has apparently emigrated to Australia and the other is already dead – from natural causes. So that leaves you, old chap, because although you were only ever a "spectator" – as you rightly claim – I have no recollection of you lifting so much as a finger to *prevent* the assaults. Hardly the behaviour of someone who purported to be my friend.'

OK, that was true, and call me a coward, but what was I supposed to have done? Some of these guys were way bigger than me, and I knew damn well that

247

I'd've got a lot worse than Danny if I'd tried to step in. It doesn't make it right, but that's how it was.

'So why wait till now if you've been gagging for revenge all this time? It's not that you haven't had plenty of opportunity in all the years we've known each other.'

'Oh, believe me, I've thought about it more times than you can possibly imagine. But revenge, as the saying goes, is a dish best served cold. – Actually, that's a load of bollocks. The real truth is that what happened to me is not something that's easily forgotten. Not that I've dwelt on it constantly, of course. The periodic flashback perhaps, usually triggered by... well, the smell of disinfectant, for example. And on those occasions, I cannot deny that the thirst for revenge is all but irresistible.' Danny sighed and briefly turned his gaze skyward and then back at me again. 'And yet, I did resist, and the moment would eventually pass – until, that is, a chance encounter with the aforementioned Christopher Delaney. Didn't recognise me from Adam, let alone remember my name, but why would he after all this time and given that my face was more often than not obscured from his view by being buried in the depths of a lavatory bowl? Such a cruel quirk of Fate – cruel for him at any rate – that his poor mother had passed away that very morning, and of all the funeral parlours in all the world, he should happen to walk into mine.'

Danny obviously derived some amusement from this last remark. I, less so.

'So you decided to kill him,' I said.

'Made up my mind virtually on the spot, dear boy. Odd in a way, because as you're aware yourself, I've sometimes found it necessary to... physically reprimand those who have displeased me in some way, but *murder*? Well, that's a whole different thing altogether, isn't it? I'd never have thought I had it in me, to be perfectly honest, but do you know what? I was genuinely surprised at how much I enjoyed the whole process. The careful and detailed planning was nearly as pleasurable as the execution itself. Hah! "Execution". How appropriate.'

He paused for several seconds while he appeared to be reliving the event in his mind and with evident satisfaction.

'And after Delaney,' he continued, 'the logical progression was inevitable, although I have to confess to more than a modicum of hesitation in your own case, Simon.'

'Oh yeah?'

'Hand on heart, and mainly for the reasons you put forward earlier that you were not one of the perpetrators of my mistreatment *per se*, I struggled to justify the notion of outright and cold-blooded murder. And that, you see, is where my little plan came in. If you and the Greek had done what I'd hoped and snuffed each other out, your death would have sat far more lightly on my conscience. But hey ho, we all have our cross to bear, and Fate, it seems, has once again intervened and decreed that my conscience will have to bear this burden after all. – Sanjeev, my boy, if you'd be so kind as to arrange our other friends into a neat, orderly line, we can get started. It seems to have turned awfully chilly, and I'm becoming rather eager to seek out a somewhat warmer environment.'

Not for the first time in the last couple of days, the voice in my head was screaming at me to do something. Say something. Any bloody thing if only to cling on to a few more precious minutes of life.

'This is crazy,' I said. 'For a start, you make it sound like you were an innocent victim in all this, but it wasn't like that at all, was it? OK, maybe a few of the lads went a bit over the top sometimes, but it wasn't as if you didn't bring a lot of it down on yourself. Whatever they did, you just wouldn't stop nicking stuff from other kids, including some of *them*. Sticking your head down the bog was—'

A sharp, stinging pain to the side of my face brought an abrupt end to the sentence as Danny hit me hard with the back of his hand. I staggered backwards but managed to stay on my feet.

'Enough!' he yelled, no longer smirking, and his fake posh accent suddenly disintegrating. 'I haven't got time to fuck about.'

He prodded me in the ribs with the muzzle of his semi-automatic, then grabbed me by the shoulder and turned me round. With the gun now digging into the middle of my back, I had little choice but to walk towards the row of Alan, Carla, Toby, Tess and her granddad, who were now standing side by side with Sanjeev covering them with his rifle.

'Place of honour, I think,' said Danny, the posh accent having been reinstated, and he used the gun to manoeuvre me towards the centre of the row.

The others shuffled sideways, and I filled the gap between Carla and Toby. I turned to face the same way and watched as Danny went to join Sanjeev about five or six yards in front of us.

They always reckon that your whole life is supposed to flash before your eyes in a situation like this. Not in my case, it didn't. Or maybe it did, and I was too distracted by Carla's shrieking in my ear to notice. Great. My last living moments filled with her bellyaching.

I could see Danny's mouth opening and closing, and I managed to screen her out enough to hear what he was saying.

'…and my only regret is that I've no idea who to bill for all your funeral expenses. Oh well, *c'est la vie*. Or perhaps I should say *c'est la mort*.'

This clearly caused him some amusement, and he chuckled as he swapped weapons with Sanjeev and lifted the rifle to his shoulder. Who was going to be first? Alan, by the look of it, and Sanjeev was taking aim with the semi-automatic at… Tess's granddad? More than likely Danny wanted to save me till last to prolong the agony. Still, at least then I'd have a couple of seconds' peace after they'd shut Carla's trap for good. Unbelievable that she was still yakking on nineteen to the dozen when she was moments away from death.

But all of a sudden, I realised that it wasn't me she was yelling at. She'd taken a step forward and was jabbing an irate finger at Danny.

'Listen, you, I don't know what the hell this is all about, but whatever it is, it's got nothing to do with me and my nephew. If you want to kill my worthless shit of a husband, then fine. Go ahead. You'd be doing me a favour. But just leave us out of this, OK?'

'I've no idea who this woman is,' said Tess's granddad, also taking a step forward, 'but she's absolutely right. If you people want to slaughter each other, then go ahead. Good riddance, I say, but killing my granddaughter and me isn't going to achieve anything.'

'All we're here for,' said Tess, moving to the old

man's side and choking back the tears, 'is to scatter my grandma's ashes, so at least you could have the decency to—'

'Will - you - all - just - shut - the - fuck - up!' Danny roared, his rifle lowered to waist height since the beginning of Carla's outburst.

An instant silence descended, and even Carla meekly complied when Danny fired a shot into the air and ordered everyone back into line.

'Thank you,' he said. 'And not that I feel any need to explain myself, but if you really want to know why I can't let any of you live, I can sum up my impeccable reasoning in a single word. Witnesses.'

There was a beat of a pause, and then he raised the rifle to his shoulder again and took aim.

Jesus Christ, the bastard had changed his mind. The bloody thing was pointing directly at *me*. Shit, shit, shit. Now what? Pray? No time. No time. This was it. This was the end. No, I hadn't had a good fucking innings. This was way too soon.

Hang on. Everything had gone black. Was this how it happened? Before you even hear the shot?

'No, it's because you've got your eyes shut, you dick.'

Oh, terrific. Not Carla after all, but the last voice I was gonna hear was the one in my head.

Kraakk!

Kraakk!

Two shots, but I was still standing. Christ, surely Danny couldn't have missed from that distance.

Slowly, slowly, I peeled open an eyelid, expecting the thudding pain in my chest at any moment.

Eh?

I opened the other eye.

Danny was on his back, spreadeagled on the ground with arms and legs flung out in all directions, but completely still. A few feet away, Sanjeev writhing on the floor, clutching at his gut and screaming his head off.

What the…?

I looked left and right along the line. Everyone else was upright, all staring at the probably dead Danny and the definitely wounded Sanjeev.

'You all OK?'

The voice came from some way off, and I turned towards it just as a figure emerged from behind one of the dilapidated walls fifty or sixty yards away. He was waving a rifle above his head as he trotted down the slope towards us.

Scratch.

Thank God he wasn't allergic to guns.

SOME WEEKS LATER

Everything about Bernard's apartment was immaculate and arranged on a kind of grid system. In the living room, each item of furniture was set either at right-angles or parallel to one of the four walls. A small pile of magazines, a neatly folded newspaper, two hardback books and his spectacles case were similarly positioned, exactly parallel to the edges of the low, wooden coffee table.

Even though it hadn't needed it, Bernard had given the entire flat a thorough clean in preparation for Tess's arrival, and as the morning sun streamed through the living room windows, not a single speck of dust could be seen floating through the air. The air, dust free but with a heavy scent of wood polish and the merest hint of disinfectant.

Bernard was standing with his back to the room and staring at the empty cremation urn in pride of place, dead centre on the gleamingly polished marble mantelpiece. He lifted his gaze slightly to the large, framed colour photograph on the wall above it. Him and Tess, both holding the urn, and seconds before committing Dottie to her final resting place on the top of Blackrigg Law. The young lad had taken the photo. Tony or Toby? Bernard couldn't remember.

He tilted his head from side to side and squinted. Then he took a step back and repeated the process before reaching out and rotating the picture half a degree clockwise.

'Blimey,' said Tess.

Bernard turned to face her. She was perched on the edge of a beige Draylon armchair at right-angles to the fireplace and studying the single sheet of paper she held in both hands.

'Couldn't have put it better myself,' he said.

Tess gave the sheet of paper a little flourish. 'I mean, obviously no amount of money could ever compensate for losing Granny, but even so…'

She let the sentence hang in the Pledge-scented air and slumped back in the chair, taking a deep breath and exhaling slowly. Bernard took the paper from her and briefly skimmed the contents, even though he'd read the piano delivery company's letter so many times before that he almost knew the wording off by heart.

'I know one thing, though,' he said, carefully folding the letter and tucking it behind the urn on the mantelpiece.

'Oh? What's that then?'

'I won't be buying a bloody piano with it, that's for sure.'

It was as if he was addressing the words to the cremation urn itself, and when he turned round, he and Tess smiled at each other and laughed.

'Right then,' he said with a clap of his hands and vigorously rubbing his palms together. 'I think this

255

calls for a drink. What'll you have?'

'Anything as long as it isn't Coke.'

* * *

The Acropolis Restaurant wasn't exactly heaving with customers, but it was busy enough for Dimitri's liking. Since Nikos was dead and Kosta and Tacky were on remand, awaiting trial for a string of drug-related offences, that only left the third brother, Vasilis, to take over the business. But as Vasilis was also wanted by the police and had done a runner with as much of the restaurant's liquid assets as he could gather together in a hurry, Dimitri had had the unwelcome responsibility thrust upon him.

Unlike his Uncle Nikos, however, there was to be no slobbing around and stuffing his face at the corner table for Dimitri. With almost nothing left in the kitty after Vasilis's disappearance, running the restaurant with barely a skeleton staff had been the only option to save it from going under. This was why Dimitri was now threading his way between the tables, balancing an enormous tray at shoulder height on his upturned palm.

The new, semi-regular occupants of Nikos's corner table looked up at him as he approached. None of them were smiling, although Toby's hint of a smirk was a clear enough indication of how much he was relishing being waited on by his former nemesis and jailer.

Dimitri served Toby's mother, Melanie, first, then Carla's son, Brad, and even put a plate of food in front of the empty chair where Carla's daughter, Emma, should have been sitting. Toby, he kept till last.

'What's this?' said Brad, leaning forward with his face six inches above his plate of calamari.

'Calamari,' said Dimitri. 'Like you ordered.'

'No, I didn't. I asked for kebabs.'

Dimitri tucked the empty tray under his arm and stared at the kid, the muscle in his jaw twitching with the intensity of his irritation.

'He did actually, Dimitri. Definitely kebabs,' said Melanie.

She was a couple of years older than Carla, but they could have been twins – in looks if not in demeanour. Maybe he didn't know her that well as yet, but of the two sisters, Melanie was by far the calmer personality.

Dimitri didn't answer but snatched up Brad's plate and stormed off towards the kitchen, slamming through the swing doors into an inferno of heat and steam. He peered through the dense haze until he located Carla, who was noisily juggling various pots and pans around on a range of gas hobs. He called out her name, but she either didn't hear him over the din or chose to ignore him. Probably the latter, he thought, so he marched up behind her and tried again.

'Your kid is driving me fucking crazy.'

Carla spun round, a saucepan in one hand and a ladle in the other. The sweat was pouring off her, some of it into the pan and some onto the full length apron which may once have been white but was now far more befitting an eighteenth century surgeon before the benefits of hygiene had been discovered.

'What is it now?' she snapped.

Dimitri nodded down at the plate of food in his hand. 'First he tells me he wants calamari, and now he says he wants kebabs.'

'Dimitri, I really don't have time for this shit right

now,' she said and turned back to the stove, glancing her wrist against an enormous bubbling saucepan in the process. 'Ow! Jesus! Now look what you made me do.'

'And what about Table Six's moussaka? They've been waiting ages,' said Dimitri, ignoring her injury but having the good sense to take a full step backwards out of range.

'Well, they'll just have to wait a bit longer, won't they?' said Carla, sucking her wrist while stirring the contents of the offending pan with the other hand. 'Slowly-slowly, as you Greeks are so fond of saying.'

Dimitri opened his mouth to speak, thought better of it and headed back out of the kitchen. But just before he reached the double swing doors, they flew open and in came the Acropolis's only other waiter, bearing yet another plate of uneaten food.

'Table Three says this isn't cooked,' he said. 'Cold anyway.'

Dimitri dipped his finger into the vegetable stew and tasted.

'Christ almighty, Carla. What the fuck are you doing? I'm trying to run a business here, and you can't even—'

He and the other waiter ducked a fraction of a second before a frying pan hurtled over their heads and clattered into the door behind them.

* * *

It was like everything had come full circle. There I was, once again, lying in an open coffin in Danny's funeral parlour with my arms folded across my chest and my eyes tight shut, enjoying the peace and quiet and the sheer comfort of the padded velvet lining. Except it wasn't *Danny's* funeral parlour any more on account of him being six feet under in one of his own coffins. It had been a bit of a steep learning curve getting the hang of the undertaker lingo and all the other stuff, but this had become a top priority since I'd become the new owner of the business with Alan and Scratch as equal partners.

As soon as the dust – and ashes – had settled after the Scottish hilltop massacre, I'd filed for divorce on the grounds of adultery. Carla had agreed not to contest it as long as she got custody of Brad and Emma, which was fine by me once I'd established that I'd get whatever visitation rights I wanted. Now that my big secret was out and I was no longer just Boring Old Bank Manager Dad, it was much as I'd suspected, and I'd picked up quite a few brownie points in their eyes, especially Brad's. But even Emma treated me to the occasional conversation and, try to disguise it though she did, actually seemed pleased to see me whenever we met up.

By the time I'd got back from Scotland, Carla and the kids had already packed some clothes and gone off to play happy families with Carla's Greek toyboy, and since pretty much everything was in my name, I got straight on with putting the house on the market. I could say that I couldn't bear to live there a minute longer than I had to because the place held too many difficult memories, but that would be total bollocks. The fact was that I'd always hated the leafy suburbia lifestyle and all the fucked-up, po-faced fur coat and no knickers bullshit that went with it. At long last, I had the means of escape, and I grasped it with both hands and without a moment's hesitation.

The house sold quickly, and even after the hefty mortgage was repaid and I'd settled Carla's remaining, not insubstantial debts as part of the divorce settlement, I was left with quite a tidy sum. Danny's parlour – with "spacious and elegantly furnished apartment above" – was up for grabs and at a relatively knockdown price, so I thought, Why not?

To be perfectly honest, I'd never been what you might call a roaring success at the bank robbing lark – brief though it was – so I decided it was maybe time I went legit. For a while anyway. Perhaps until a cast iron, golden opportunity presented itself. And so it was that, with the money from the sale of the house, Danny's ten grand debt written off and the meagre savings Alan and Scratch had scraped together, we managed to persuade one of the banks that we were worth investing in. The ultimate and rather beautiful irony was that the branch that agreed the loan was the very one that we'd failed to knock off at the beginning of this whole sorry tale.

'You still awake in there, Max?'

It was Alan's voice, and I opened my eyes to see first his neck brace and then his face a dozen or so inches above mine.

'How many of these we got in stock?' I said.

Alan straightened up and shrugged. 'Couple, I think.'

'Better get some more in then. This one's a beauty.'

I sat upright in the coffin and spotted Scratch about six feet away, dabbing at his eyes with a handkerchief.

'You all right, mate? I'm not dead yet, you know.'

Scratch sniffed a couple of times and then let out a series of three Richter-scale sneezes.

'Must be the wood polish or something,' he said.

Not surprisingly, Scratch hadn't been the easiest to convince when I'd first suggested taking over Danny's funeral director business. His phobia about anything even vaguely related to death and dying was a major obstacle, of course, but Alan and I had worn him down eventually, albeit by making a number of concessions. These included never calling upon him to act as a pallbearer – 'I ain't going that close to a real life fucking stiff' – and on no account was he ever going to set foot in the basement of the parlour – 'Putting makeup on corpses? That's just bloody weird, that is.'

With Scratch almost doubled over by a second fit of sneezing, Alan, as per usual, couldn't resist a dig about the poor bloke's many and varied allergies. Also true to form, Scratch retaliated with some snarky remarks about Alan's neck brace and these days had the additional ammunition of, 'You'd be pushing up the daisies right now if it wasn't for me, you ungrateful prick.'

Mercifully on this occasion, the bickering was cut short by the appearance of Toby from the storeroom at the front of the parlour, bearing a tray with four steaming mugs of tea. He'd apparently taken quite a shine to us since his ordeal – which, according to him, had been "awesome" – and he'd often call in after he'd finished school for the day just to "hang out", as he put it.

'Aunty Carla was asking after you last night,' he said as he handed me my tea.

'Oh yeah?' I said, instantly on the defensive.

'Well, not *asking* exactly. More like… bitching really. How she should have got more out of the divorce settlement and what a tightarse you'd been.

261

Stuff like that mainly.'

'Do I take it that all is not well at Shit Kebabs Are Us?'

'You could say that, yeah.'

'Brad and Emma all right?'

'Didn't see Emma. Brad seems OK though. His latest hobby seems to be winding up that Dimitri twat.'

Good lad, I thought, and took a sip of my tea.

'Jesus,' I said, wincing at the taste. 'You put sugar in this?'

'Yeah, course. Two spoonfuls.'

I took another more tentative sip, and it still didn't taste right at all. 'Definitely no sugar in this, Toby.'

'Yes there is,' he said, all pissy like. 'Plastic Tupperware box next to the kettle with a label on it marked "Sugar".'

The third sip was already in my mouth, but it didn't stay there for long.

THE END

DEAR READER

Authors always appreciate reviews – especially if they're good ones of course – so I'd be eternally grateful if you could spare the time to write a few words about *Cremains* on Amazon, Goodreads or anywhere else you can think of. It really can make a difference. Reviews also help other readers decide whether to buy a book or not, so you'll be doing them a service as well.

MAILING LIST

If you'd like to be kept informed of new posts on my website, my new books, special offers on my books and other relevant information, please click on the link below and add your details.

Don't worry, any emails I send you will be few and far between, and I certainly won't be sharing your details with any third parties. You can also easily unsubscribe at any time.

http://eepurl.com/cwvFpb

AND FINALLY...

I'm always interested to hear from my readers, so please do take a couple of minutes to contact me via my website at:

https://rob-johnson.org.uk/contact/

ABOUT THE AUTHOR

'You'll have to write an author biography of course.'

'Oh? Why?'

'Because people will want to know something about you before they lash out on buying one of your books.'

'You think so, do you?'

'Just do it, okay?'

'So what do I tell them?'

'For a start, you should mention that you've written four plays that were professionally produced and toured throughout the UK.'

'Should I say anything about all the temp jobs I had, like working in the towels and linens stockroom at Debenhams or as a fitter's mate in a perfume factory?'

'No, definitely not.'

'Motorcycle dispatch rider?'

'You were sacked, weren't you?'

'Boss said he could get a truck there quicker.'

'Leave it out then, but make sure they know that *Cremains* is the fifth book you've written. And don't forget to put in something that shows you're vaguely human.'

'You mean this kind of thing: "I'm currently in Greece with my wife, Penny, two cats and five rescue dogs and working on a new novel and a couple of screenplays".'

'It'll have to do, I suppose, and then finish off with your website and social media stuff.'

'Oh, okay then.'

- visit my website at
  http://www.rob-johnson.org.uk

- follow **@RobJohnson999** on Twitter

- check out my Facebook author page at
  https://www.facebook.com/RobJohnsonAuthor

OTHER BOOKS BY ROB JOHNSON

LIFTING THE LID

(Book One in the 'Lifting the Lid' series)

There are some things people see in toilets that they wish they hadn't. What Trevor Hawkins sees might even cost him his life…

It was simply a matter of a broken flush, so how come he's suddenly a fugitive from a gang of psychopathic villains, a private detective, the police and MI5? 'Lifting the Lid' is a comic thriller with more twists and turns than an Escher-designed bobsleigh run.

"A superb adventure-comedy." - Jennifer Reinoehl for *Readers' Favorite*

"It's brilliant!" - Samantha Coville for *SammytheBookworm.com*

"The story is just so much FUN!" - Joanne Armstrong for *Ingrid Hall Reviews*

"The twists and turns kept me on the edge of my seat, laughing all the time." – *San Francisco Review of Books*

HEADS YOU LOSE

(Book Two in the 'Lifting the Lid' series)

The assignment in Greece might have been the answer to Trevor and Sandra's problems except for one thing. Someone was trying to frame them for murder... with a watermelon.

Trevor and Sandra's detective agency is almost bankrupt when they take on the job of looking after the ageing Marcus Ingleby at his villa in Greece. It's easy money until someone tries to frame them for murder, and Ingleby gets a visit from two ex-cons and a police inspector from his murky past.

"A highly entertaining, well-constructed screwball comedy." - Keith Nixon for *Big Al's Books and Pals*

"Masterfully planned and executed... It tickled my funny bone in all the right places." - Joanne Armstrong for *Ingrid Hall Reviews*

Shortlisted for a Readers' Choice Award 2015 (*Big Al's Books and Pals*)

QUEST FOR THE HOLEY SNAIL

(A time travel comedy adventure)

WANTED: Gainful employment of an adventurous nature but without risk of personal physical harm. (Can supply own time travel machine if required.)

When Horace Tweed places an advertisement in a national magazine, the last thing he expects is to be commissioned to travel back through time in search of the long extinct Holey Snail.

But this isn't just any old snail. The *helix pertusa* is possessed of an extraordinary and highly desirable property, and Horace's quest leads him and his co-adventurers to Ancient Greece and a variety of near-death encounters with beings both mythological and not so mythological.

Meanwhile, Detective Chief Inspector Harper Collins has her hands full trying to track down a secret order of fundamentalist monks whom she suspects of committing a series of murders – the same monks who are determined to thwart Horace in his quest.

"Fans of Douglas Adams' *Hitchhikers' Guide to the Galaxy* **will enjoy** *Quest for the Holey Snail***."** - *Awesome Indies*

"The author is a talented wordsmith with a penchant for Monty Python-esque humour... Overall, the writing is excellent." - Lynne Hinkey for *Underground Book Reviews*

A KILO OF STRING

(A memoir/travelogue)

"Fabulously funny - a real must for lovers of all things Greek."

After living in Greece for thirteen years, writer and reluctant olive farmer Rob Johnson has got used to most of the things that he and his partner Penny found so bizarre at the beginning. Most, but not all.

A Kilo of String is the story-so-far of this not-particularly-plucky couple's often bewildering experiences among the descendants of Sophocles, Plato and Nana Mouskouri with occasional digressions into total irrelevances.

"A Kilo of String **had me howling with laughter... I am so excited to have found this wonderful author."** - Effrosyni Moschoudi (author of The Lady of the Pier series)

"The author's entertaining stories, interesting anecdotes, and humor make this book an excellent read for everyone." - Mamta Madhavan for Readers' Favorite

A Kilo of String **is loosely based on Rob Johnson's podcast series of the same name, which is free to listen to and download at https://rob-johnson.org.uk/podcasts/a-kilo-of-string/**

"LIFTING THE LID"
OPENING CHAPTERS

I hope you've enjoyed reading *Cremains* and that you might be interested in reading one of my other novels. To give you an idea what to expect, these are the opening chapters of *Lifting the Lid*, which is the first in my comedy thriller series of the same name.

LIFTING THE LID
CHAPTER ONE

Trevor stood with his back to the fireplace like some Victorian patriarch but without a scrap of the authority. Although the gas fire wasn't on, he rubbed his hands behind him as if to warm them. His mother sat in her usual chair by the window, staring blankly at the absence of activity in the street outside.

He knew exactly what her response would be. It was always the same when he told her anything about his life. Not that there was often much to tell, but this was different. This was a biggie. Almost as big as when he'd told her about Imelda's—

'It's of no concern to me.'

There we go. And now for the follow-on. Wait for it. Wait for it.

'I'm seventy-eight years old. Why should I care? I could be dead tomorrow.'

Trevor screwed up his face and mouthed the words

of his mother's familiar mantra, but it became rapidly unscrewed again when she added, '…Like Imelda.'

'Don't,' he said. 'Just don't, okay?'

'No concern to me,' said the old woman with a barely perceptible shrug.

In the silence that followed, Trevor became aware of the ticking of the pendulum clock on the mantelpiece behind him. It had never been right since his father had died, so he checked his watch instead. 'You won't be... ' and he hesitated to say the word, ' ... lonely?'

If his mother had had the energy or inclination to have laughed – derisively or otherwise – she would have done, but she settled for the next best option and grunted, 'Hmph.'

Trevor knew from experience that the intention was to pick away at his already tender guilt spot, and he looked around the room as if he were searching for the nearest escape route. His mother still referred to it as "the parlour", perhaps in a vain attempt to attach some kind of outmoded elegance to a room which, to Trevor's eye at least, was mildly shabby and darkly depressing even on the brightest of days. It was festooned with fading photographs of people who were long since dead, interspersed here and there with pictures of his more recently deceased brother and his very-much-alive sister. Of Trevor, there only the one – an unframed snapshot of him and Imelda on their wedding day.

He became aware of the clock once again and cleared his throat. 'So... er... I'll be away then.'

This time, the shrug was accompanied by the slightest tilt of the head. 'No concern to me,' she said.

Again, he glanced at his watch. 'It's just that I have

to—'

'Oh get on if you're going.'

Trevor stepped forward and, picking up his crash helmet from the table next to his mother, kissed her perfunctorily on the back of the head. For the first time, she turned – not quite to face him, but turned nevertheless.

'Still got that silly little moped then,' she said, repeating the comment she'd made when he had first arrived less than an hour before.

'Scooter, mother. It's a scooter. – Anyway, how could I afford anything else?' He was thankful she couldn't see the sudden redness in his cheeks or she would have instantly realised that he was lying.

He kissed her again in the same spot, and this time she seemed to squirm uncomfortably. For a moment, he followed her line of vision to the outside world. – Nothing. He tapped his helmet a couple of times, then turned and walked towards the door. As he closed it behind him, he could just make out the words: 'Your brother wouldn't have gone.'

Out in the street, he strapped on his helmet and straddled the ageing Vespa, eventually coaxing the engine into something that resembled life. He took a last look at the window where his mother sat and thought he saw the twitch of a lace curtain falling back into place.

'Oh sod it,' he said aloud and let out the clutch.

At the end of the road, he turned right and stopped almost immediately behind a parked camper van. Dismounting the Vespa and still holding the handlebars, he kicked out the side stand and was about to lean it to rest when he decided that some kind of symbolic gesture was called for. Instead of inclining the scooter to a semi-upright position, he looked down at the rust-ridden old machine, tilted it marginally in the opposite direction and let go. With the gratingly inharmonious sound of metal on tarmac, the Vespa crashed to the ground and twitched a few times before rattling itself into submission. Trevor took in the paltry death throes and allowed himself a smirk of satisfaction.

Pulling a set of keys from his pocket, he kissed it lightly and walked round to the driver's door of the van. The moment he turned the key in the lock, a lean-looking black and tan mongrel leapt from its sleeping position on the back seat and hurled itself towards the sound. By the time Trevor had opened the door, the dog was standing on the driver's seat, frantically wagging its tail and barking hysterically.

'Hey, Milly. Wasn't long, was I?' said Trevor, taking the dog's head between both hands and rocking it gently from side to side. 'Over you get then.'

Milly simply stared back at him, no longer barking but still wagging her tail excitedly.

'Go on. Get over.' Trevor repeated the command and, with a gentle push, encouraged her to jump across to the passenger seat. Then he climbed in and settled himself behind the steering wheel. 'Right then,' he said, rubbing his palms around its full circumference. 'Let's get this show on the road.'

LIFTING THE LID
CHAPTER TWO

The lift was dead. The grey-haired guy in the expensive suit wasn't, but he looked like he was. Lenny had him pinned against the wall by leaning his back into him as hard as he could to keep him upright – no mean achievement since, although built like a whippet on steroids, Lenny was little more than five feet in height and well into his fifties.

'Come on, Carrot,' he said. 'What you messin' about at?'

Carrot – so called because of his ill-fitting and very obvious ginger toupee – jabbed at the lift button for the umpteenth time. 'Lift's not working. We'll have to use the stairs.'

'You kidding me? With this lard-arse?'

'So we just leave him here, do we?'

Lenny's heavily lined features contorted into a grimace. 'How many flights?'

'Dunno. Couple maybe?'

'Jesus,' said Lenny, taking a step forward.

The laws of gravity instantly came into play, and the Suit slid inexorably down the wall and ended up in a sitting position, his head lolled to one side and his jacket bunched up around his ears. Not for the first time, Carrot wondered why he'd been paired up with a dipshit like Lenny and even why the whining little git had been put on this job at all.

'Well you'll have to take the top half then,' Lenny said. 'Back's playing me up.'

Carrot snorted. Here we go again, he thought. The

old racing injury ploy.

Lenny pulled himself up to his full inconsiderable height and shot him a glare. 'And what's that supposed to mean? You know bloody well about my old racing injury.'

'Doesn't everyone?' said Carrot.

Although Lenny's stature – or lack of it – gave a certain amount of credibility to his countless stories about when he used to be a top-flight steeplechase jockey, nobody in the racing business ever seemed to have heard of him. It was certainly true that he knew pretty much everything there was to know about the Sport of Kings, and most of his tales of the turf had a ring of authenticity about them, so he must have been involved in some way or other but more likely as a stable lad than a jockey. Hardly anyone bothered to doubt him to his face though, probably because his vicious temper was legendary and so was his ability with both his fists and his feet. For a little guy, he could be more than handy when it came to a scrap.

He looked like he was spoiling for one right now, so Carrot diverted his attention back to the Suit.

'Grab his ankles then,' he said and manoeuvred the man's upper body forward so he could get a firm grip under his armpits from behind.

Halfway up the first flight of concrete stairs, Lenny announced that he'd have to have a rest. Even though Carrot was doing most of the work, he decided not to antagonise him and eased his end of the body down onto the steps. Truth be told, he could do with a short break himself. He was already sweating like a pig and, besides, he needed at least one hand free to push his toupee back from in front of his eyes.

Lenny leaned back against the iron handrail and

started to roll a cigarette.

Carrot's jaw dropped. 'Lenny?'

'Yeah?'

'What you doing?'

'Er…' Lenny looked down at his half completed cigarette and then back at Carrot. 'Rollin' a fag?'

His expression and tone of voice rendered the addition of a "duh" utterly redundant.

'We're not in the removal business, you know.' Carrot nodded towards the Suit. 'This isn't some bloody wardrobe we're delivering.'

Lenny ignored him and lit up. He took a long drag and blew a couple of smoke rings. Putting the cigarette to his lips for a second time, he was about to take another draw when he hesitated and began to sniff the air. 'What's that smell?'

'Er… smoke?' Two can play the "duh" game, thought Carrot.

'It's like…' Lenny's nose twitched a few more times and then puckered with distaste. 'Ugh, it's piss.'

'Dumps like this always stink of piss.'

'No, it's more…' Lenny carried on sniffing, his eyes ranging around to try to identify the source of the smell. 'Oh Jesus, it's him.'

Carrot looked in the direction he was pointing and, sure enough, the dark stain which covered the Suit's groin area was clearly visible despite the charcoal grey of the trousers. 'Oh for f—'

'Bugger's wet 'imself.'

'I can see that.'

Lenny took a pull on his cigarette. 'Fear probably.'

'Don't be a prat. The man's out cold. He doesn't know if it's Christmas Day or Tuesday.'

'Maybe it's like when somebody has their leg cut

off – or their arm. They reckon you can still feel it even though it's not there any more.'

Carrot stared at him, unable to discern any logical connection between amputation and pissing your pants.

'You know,' Lenny continued, apparently aware that further explanation was necessary. 'It's like your subconscious, or whatever, doing stuff behind your back without you realising.'

'I think it's far more likely it's a side effect of the stuff we injected him with.'

'Could be,' said Lenny, and he took a last drag on his cigarette before lobbing it over his shoulder into the stairwell.

'Ready now?' Carrot made no attempt to disguise the sarcasm in his tone.

'I'm not taking the feet this time though. My face'll be right in his piss.'

Carrot squeezed his eyes shut and counted to three. 'You want to swap?'

'Not necessarily. We could try taking an arm each.'

Because of the substantial difference in their heights, Carrot knew that this meant he would be taking most of the weight again, but he also realised there was no point in arguing. The priority was to get the guy up the stairs and into the flat before somebody spotted them.

LIFTING THE LID
CHAPTER THREE

The time wandered by, and the miles slid comfortably under the tyres at a steady fifty-five. Battered though it was, the converted Volkswagen Transporter was only twelve years old and could have gone faster, but Trevor was in no particular hurry. He was enjoying the ride, happy to be away and with the road stretching before him to an unknown destination. Milly seemed equally contented and alternated between sitting upright on the passenger seat, staring fixedly ahead, and curling up to sleep in the back.

It was Trevor's first real trip in the camper, and he liked the idea of having no fixed itinerary. After all, he reasoned, wasn't that the whole point of having one of these things?

To say that he had bought it on a whim would have been a gross distortion of the truth. Trevor didn't really do whims. His idea of an impulsive action was to buy an item that wasn't on his list when he did his weekly shop at the local supermarket. Even then, there would have to be a pretty convincing argument in favour of dropping the quarter-pound packet of frozen peas, or whatever it might be, into his trolley. Half price or two-for-one were minimum requirements.

The camper van hadn't fulfilled either of these criteria, and to begin with, he'd toyed with the idea of a motorbike. Something a bit flash, like a Harley. He'd have needed a halfway decent tent of course. A simple bedroll and sleeping out under the stars were all very well in Arizona or wherever but totally inadequate over here – unless you were one of those rufty-tufty outdoor survival types with an unnatural fixation about the SAS. He'd never understood the attraction of deliberately putting yourself in a situation where it was more than likely you would either starve or freeze to death or be attacked by a large carnivore or stung by something so venomous you'd have seconds to live unless you applied the appropriate antidote in time or got your best friend to suck out the poison. No, Scottish midges were about as much as he was prepared to tolerate, but even then he'd make damn sure he had a plentiful supply of insect repellent with him.

A hermetically sealable tent and a good thick sleeping bag would be indispensable as far as Trevor was concerned and, if space permitted on the Harley, an airbed – preferably with a pump which operated off the bike's battery. It had all started to make perfect sense until a small problem finally occurred to him. What about Milly? She was too big to ride in a rucksack on his back, and as for the only other possible option, the very idea of a Harley with a sidecar made him squirm with embarrassment.

A car was far too ordinary for his purposes, so a camper van had seemed to be the next best thing if he couldn't have a Harley. It still had a kind of "just hit the open road and go where it takes you" feel to it, and he'd once read a book by John Steinbeck where he set off to rediscover America in a camper with an enormous poodle called Charley.

The whole decision-making process had taken months of what Imelda would have called "anally retentive faffing", but which Trevor preferred to consider as an essential prerequisite to "getting it right". In his defence, he would have argued that it wasn't just about buying a van. There had been much greater life choices involved, such as whether to pack in his job at Dreamhome Megastores.

As it turned out, that particular decision had almost made itself for him. The company was in a bit of financial bother and was having to make cutbacks, so he and several of his colleagues had been offered voluntary redundancy. Although not exactly generous, the severance package was certainly tempting enough to cause Trevor a run of sleepless nights. But it wasn't until his annual staff appraisal that he'd finally made up his mind.

He had sat across the desk from the store manager and studied the thin wisps of hair on top of the man's head while he read out a litany of shortcomings and misdemeanours from the form in front of him.

'This simply won't do, Trevor. Really it won't,' Mr Webber had said, finally looking up and removing his glasses. 'I mean, there have been more customer complaints about you than any other member of staff.'

'I don't know why. I'm always polite. Always try and give advice whenever I—'

'But that's exactly the problem, Trevor. More often than not, the complaints are *about* your advice. We've had more goods returned because of you than... than...' The manager had slumped back in his chair. 'Good God, man, have you learned nothing about home maintenance and improvement in all the... What is it? Fourteen years since you've been here?'

'Fifteen.' And in all those long years, he'd never once heard Webber use the phrase "do-it-yourself", let alone its dreaded acronym.

'Quite honestly, I'm at a loss as to know what to—'

This time, it was Trevor who had interrupted. He couldn't be sure that he was about to be sacked, but he'd already had his quota of verbal and written warnings and thought he'd get in first with: 'About this voluntary redundancy thing...'

And that was that. Decision made and not a bad little payout. Added to what he'd squirreled away over the last couple of years or so, he could buy the van and still have enough left to live on for a few months as long as he was careful. He'd have to look for another job when the money did run out of course, but he was determined not to worry about that until the time came. At least, he was determined to *try* not to worry about it.

'What the hell, eh, Milly? This is *it*,' he said and shoved a tape into the cassette player.

He caught sight of the dog in the rear-view mirror. She briefly raised an eyebrow when the opening bars of Steppenwolf's *Born to be Wild* bellowed from the speakers above her head. Then she went back to sleep.

Trevor tapped the steering wheel almost in time with the music and hummed along when the lyrics kicked in. A song about hitting the open road and just seeing where it took you seemed particularly appropriate for the occasion, and when it got to the chorus, he'd begun to lose all sense of inhibition and joined in at the top of his voice.

Moments later, the van's engine spluttered and then abruptly died.

LIFTING THE LID
CHAPTER FOUR

Carrot and Lenny hauled the Suit to his feet and, with an arm slung around each of their shoulders, half carried and half dragged him up to the first floor landing. As Carrot had predicted, Lenny's contribution amounted to little more than providing a largely ineffectual counterbalance, and by the time they'd lurched and staggered to the top of the second flight of steps, every muscle in his neck and back was screaming at him to stop whatever he was doing.

'I'm gonna have to… have a break for a minute,' he said, fighting for breath as he altered his grip and lowered the Suit to the ground.

'Come on, mate. We're nearly there now,' said Lenny, but his words of encouragement were meaningless, given that he did nothing to prevent the Suit's descent.

Carrot groaned as he sat him down against the frame of the fire door and so did the Suit.

''Ang on a sec. He's not coming round, is he?' Lenny squatted like a jockey at the start gate and brought his face to within a few inches of the Suit's. 'He is, you know.'

The muscles in Carrot's back grumbled as he crouched down to take a closer look and spotted the faintest flicker of the eyelids.

'You can't have given him enough,' said Lenny.

'What?'

'The injection.'

'Yeah, stupid me,' said Carrot, slapping his palm

against his forehead. 'I should've allowed extra time for all your fag breaks.'

Even though he resented Lenny's accusation, he'd worked with him on several other jobs and was used to getting the blame when things went wrong. Not that this was surprising since Lenny always avoided making any of the decisions, so any cockups were never his fault.

'We'll have to give him another shot,' said Lenny.

"We" meaning "you", Carrot thought and shook his head. 'Stuff's still in the van.'

'Jesus, man. What you leave it there for?'

Carrot bit his lip, aware from his peripheral vision that Lenny was staring at him, but he had no intention of shifting his focus to make eye contact. The Suit's eyelids were twitching more rapidly now and occasionally parted to reveal two narrow slits of yellowish white. Maybe the guy was just dreaming, but it was two hours or more since they'd given him the shot, so—

'Better bop him one, I reckon,' said Lenny.

It was Carrot's turn to stare at Lenny. 'Bop him one?'

'Yeah, you know…' He mimed hitting the Suit over the head with some blunt instrument or other and made a "click" sound with his tongue. 'Right on the noggin.'

Carrot continued to hold him in his gaze while he pondered which nineteen-fifties comedian Lenny reminded him of, but he was shaken from his musing by a strange moaning sound. The Suit's eyes were almost half open now.

END OF FIRST FOUR CHAPTERS OF 'LIFTING THE LID'

To read on, please go to:
http://viewbook.at/Lifting_the_Lid

Printed in Great Britain
by Amazon

40981495R00162